Published by M.L. Hamilton

Editor: Ayesha E.B.

Cover Design: Volodumur Volianyuk at Miblart

PROLOGUE
FRESH BLOOD

The night air was crisp and still, the moon hanging high in a cloudless sky, casting an eerie glow over the darkened forest below. An unnatural fog had settled in, shrouding the forest in a heavy gray veil that muffled sounds and obscured vision for more than a few feet. Somewhere in the distance, a lone owl hooted, its haunting call piercing the otherwise dead silence.

A young woman raced through the trees, her breath coming out in panicked white puffs that dissipated into the cold air. She stumbled over gnarled roots and low bushes, thorns and branches tearing at her clothing and cutting thin lines across her flesh. Blood trickled from the cuts, leaving small droplets on the leaves she brushed past in her frantic flight.

Terror shone in her alarmed eyes, the hazel irises barely visible in the dark. Her auburn hair was wild and tangled from her mad dash through the woods. She had no idea how long she had been running or how far she had come since the moment she first sensed the lurking presence in the shadows behind her.

She was walking home alone from a night out with friends, taking her usual shortcut through the woods near her house, a path she had taken a hundred times before. But tonight, an instinctive chill crept over her, the feeling that unseen eyes were watching her every move. When she glimpsed a tall, formidable silhouette emerging from the trees, she turned and fled into the forest without looking back.

Exhaustion threatened to overwhelm her, but she dared not stop. Every time she paused to catch her breath, she could hear subtle sounds approaching - the snap of a twig, the rustling of leaves where there was no wind. The sounds spurred her tired legs back into motion, driving her deeper into the dark, shrouded maze of trees.

Finally, just as she was about to collapse, she stumbled into a small clearing illuminated by glimmers of moonlight filtering through the canopy. Gasping for breath, she spun around and peered into the surrounding forest for any sign of her pursuer. Nothing. Had she lost them in the darkness?

Before relief could set in, a heavy weight slammed into her from behind. She was thrown hard to the damp forest floor, the air forced from her lungs in a choking gasp. Dazed, she tried to scream, but a gloved hand clamped over her mouth, muffling her cries.

She struggled in blind panic, only to have her attacker roughly flip her onto her back and straddle her, their far greater size and strength pinning her down. She froze as the moonlight glinted off a long, curved knife held aloft.

A scream rose in her throat, but the attacker's hand remained clamped over her mouth, muffling any sound to a barely audible whimper. With their free hand, her attacker methodically tore open the front of her shirt, exposing the soft flesh of her torso.

She struggled violently, trying to buck and kick, but it was useless. The attacker held her down effortlessly, like an adult restraining a misbehaving child. The knife flashed and plunged down. She arched her back and let out a gurgling scream into their palm as the blade sliced along her abdomen.

The villain worked slowly, carefully, carving intricate symbols into her flesh. Blood welled from each cut, running down her sides in crimson rivulets. Her throat was raw from screaming, her strength waning as she lost more and more blood. Her weak twitches became mere tremors, like a leaf trembling in an autumn wind, as the knife continued its gruesome work.

Finally, they withdrew the blade and appraised their handiwork. The woman's torso was a horrifying display of arcane runes and symbols, etched in red. She whimpered, praying that her suffering was over. Then they grabbed her ankles and dragged her limp body across the forest floor.

She clawed feebly at passing rocks and roots, leaving a smeared trail of blood as she was dragged to the center of the clearing. The woman lay limp and bleeding as her tormentor slowly surveyed the area.

After a moment, the scourge walked purposefully to four slender birch trees at the edge of the clearing. With disconcerting ease, they grabbed the trunk of the first tree and bent it until the top nearly touched the ground. The woman watched through dazed eyes as they produced a coil of rope, tossing one end over a high branch before tying the other end to a wooden stake and driving it into the soft earth with a hammer.

The assailant returned to the bent tree and added a series of intricate knots along the taut length of the rope. They gave an experimental tug and nodded in satisfaction as the bindings held firm. One by one, they repeated the process on the remaining three trees, encircling the clearing with bent birch trunks anchored to the ground.

With their grisly preparations complete, they turned their attention back to the woman. With ruthless efficiency, they grabbed her ankles and dragged her across the ground to the center of the trees. She whimpered, her foggy mind slowly comprehending what they had planned.

They looped ropes around her wrists and ankles and pulled them tight. She now lay splayed on her back between the four bent trees, her limbs immobilized by the ropes leading to each staked tree.

She struggled one last time, but it was useless. Her attacker stood silently over her for a moment, watching their work. Then they drew a knife from their belt. The woman's eyes filled with dawning terror as she realized her fate. She tried to scream, but could only manage a hoarse sob as the knife sliced through the rope.

The birch snapped upright with a sudden, violent force. The sudden snap echoed like a rifle shot, cutting through the silence of the forest. The woman's leg was wrenched sideways, far beyond its natural limit. There was an audible pop as her hip dislocated, the ball joint ripping from the socket.

Her mouth opened in a soundless scream as her leg continued to twist violently, bones grinding at unnatural angles beneath torn skin and shredded muscle. Crimson bloomed across the shredded fabric of her jeans as searing pain shot through her nervous system. Only then did the piercing wail tear from her throat, a primal sound of agony that sent birds fleeing from the canopy above.

But her torment was far from over. The killer waited only a few seconds for her screams to fade to whimpering gasps before he sliced through the next rope. Again, the tree recoiled with a snap, jerking her arm up and back, eliciting another stomach-churning chorus of cracks and pops as bones fractured and shifted.

Each cut rope sent a fresh wave of blinding agony through her ravaged body. A guttural, animalistic shriek tore from her raw throat, eyes bulging until the tendons in her neck were visible beneath the skin. With clinical precision, the killer maintained a pace that allowed just enough time for her screams to fade before initiating the next round of torture. Each subsequent torturous cycle took more of her breath away, reducing her deafening screams to hoarse, desperate whimpers.

By the time the last rope fell, the woman was barely conscious, her throat dry and strained from screaming. Her limbs dangled limply in directions nature had never intended, muscles and skin torn, bones protruding at jagged angles. Her mind had retreated, unable to endure the intensity of the pain her nerves were transmitting.

The killer stood slowly, assessing their work with cold satisfaction. The woman's mutilated body now hung between the trees like an obscene puppet, its limbs dramatically distorted. With a slight nod, they turned and disappeared silently into the shadows between the trunks, leaving the gruesome scene behind.

An eerie silence settled over the forest as the thick fog crept back in, its misty tendrils slowly enveloping the horrific spectacle. The trees seemed to recoil from the atrocity hanging between them, their branches trembling slightly in the cold night air. As the pale mist thickened, it began to obscure the gory details - the unnatural angles of shattered bones, the ragged strips of flesh hanging like macabre streamers.

Soon the fog engulfed the scene, muffling all sound except the mournful creaking of the ropes as they strained against the dead weight they carried. The night breeze sighed through the leaves, causing the grisly remains to sway gently, a final indignity to the broken vessel that once held a human soul.

CHAPTER ONE

CITY OF SHADOWS

The rain fell in a steady drizzle as I made my way through the neon-lit streets of Silvergate, the city lights reflecting off the wet pavement and casting a kaleidoscopic glow on the surroundings. The cold rain seeped under my collar as I trudged through the streets. I watched the usual nightlife suspects emerge from the shadows - the working girls staking their claim on familiar street corners, the gamblers and hustlers looking for an easy score, and the homeless huddled in filthy alleys.

I've been walking these streets since I was a kid, growing up in the heart of Silvergate's gritty underbelly. Even then, I could feel the pulse of the city, its lifeblood coursing through the veins of every alley and street. The sounds of the city were my lullaby - the wail of police sirens, the raucous laughter emanating from dive bars, the distant rumble of trains snaking through the industrial district.

As a kid, I'd wander these streets for hours, memorizing every crack in the sidewalk, every tag on the walls. I knew the shortcuts and the hiding places, the places where the local gangs gathered to settle scores or make deals. The city was my playground, my classroom, my home.

But even then, I could sense the darkness lurking beneath the surface. I saw it in the haunted eyes of the addicts, in the bruises on the faces of the working girls, in the whispers of unsolved murders and corrupt cops.

It was a darkness that seeped into your bones, a rot that festered at the core of the city.

I've spent three decades pounding this beat, first as a civilian and now as a detective. The players changed, but the game remained the same - yet something about this night felt different. A shadowy, ominous feeling crept beneath my skin, it cold grip refusing to let go.

There had been three murders in as many months, gruesome, barbaric killings that pointed to the work of a seriously twisted individual. Leadership was pushing me hard to close this case before panic grabbed the city by the throat and squeezed. But the crime scenes yielded few clues, and the murders seemed random and without pattern. The kind of investigation that had the potential to either catapult a detective's reputation into the stratosphere or shatter it beyond repair had landed squarely in my lap. And I wasn't about to let it break me.

I paused under the glowing sign of the Blue Lantern, seeking a moment's respite from the chilly night air. Stepping inside, I was enveloped in the familiar trappings - the warm light, the smell of whiskey and stale beer, the murmur of hushed conversation. It was an oasis, a refuge for those who walked the thin blue line, far removed from the harsh realities waiting just outside the door.

"Well, if it ain't Detective Black!" boomed a voice from behind the bar. "Come on in and warm those bones."

I couldn't help but smile. Jack Sullivan, or "Sully" as everyone called him, had been a grizzled beat cop long before I joined the force, and he'd taken me under his wing as a rookie. His weathered face, creased with laugh lines and old scars, was a map of a life lived on the front lines of law enforcement. After he retired, he'd put his pension into opening the Blue Lantern - a cop bar for cops, no questions asked. Sullivan was like a second father to me - a mentor who'd taught me more about being a good cop than any academy ever could.

"How you doing, Sully?" I said, sneaking up to the bar and taking off my soaked coat.

"Oh, just trying to keep this place out of the clutches of bureaucrats and pencil pushers," he said with a wry smile. "Let me get you a drink to take the edge off. You look like you could use one."

I nodded gratefully as Sully poured me three fingers of Irish whiskey. The liquid warmth spread through me, soothing frayed nerves and steadying my resolve. As much as I needed a clear head for this case, I wasn't too proud to admit that I required a little liquid courage every now and then.

Out of the corner of my eye, I noticed a familiar figure slide onto the stool next to me. Detective Jenna O'Malley, my partner, fixed me with a knowing look. Her small stature belied an inner strength and tenacity that had made Jenna one of the pioneering women in Silvergate's detective force. Her dark hair was pulled back in a practical ponytail, and her sharp eyes missed nothing as they scanned the room.

Jenna had faced her fair share of hurdles along the way, battling not just criminals but also the skepticism of some of our less enlightened colleagues. But she'd met every challenge head-on, earning the respect of even the most hardened veterans on the force. I'd never met anyone sharper or more dedicated to the job. We'd bonded over late nights poring over case files, and over time, she'd become the closest thing to a sister I'd ever had.

"Starting without me, I see," O'Malley said wryly, nodding at my drink. Her voice carried a hint of amusement, but I could hear the underlying tension. This case was wearing on her too.

"Just trying to take the edge off. This case..."

My voice faded into the buzz of the bar as I met Jenna's gaze. No words were needed - her eyes reflected the same weariness and frustration I felt in my bones. The bond between us transcended mere conversation. Countless stakeouts and hard-fought cases together had forged an almost telepathic understanding, an instinctive connection that only true partners could understand.

"I know, but we'll get him, James. We always do." Her voice was soft but filled with determination. She placed a reassuring hand on my arm, and I felt some of the tension drain from my shoulders.

I reached over and gave Jenna's shoulder a appreciative squeeze, feeling the dependable strength in her frame. With her unwavering presence at my side, an unshakable pillar of support, I felt emboldened enough to stare down the devil himself and not flinch.

We sat in silence for a few moments, sipping our drinks. My eyes wandered over the memorabilia that adorned the walls - the fading photographs of cops from generations past, their bright smiles belies the darkness they waded through each day. A familiar twinge of sadness pierced me as I lingered on those frozen moments of simpler times, when the job still held a sense of optimism and pride.

I thought of the fresh-faced rookies in those photos, oblivious to the toll this work would take on their souls over the years. The crumpled bodies, the anguished cries of grieving relatives, the futility of trying to stem the endless tide of violence and depravity. No one could be truly prepared for the things we've seen. The things that keep us awake at night, that haunt us.

My eyes lingered on one portrait in particular, a kindly officer with his arm slung proudly over his partner's shoulder, their faces beaming with the optimism and camaraderie of those early days on the force. It was a stark reminder of the bonds we forge in this line of work, the unspoken understanding that we would lay down our lives for one another without hesitation.

One day, this place may honor my own service, my own sacrifice, I realized with a pang that resonated deep in my chest. It was a sobering thought, the fragility of life laid bare against the unforgiving nature of our chosen path. We willingly put it all on the line every day, donning the badge and the burdens that come with it, knowing that we may not make it home to our loved ones. And yet we soldier on. Someone has to stand at the gates of hell itself to keep the demons at bay.

I couldn't afford to dwell on such morbid thoughts, not with a killer still on the loose, leaving a trail of blood and suffering in their wake. I tossed back the last of my whiskey, savoring the smoky heat as it burned a path down my throat, hardening my resolve like tempered steel.

I stood abruptly, the scrape of my chair against the worn floorboards cutting through the somber atmosphere like a gunshot. I turned to O'Malley, my eyes alight with a fierce determination that burned away any lingering traces of melancholy. "Let's go hunting."

Beside me, O'Malley nodded, her sharp eyes mirroring my resolve. A sense of relief washed over me as I reentered the rain-slicked streets. The familiar scent of wet asphalt and the distant hum of the city surrounded us as we made our way to the car.

The patrol car sat waiting under the dim glow of the streetlights, its glossy exterior reflecting the weary cityscape. O'Malley slid into the passenger seat, her movements fluid and practiced. I settled into the driver's seat, the worn leather creaking under my weight.

The crackle of the radio pierced the heavy silence that had settled over our patrol car as we idled at a traffic light.

The sudden burst of static made me jump, breaking the tense silence that had filled the squad car. My partner O'Malley glanced over at me, her eyes narrowed as she listened intently to the dispatcher's voice coming through the speakers.

"All units, we have a 10-16 in progress at the Cypress Arms Apartments on East 112th. Officers requested."

A domestic disturbance. I felt my jaw instinctively clench. It was never an easy situation to walk into, with emotions running high and tensions heightened behind closed doors. But it was our duty to respond, to intervene before the violence escalated beyond the point of no return.

I turned on the sirens and stepped on the accelerator, expertly weaving through traffic as O'Malley radioed our ETA back to dispatch. The streets were slick with rain, reflecting the glow of neon signs and traffic lights as we sped through the city's winding veins. We'd been partners for years now, and I knew I could count on her to have my back. No matter what, we'd face it together.

My hands gripped the wheel tightly, the tension evident. A disturbance in these run-down apartments usually meant hard drugs were involved.

Beside me, O'Malley was on high alert, one hand casually resting on the shotgun rack as her sharp eyes scanned the dark streets. She knew as well as I did that these kinds of calls had a way of going south fast.

The wail of sirens echoed off the dilapidated brick walls as we pulled up to the Cypress Arms complex. Even at this hour, residents loitered in the courtyard - hollow-eyed addicts and weary mothers trying to tuck children safely inside. They parted silently as we passed, our footsteps ringing on the cracked walkway.

Muffled shouting came from the second floor. I drew my Beretta 92D sidearm and nodded to O'Malley before climbing the stairs, my senses heightened for any sudden movement. The shouting grew louder as we approached the door of Unit 204. I could make out the voice of a man and a woman engaged in a heated argument, their words indistinct but their emotions running high.

I pounded my fist on the scarred wooden door, the sound echoing through the empty hallway.

"Silvergate PD! Open up!"

The commotion inside stopped abruptly. Heavy footsteps approached, and the door was flung open by a wild-eyed man I instantly recognized as Vince DeLuca, a low-level dealer with a rap sheet as long as my arm. His bloodshot eyes narrowed at the sight of me.

"DeLuca," I growled. "You want to explain the ruckus?"

He feigned innocence. "Ruckus? Just havin' a chat with my lady here."

His breath reeked of booze. I peered past him. A frightened woman huddled against the wall, her arms wrapped protectively around herself. Mottled bruises were already forming on her face.

Rage simmered in my gut at the sight of her battered face, fury roaring through my veins. Every fiber of my being yearned to grab DeLuca by the scruff of his neck and smash his skull into the drywall, to feel the satisfying click of the cuffs around his wrists.

Bitter experience had taught me the futility of such actions. Like a cockroach, he'd be back on the streets within hours, and she'd bear the brunt of the consequences. The scales of justice were skewed, the system broken beyond repair, and I was just another helpless pawn, my hands tied by the very laws I had sworn to uphold.

O'Malley placed a gentle hand on the woman's shoulder, her voice soft. "Ma'am, do you need medical attention?"

The woman's eyes darted anxiously to DeLuca before she silently shook her head. My jaw clenched. How many times had she silently endured his abuse?

DeLuca sneered. "See? We're all good here. So why don't you pigs get the fuck out of my apartment?"

Every instinct screamed at me to put this rabid animal down. To end his reign of terror, to spare his victims any more pain. For a brief, wild moment, I thought about crossing that line, taking justice into my own hands.

But I forced myself to breathe, to control the rage that threatened to consume me. As much as it tore at me, I had to play by the rules. Anything else and I'd be no better than the scum I hunted.

"This isn't the end, DeLuca," I snarled through gritted teeth. "Step one inch out of line and you'll be behind bars before you can blink. You got that?"

His sneer was like acid as he slammed the door, nearly catching my nose. The dingy hallway seemed to close in around me as O'Malley and I retreated. I could feel her gaze drilling into the back of my skull, her unspoken question thickening the air between us until it was hard to breathe.

Why didn't you stop him?

I wished I had an answer for her. For myself. But the bitter truth was that my hands were tied by laws that predators like DeLuca could easily exploit. Lowlifes who had somehow managed to slip through the cracks of our flawed legal system, sidestepping the courts countless times.

As we stepped back out into the cool night air, I took a deep breath, trying to clear the rage that burned in my lungs. Cases like this always left a bitter taste in my mouth, a tinge of fury at my inability to truly bring predators like DeLuca to justice. I had to trust that justice would triumph in the end, even as the shadows crept closer, threatening to swallow us whole.

If I ever stepped over that line, surrendering to sheer vengeance instead of upholding the law, then hope would be extinguished. And without hope to sustain us, what meaning did any of our actions have? We'd become just another part of the relentless machinery of corruption.

I had to hold on to the light, no matter how dim it seemed with each passing day. To work within this flawed system while striving to fix it. I placed a hand on O'Malley's shoulder and locked eyes with her conflicted stare.

"One day at a time, partner. One day at a time."

In the end, that was all either of us could do. Continue to walk the path laid before us, even when lost deep in the shadows. Trusting that if we stayed true, the light would guide us home.

As I slid behind the wheel, I noticed that my hands were shaking almost imperceptibly. Whether from the adrenaline rush or sheer anger, I couldn't tell. I reached into my coat pocket and pulled out the silver flask I kept for occasions like this. The burn of the whiskey in my throat always helped steady my nerves. It was a bad habit, perhaps, but in this line of work, each of us had our own ways of coping with the darkness.

O'Malley shot me a knowing look, but remained silent as I screwed the cap back on the flask and slipped it into my pocket. She had never judged me for it. As partners, we each carried our share of demons that weren't easily exorcised.

I took a deep breath as I pulled the patrol car away from the curb, trying to focus my thoughts. But the unease still clung to me, impossible to shake. There was something in the air tonight, a sense of dread I couldn't quite put my finger on. Like a shadow I kept catching out of the corner of my eye, only to find nothing there when I turned to look.

"You okay?" O'Malley asked, her dark eyes searching my face with concern.

"Yeah," I murmured. "Just one of those nights, I guess."

She nodded in understanding and looked back out the window. We drove on in silence through the rain-slicked streets, each of us lost in our own thoughts. But the knot in my stomach remained, souring every swallow.

I couldn't shake the feeling that something was wrong in Silvergate lately. The last few months had seen a disturbing increase in gruesome murders, with no leads or suspects. At first, the brass dismissed it as a mere coincidence, some transient causing trouble before moving on. Even then, my instincts told me there was something more at work. Something far more sinister than your average deranged killer.

My instincts proved correct as more butchered bodies began to appear, their wounds eerily reminiscent of the previous killings. The brass now had no choice but to face the grim reality - a monster stalked the shadows of Silvergate, leaving a trail of carnage in its wake. This was no mere coincidence or the work of a lone madman. No, something far more malevolent had crept into our city, and it was looking for more innocent blood to spill.

Not for the first time, I wondered if the shadows encroaching on this city ran deeper than any of us realized. Perhaps the bright lights and gleaming towers hid an underbelly few dared to confront. One beyond the reach of traditional law and order.

A flicker of movement in the rearview mirror made me tense reflexively, but it was only a stray dog scavenging for scraps. I forced myself to exhale slowly, trying to clear the dark path my thoughts had taken. Being a cop naturally lent itself to paranoia, always seeing threats lurking in every shadow. But I couldn't let it distract me from doing my job. There were enough real monsters out there without borrowing imaginary ones.

Still, I couldn't completely silence the doubts that nagged at the back of my mind. The feeling that I was missing something important, some crucial piece of the puzzle. I glanced at O'Malley, wondering if she felt the strange foreboding feeling that seemed to creep through the night air. But her face remained impassive, her posture relaxed in the passenger seat beside me.

Maybe it was just the lateness of the hour that got to me. God knew we hadn't had enough rest these past few weeks. I decided to put my concerns aside for the night. A few hours of sleep would provide much-needed perspective and wash away the shadows that clouded my thoughts.

The glowing sign of the precinct emerged from the rain ahead of me, evoking mixed feelings. While it represented a refuge of sorts, it also contained a mountain of paperwork awaiting us inside. But the promise of hot coffee and a warm desk chair drove me forward.

I pulled the cruiser into the parking lot and turned off the engine with a sigh, my breath fogging the air. The knot in my stomach had loosened, but not completely disappeared. I glanced over at O'Malley, who gave me a tired smile that I instinctively returned. No matter what lay ahead, we'd face it together.

"Ready to battle the paperwork dragon?" she quipped, pushing open her door.

"After you, partner," I said wryly, getting out of the driver's seat. Maybe she was right and I was just overly tired, grasping at phantoms conjured up by an exhausted mind. Either way, the reports wouldn't finish themselves.

With a tired, shared look of understanding, we went inside to finish another long shift. The specter of doubt still lingered at the periphery, but I pushed it down forcefully. Whatever this unease portended, it could wait until morning. Tonight the call of duty beckoned, mundane but no less vital. And we would answer it, as we always did.

Until dawn chased away the shadows, the task remained unfinished.

CHAPTER TWO

BEHIND THE BADGE

The precinct buzzed with activity despite the late hour. Phones rang, keyboards clacked, and the air was filled with the murmur of overlapping voices. The organized chaos of the night shift, a scene that always made me feel a sense of belonging. I nodded to the officer at the front desk as we passed, the corners of my mouth turning up involuntarily. It felt good to be back, surrounded by colleagues who were like an extended family. People who understood the particular madness that came with devoting your life to the badge.

O'Malley gave my arm a playful nudge as she turned toward the break room. "Coffee?"

"Please," I said. A kick of caffeine always tantalized my tired mind, the perfect antidote for bone-deep exhaustion. O'Malley laughed knowingly and disappeared through the door as I made my way to my desk.

I sank gratefully into my chair with a tired groan, leaned back, and closed my eyes for a moment. My body ached, less from physical exertion than from sheer mental fatigue. The nagging feeling of unease from earlier still lingered at the edges of my mind, impossible to completely dismiss. With a sigh, I sat up and opened the top folder from the stack on my desk. No rest for the wicked. Or the righteous, it seemed.

"Working hard or hardly working?" a wry voice spoke behind me.

I glanced up to see Marcus Jones and Theo Ramirez leaning against the door of my office, arms folded across their broad chests.

"Hey, Jones, Ramirez," I greeted them.

A crooked grin tugged at my lips as I met their gaze. "You know me, boys. Sleep is for the weak." The joke rolled off my tongue with practiced ease, but beneath the veneer of humor, I recognized the same soul-deep exhaustion etched into the lines of their faces, an all-too-familiar companion these days.

"Don't worry, I'll leave the hard work to you two tonight."

Ramirez let out a chuckle. "Good one, Black. Writing your own comedy routine now?"

I flashed a weary grin in return. Jones, Ramirez, and I went way back, having come up through the academy together years ago. We'd been partners for a while before finally going our separate ways. But a lasting bond had been forged between us in those chaotic early days that had stood the test of time. These men had saved my hide more times than I could count. I trusted them with my life.

"How did the call go?" Jones asked, jerking his chin at the file I'd opened. Straight to business, then.

"About as you'd expect," I sighed, scrubbing a hand across my stubbled jaw. "Neighbors reported a disturbance at the residence of one Vince DeLuca. Claims of yelling and sounds of a physical altercation."

Ramirez snorted and shook his head. "Let me guess. You showed up to find DeLuca drunk off his ass after smashing some of his girlfriend's stuff."

I grimly confirmed Ramirez's guess. The scene with DeLuca was all too familiar. The man had an extensive rap sheet of slinging dope, fights with his girlfriend, and drunken disturbances that spanned a tree's worth of paper. "Barely lucid when we got there. The apartment was trashed along with his girlfriend. She still refuses to press charges."

"That woman needs to wise up and ditch that piece of shit." Jones's voice hardened. He had even less tolerance for abusers than I did.

"No argument here," I agreed. "With no one pressing charges, all I could do was threaten DeLuca with a ticket to County if he ever crossed the line."

Ramirez rubbed his chin thoughtfully. "We've got to get this piece of trash off the streets for good, though. Build a case against him."

"I know Ramirez. We'll do what we can."

And it was true. But sometimes our best efforts still weren't enough for justice to be served. The bitter truth at the heart of so much police work. We did what we could with the tools we had. Even if it felt like trying to chip away at a mountain with a teaspoon.

O'Malley returned then, breaking the dark turn my thoughts had taken. She handed me a steaming mug with a sympathetic smile, keeping one for herself.

"Hey Jones, Ramirez," she greeted them warmly. "What brings you two by?"

"Just checking in on you newbies," Ramirez said with a wink. "Black filled us in on the DeLuca call. That guy really needs to be locked up."

O'Malley's expression clouded. "No kidding. I hate to leave his girlfriend in that situation, but she won't press charges or accept help." Her frustration was palpable. O'Malley took the victims' suffering personally, fueled by deep wells of empathy.

"We'll get him sooner or later," Jones assured her gently. "Scumbags like that always screw up eventually."

O'Malley didn't look convinced, but she nodded. We stood in solemn silence for a few moments, united in our desire to protect the weak. But also equally resigned to the sad reality that sometimes there were no good options. Just slightly less-bad ones.

I cleared my throat harshly, hoping to move on to a less somber topic. "Have either of you heard back from the lab on those runic symbols from the last Rune Killer scene?"

Ramirez perked up slightly, welcoming the change of subject. "Yes. I wanted to catch up with you about that. The lead analyst called in her preliminary findings earlier."

He pulled a folder from under his arm and handed it to me. I flipped through the contents while he summarized the report.

"Still no matches in any of the criminal databases, unfortunately. But the analyst was able to confirm that the use of the symbols is consistent with some kind of ritualistic practice."

"Any indication of their purpose?" O'Malley asked. "Are they meant to accomplish something, or are they just for show?"

Ramirez shook his head. "Too early to tell, really. They could have some deeper meaning, or the killer could just be tapping into occult imagery. The lab needs more examples to make any definitive conclusions."

"You would think that three bodies all bearing similar markings would be more than enough material to flesh out their analysis," I remarked.

I stared down at the strange glyphs and sigils, a chill running through me despite the overheated room. They seemed to writhe on the page, mocking our efforts to impose reason or meaning on such madness. What dark compulsions drove the Rune Killer to adorn his horrific crimes with these designs? A desperate cry for attention? Delusions of grandeur? Or were the runes themselves imbued with a deeper power, somehow directing his actions?

A knock on my office door broke the silence. I glanced up to see Chief Thompson standing in the doorway, his craggy features set in their usual dour expression. The one he reserved specifically for me. Jones, Ramirez, and O'Malley knew better than to stick around and excused themselves.

"Chief," I greeted neutrally, closing the folder. "What can I do for you?"

He stepped inside, closing the door firmly behind him. Never a good sign. "You can explain to me why one of my best detectives is wasting time and resources chasing ghosts instead of making real progress on this case."

I stiffened. "With all due respect, I'm following every viable lead. The occult angle can't be dismissed."

Thompson scowled and crossed his arms over his chest. "You mean that mystical nonsense those eggheads cooked up in the lab? The Mayor's pressuring me to produce tangible results, and you're sitting here studying ancient symbols and rituals."

I took a slow breath, struggling to keep my voice level. "The symbols at the crime scenes are our only solid leads right now. Evidence that the killer deliberately left behind. We need to determine their meaning if we want to get inside their head."

The chief jabbed a finger at the folder. "What I need is physical evidence that can identify a suspect and support charges in court. Not mystical theories of ritual magic." His tone made it clear what he thought of such notions.

My jaw tensed despite my best efforts to remain calm. We'd had this argument too many times. "Chief, dismissing any possibility out of hand is short-sighted. We need to follow the evidence no matter where it leads."

Thompson's scowl deepened, his craggy face turning an alarming shade of red. I braced myself for the tirade to come.

"The only place this evidence leads is down a rabbit hole of hocus-pocus nonsense!" He jabbed his finger at me again. "I want you to drop this voodoo bullshit and refocus your efforts on identifying real, concrete leads that can break this case."

I sprung to my feet, matching the chief's confrontational stance. "I can't ignore what may be the killer's only defining characteristic! My gut tells me these symbols are the key to unraveling his motivations."

"Well, your gut isn't getting the job done!" Thompson roared. "This isn't one of your philosophical debates at the Academy. Out here, results count, not abstract theories."

He leaned over my desk, his face inches from mine. "Wrap your head around that, or turn this case over to someone who can separate fantasy from reality long enough to catch this psycho. Are we clear, Detective?"

I held the chief's burning gaze, jaw clenched. Every instinct screamed at me to push back, to make him understand the potential significance of the runic symbols. But years of experience kept me in check, just barely. Picking this fight would only undermine the investigation in Thompson's eyes. However misguided I found his position.

With a monumental effort, I relaxed my stance and stepped back. "Understood...sir. I will reevaluate my approach and focus on the physical evidence."

Thompson eyed me for a moment, as if gauging my sincerity. Then he gave a curt nod and turned toward the door. "Make sure you do," he tossed over his shoulder before disappearing down the hall.

I sank back into the worn leather chair behind my desk, scrubbing my face with a frustrated hand. As much as I hated to admit it, Chief Thompson had a point. If we had any hope of convincing a jury to convict the killer, we needed hard, irrefutable evidence. Fingerprints, DNA, murder weapons – the kind of hard evidence a jury would expect.

I just couldn't shake the sinking feeling in my gut that dismissing those strange runic symbols so easily was a grave mistake. One that might allow the perpetrator the media had dubbed "The Rune Killer" to remain free to take more innocent lives.

My eyes drifted back to the pile of glossy crime scene photos spread out on my desk, those cryptic glyphs staring back at me. Mocking me.

The Chief expected a conventional investigation, focusing on physical evidence and building a logical suspect profile. But my instincts - honed by over a decade navigating the dark underbelly of this city - screamed that something deeper was at play here. Something that defied natural explanation.

I leaned forward, studying the images, willing the symbols to reveal their secrets. There had to be a way to follow the tangible leads the Chief demanded, while also following the eerie hunch that twisted my gut. I just had to find the right approach, the perfect angle that would allow me to illuminate the truth.

Shadows lengthened across my office walls as the day slipped into dusk, the muffled sounds of traffic drifting up from the streets below. I knew the key to untangling this mystery lay just out of reach, concealed in the murky void between established facts and maddening unknowns. I would dig it up, drag it into the searing light. I had no choice. Not with the Rune Killer still out there, ready to drag more unsuspecting victims into a web of broken bodies and fresh blood.

The doors to the precinct slid shut behind me with a muted hiss, cutting off the constant noise that filled its walls. In the abrupt silence that followed, the events of the day seemed to catch up with me all at once, their accumulated weight settling on my shoulders. I let out a weary sigh and began the long trudge back to my apartment, my shoes scuffing against the worn pavement.

Another day had come and gone, with little to no progress to show for the endless hours spent poring over files, conducting interviews, and chasing down the tiniest of leads. The Rune Killer continued to elude us, their true motives shrouded in sinister runic symbols and vulgar murders.

Despite our best efforts, we seemed no closer to stopping them, or even understanding the dark compulsions that drove their actions.

As I left, the Chief's words from earlier echoed through my mind. His impatience and skepticism at my focus on the mystical elements of the case still grated, even hours later. Could he be right? Was I wasting time and resources by not dismissing the occult angle outright? Or did the answer to stopping this killer lie somewhere in the spaces between the earthly and the otherworldly?

I pushed the questions from my mind as I approached my apartment building, the massive brownstone rising before me. Its stately facade stood in stark contrast to my dark thoughts, the warm light spilling from its windows offering a silent reprieve. Home. Or the closest thing I had to one these days.

The interior of my apartment was shrouded in shadows as I unlocked the door and stepped inside. I shrugged off my coat and threw my keys on the table by the door, not bothering with the lights. The dark spaces suited my mood tonight. I moved through the inky rooms with the ease of long familiarity, heading straight for the liquor cabinet and pouring myself two fingers of whiskey.

The alcohol burned pleasantly as it slid down my throat, a balm for my weary mind and spirit. I knew drinking alone like this wasn't healthy, but lately, it seemed like the only reliable way to get away from the stresses of work. If only temporarily.

I carried my glass over to the sofa and sank down with a tired groan, resting my head on the back cushion and closing my eyes. The silence enveloped me, broken only by the low hum of the refrigerator and the occasional bustle of traffic outside. It was far too quiet with just me here. My thoughts drifted, as they often did on these lonely nights, to Samuel, my younger brother.

His restless energy and enthusiasm, his passion for art and beauty, balanced my naturally stoic and cynical disposition. But that was before.

Before the incident that had irrevocably changed the course of both our lives. The memories of that terrible event still haunted me, intertwined with guilt and the pain of Samuel's absence.

He now lived in a care facility across town. I still visited him regularly, but our relationship remained strained, burdened by our shared trauma and my contribution to the horrors inflicted by cruel chance. He would likely spend the rest of his days struggling with the damage done to his once brilliant mind. While I continued to search for meaning through my work, neither of us was able to fully move beyond the tragic events of our past, me emotionally and him physically.

I took another stinging sip of whiskey, embracing the numbness it brought. In a way, I envied Samuel. His fractured psyche and tenuous grip on reality shielded him from fully comprehending the injustices and disappointments of our harsh world. He floated through life in a fog of muted colors and blurred edges that provided a semblance of peace. While I felt the sharp sting of life's thorns with each new failure or disillusionment.

With a shake of my head, I pushed those gloomy thoughts aside and sat up. Wallowing in past regrets and self-pity wouldn't get me any closer to stopping the Rune Killer.

I downed the last of my drink and set the empty glass down with a definitive clink. The alcohol hummed pleasantly through my veins, acting as a buffer between me and my bleak thoughts. Tomorrow I would start anew. There had to be a clue, some thread we'd overlooked that could lead to a break in the case. And I would find it. I had to, before the Rune Killer could take another life.

One day at a time, that's all I could manage right now. The doubts crept in, but I pushed them aside, clinging to the instincts that had never let me down before. If I could just stay sharp a little longer, maybe the twisted logic behind these depraved murders would finally unravel.

I stood slowly, fatigue creeping through my body. But my mind still buzzed with a restless energy. I knew sleep would be hard to come by tonight. As was often the case these days, my overactive thoughts kept me awake into the early hours of the morning.

With a sigh, I made my way through the darkened apartment to my office. If rest wasn't coming, I might as well try to make the most of the extra hours. There were files to review, research to do, leads to follow. The hunt for the elusive Rune Killer wasn't over. Not yet. Not as long as I had any fight left in me.

The search continued, as it always would. No matter how heavy my steps grew or how dark my thoughts became, I had to keep going. Move forward. The next clue was out there somewhere, waiting, and I would find it. I had to believe that.

I sat down at my desk and turned on the lamp. The files and notes seemed to look at me reproachfully in the yellow light. So much to do, so far to go. But I wasn't finished yet. No matter how long it took, I would keep fighting. For my brother. For the victims. And for myself. I owed it to all of us.

The rest of the world faded away as I lost myself once again in the details of the case. Searching for the one overlooked clue that could unravel this dark mystery. It was here somewhere, and I would find it. That much I had to believe. The thought of failing, of letting the killer slip through my fingers, sent a chill through me. I clenched my jaw, refusing to let that possibility take root. Giving up was not an option. Not when I'd sacrificed so much. Not when the stakes were so high. I had to see this through, whatever it took. For the lives lost. For the families torn apart. And for the shadow, this case had cast on my own soul. There was no other choice.

CHAPTER THREE

AN OMINOUS CASE

I took a deep breath as I stood in front of the team, surveying the sea of expectant faces gathered in the precinct bullpen. Morning light streamed in through the windows, casting a pale glow over the room as another day of investigating the Rune Killer began.

The anticipation hung heavy, mingling with the aroma of freshly brewed coffee that permeated every corner of the bullpen. Their eyes bored into mine, their faces painted with a mixture of cautious optimism and unease that I knew all too well. They were counting on me to guide them through this labyrinthine case, to unravel the twisted threads the killer had left in his wake. I straightened my shoulders, ready to carry the burden of their trust and lead them through the dark days ahead.

"Alright everyone, let's get started," I said, my voice echoing off the walls of the cramped briefing room. I surveyed the sea of expectant faces before me, noting the dark circles and haggard expressions that mirrored my own. We were all running on fumes, fueled by a potent mix of caffeine and determination.

"I know we're all anxious to find new leads after the murder of Tyler Walsh five nights ago. The brutality of the crime scene has shaken us all, and the community is demanding answers. But first, let's review what we know about the case so far, so that we can move forward with a clear understanding of the facts.

I turned to the whiteboard, which was covered with crime scene photos, maps, and notes about the investigation.

"There have been three victims so far," I began. "Amanda Myers, Christopher Booth, and now Tyler Walsh. All killed in a similarly gruesome manner, with strange runic symbols carved into their flesh."

I tapped on the first image.

"The first victim, Christopher Booth, was found in a remote clearing just outside the city limits." I turned and pointed to the picture of Booth's body sprawled on the ground. "Notice the limbs pinned down with stakes. The killer tore open his back, snapping the ribs outward to resemble bloody wings. This method is known as the "blood eagle" - a brutal Viking execution. Booth's lungs were removed and salted, resulting in death by asphyxiation."

I gestured to the runic symbols carved into his flesh. "Also note the intricate markings on the arms and torso. These appear on all the victims."

Returning to the board, I pointed to the photo of Amanda Myers. "The second victim, Amanda Myers, was discovered deep in Silvergate Forest. Her body was hanging between birch trees, limbs badly mangled from violent wrenching. The coroner's report showed dislocated joints, torn ligaments and muscles from extreme force."

I tapped on the image showing her exposed midsection covered in runes. "More of the distinctive markings were etched across her exposed midsection."

"And finally, victim number three - Tyler Walsh." The picture showed Walsh's body with a large wire cage attached to his torso along with a portable heating element. "Found in an uptown parking garage. The victim's gaping torso was marred by bite and claw marks. Upon examination, it was determined that the rats trapped in the cage had burrowed their way through Mr. Walsh to escape the searing heat of the hot plate."

"The first two victims, Booth and Myers, were both found on the outskirts of town. But Walsh's body turned up here-" I circled a location on the map "-in an uptown parking garage. The change in location is significant. It shows the unsub is evolving, getting bolder."

"And we're no closer to finding out why these people were targeted," Officer Chen said, frustration clear in her voice.

"Not yet," I admitted. "But we've been digging into their backgrounds, their finances, their social connections. There has to be some connection between them that can help us establish a motive."

I put the headshots of the victims side by side.

"Myers was a bank teller, Booth an auto mechanic. And Walsh was a wealthy businessman. No obvious connections between their occupations or social circles that we can see. But I'm hoping forensics will turn up new evidence to connect the dots."

Chief Thompson had been pushing hard for new leads. But so far, the murders seemed random, the mysterious runes our only real clue. We needed a break in the case soon, before the killer struck again.

"What about the physical evidence from the crime scenes?" Officer Ramirez asked.

I shook my head. "Whoever is doing this is covering their tracks well. We didn't find any fingerprints, DNA, or anything else besides the carved symbols. They're meticulous."

"So where does that leave us?" Chen asked.

"Going over every detail with fresh eyes," I said. "Re-interviewing the victims' family and friends. Tracking their digital footprints for any activity that seems unusual or suspicious. If we look hard enough, the connection between these victims is there. We just have to find it."

I watched as my team scribbled furiously on their notepads, hanging on my every word. A change had come over them as I spoke - their posture straightened, their eyes sharpened with rekindled resolve. The very air in the room seemed to hum and spark with possibility, the suffocating despair of dead ends giving way to the invigorating promise of fresh leads to pursue.

"I need every available officer to canvass known associates of the victims," I said. "Somebody out there knows something. We just need to ask the right questions to shake them loose. I know it's painstaking work, but it's our best shot at a lead right now. Let's go out there and find it."

The officers began to gather their things, muttering as they left to follow up on assignments. We were stalled for now, but eventually, even the most meticulous killer would slip up. And when they did, we'd be there, ready to strike. The Rune Killer's days were numbered. They just didn't know it yet.

Determination blazed through my veins, fueling the relentless pursuit that had consumed these long months on the case. No matter how meticulously the killer had tried to hide the truth, my team would dig it out and drag it into the light. It would take every ounce of our collective tenacity and perseverance, but I had no doubt that we were up to the task. This killer would soon learn that we were just getting started.

I rubbed my eyes, the fluorescent lights of the precinct burning into my retinas as I walked back to my desk. The weight of the case seemed to grow heavier with each passing day, and the lack of progress was taking its toll.

Just as I was about to sit down, Officer Chen approached me with a grim expression. "Detective Black, we have another one."

I felt the world fall out from under me. "Where?"

"Abandoned warehouse on the south side. Patrol officers responded to an anonymous tip and found the body. Same M.O. as the others."

I nodded and grabbed my coat. "All right, let's go. O'Malley!" I called to my partner across the bullpen. "We've got a fresh scene. You're with me."

O'Malley looked up from her paperwork, her eyes widening as she took in the news. She quickly gathered her things and joined me as we headed for the car.

The drive to the scene was filled with anticipation, only the intermittent crackle of the police radio breaking the strained silence. My fingers dug into the steering wheel with an iron grip.

"They're not slowing down," I said. "If anything, they seem to be escalating."

O'Malley nodded, her jaw tensing. "We're going to have to catch a break soon. I don't know how much more of this I can take."

I understood the feeling all too well. Each new victim was a reminder of our failure, a life lost because we couldn't stop the killer in time.

We arrived at the warehouse, the flashing lights of the patrol cars casting an eerie glow over the dilapidated building. I parked the car and we made our way inside, ducking under the yellow crime scene tape.

The responding officers were already on the scene, their faces grim as they took in the gruesome sight before them. I approached the officer who was taking notes on his pad.

"What do we know so far?" I asked.

Officer Reynolds shook his head. "Not much. Victim is a Hispanic male, mid-30s. Same symbols carved into his skin as the others. Looks like he's been here a while, judging by the state of decomposition."

He hesitated before adding, "I got to warn you though, this one's... it's bad. Worse than anything we've seen before. Hope you haven't eaten recently."

I nodded, steeling myself for what I was about to see. "I appreciate the warning. Let's take a look."

As we entered the warehouse, the first thing that hit me was the overwhelming stench - the sickly sweet, cloying smell of rotting flesh. Swarms of flies buzzed around the scene, their insistent droning cutting through the heavy silence. In the center of the morose room stood the victim, illuminated by a halo of pale light streaming through a broken window.

He was stripped bare, railroad spikes driven through his limbs. Heavy weights were attached to each spike by rope, giving the victim considerable heft and a constant, agonizing tension on the limbs.

Most horrifying of all was the thick wooden stake driven upward between his legs. It was clear that the increased weight on his limbs had caused him to slowly slide down the stake over time until it fully impaled him, emerging through the empty space of his collarbone.

Dark rivulets of bodily fluids and excrement stained the shaft of the spike, merging into a putrid mass crawling with maggots. The pooling fluids dripped steadily to the ground below, where they mingled with congealed blood.

Runic symbols had been carved into his skin, which now took on a blackened, leathery appearance, obscured in places by decay.

As I studied the body, goosebumps involuntarily spread over my body. It was as if the temperature had dropped ten degrees in an instant. I looked around, trying to locate the source of the draft, but found nothing.

O'Malley noticed my discomfort. "Are you all right?" she asked, concern etched into her face.

I shook my head, trying to clear the strange sensation. "Yeah, I just got a weird feeling. Like someone walked over my grave."

I turned my attention back to the body, pushing aside the unease that had settled in. There would be time to analyze this later. Right now we had a job to do.

I began methodically cataloging the details of the scene, looking for anything that might give us a clue as to the killer's identity or motive. But just like the others, this scene was frustratingly clean. No hair, no fibers, no fingerprints. Just another life snuffed out by a faceless monster.

As I continued to examine the body, my eyes were drawn to the victim's face. Looking closer, I noticed that their mouth seemed to be stuffed with some kind of cloth. Cautiously reaching in with a gloved hand, I began to pull out the wadded material.

As I pulled the gag free, a small metallic object slipped from their mouth and hit the floor with a faint thud. I crouched down and retrieved the object for closer inspection. Holding it up to the light revealed it to be some sort of coin or medallion, tarnished with age.

Strange symbols were etched into its surface, similar to those carved into the victims' skin. My heart raced as I realized what I was holding, a surge of adrenaline electrifying my body. This coin represented the first real piece of evidence we had found, a tangible link to the twisted individual behind these heinous crimes.

I turned to O'Malley and held up the coin. "Bag this. I want it sent to the lab for analysis as soon as possible."

She nodded, took the coin, and placed it in an evidence bag. "You think it's significant?"

"It has to be," I said, my mind already racing with possibilities. "The killer left this for a reason. We just have to figure out what it means."

A glimmer of hope ignited within me, but it was restrained by a looming sense of unease. Even as I savored this small victory, a chilling realization crept over me-we had barely begun to unravel the dark and sinister web that had ensnared us, a mystery far more complex and malevolent than we could possibly fathom.

I paced the length of my office, my mind racing as I tried to make sense of the new evidence. The coin found on the latest victim was a tantalizing clue, but its meaning remained frustratingly elusive.

A knock on the door interrupted my thoughts. "Come in," I called, turning to face the entrance.

O'Malley and Jones entered, their faces etched with the same weariness and determination I felt. They had been working around the clock, chasing down leads and interviewing witnesses, but so far we had come up empty.

"Any luck with the coin?" O'Malley asked, her voice filled with hope.

I shook my head. "Not yet. The lab is still analyzing it, but the preliminary report indicates it's old. Really old. Like, ancient civilization old."

Jones frowned. "What would our killer be doing with an artifact like that?"

"That's precisely what we need to find out," I mused, stroking my jaw thoughtfully. "But there's no doubt it has some significance. Could it be connected to what's driving them?"

I walked over to the whiteboard, where photos of the victims and crime scenes were pinned up in a macabre collage. The faces of the dead stared back at me, their eyes haunted and accusing, as if demanding justice from beyond the grave. I tapped my finger against the image of the latest victim, a young man whose life had been brutally cut short by the Rune Killer's twisted compulsions. His pale, lifeless features seemed to plead with me, begging for answers that remained frustratingly out of reach.

"Let's go over what we know about the victims again. There must be some connection we're missing."

O'Malley stepped forward, her eyes scanning the board. "Well, we know they were all killed in different parts of the city. Different ages, genders, races, socioeconomic backgrounds. No obvious connections between them."

"But the killer chooses them for a reason," I said, my brow furrowed in concentration. "The locations, the staging of the bodies, the runes carved into their skin. It's all too theatrical not to be part of some larger plan."

Jones nodded. "The question is, what is that plan? What is the killer trying to accomplish?"

I sighed, the strain of the case mounting evermore. "I can't say for sure, but I sense it's something big, something that goes beyond these murders."

I turned back to the board, my eyes falling on the photos of the runes. "I think the key is in these symbols. They're not just random carvings. They have to mean something."

O'Malley crossed her arms. "But what? We've run them through every database we have access to. No hits."

"Then we need to widen our search," I said, a glimmer of an idea forming in my mind. "We need to look beyond our usual sources. Consult experts in ancient languages, symbology, maybe even the occult."

Jones raised an eyebrow. "The occult? I know these killings stink of the old world, but do you think this could be ritualistic in nature?"

I shrugged. "I'm not ruling anything out at this point. We have to be open to all possibilities, no matter how strange they may seem."

O'Malley nodded, her expression pensive. "It's worth a try. I can contact some of the local heads of academia and see if they know anyone who might be able to help."

"Good idea," I said. "In the meantime, let's keep digging into the victims' backgrounds. There's got to be something we're not seeing. A connection that will lead us to the killer."

Jones and O'Malley murmured their agreement, and we set to work, poring over case files and evidence reports. The hours ticked by in a blur as we chased down every possible lead, no matter how tenuous. My vision blurred as I stared at the endless pages, the typed words transforming into a blurry sea of black on white. Exhaustion tugged at every fiber of my being, urging me to rest, but I pushed on. I couldn't afford to lose momentum, not with an unhinged killer roaming the streets unchecked, ready to strike again at any moment.

O'Malley stifled a yawn as she scrolled through the coroner's report for what must have been the tenth time, her eyes bloodshot from staring at the screen. Jones leaned back in his chair and rubbed his temples, as if to stave off the headache that came from a day of intense concentration. I probably looked as haggard as everyone else, but I couldn't rest. Not yet.

"There must be something we're missing here," I muttered, more to myself than to my colleagues. Some small detail that would blow this case wide open. But every theory or hunch seemed to hit a brick wall, every lead was a dead end.

As the clock struck midnight, the precinct grew eerily quiet. The hustle and bustle of the day shift gave way to the solemn quiet of the graveyard shift. In the distance, I could hear the dispatcher's steady intonations over the crackling radio, punctuated by the occasional static-laden response from a patrol unit. The coffee in my mug had long since gone cold, but I took a sip anyway, hoping the bitter liquid would sharpen my weary mind.

I wasn't going to give this killer the satisfaction of outsmarting us. There had to be an answer buried somewhere in this mountain of crime scene photos and paperwork.

The fading daylight filtering through the blinds cast an amber haze over the scattered files and photographs that littered my desk. I massaged my temples, trying to knead away the throbbing headache that had taken root behind my eyes. Each passing hour seemed to tighten the knot of frustration inside me as the trail grew colder and the likelihood of another body turning up increased.

Sighing heavily, I reached for the bottle of bourbon I had stashed in my bottom drawer, hoping a quick swig would provide a brief respite from the oppressive futility gnawing at my resolve.

I glanced up at the whiteboard, my eyes tracing the faces of the victims. I refused to give up. I owed it to them, to their families, to find this killer.

"I will find them," I whispered, my voice barely audible in the silence of the office. "I'm going to make them pay for what they've done."

CHAPTER FOUR

A FLIP OF A COIN

The glare of the morning sun assaulted my eyes as O'Malley and I stepped out of the station. I squinted, raised a hand to shield my face, and took a deep breath of the crisp autumn air. The chill helped clear my head, shaking off the cobwebs of a long night spent poring over case files and dead ends.

"Where to, boss?" O'Malley asked, her voice still raspy with fatigue.

"One of your contacts got back to us, put us in contact with Dr. Kensington, we're going to her office," I replied, fishing the car keys out of my pocket. "She's expecting us at nine."

O'Malley nodded and stifled a yawn as she climbed into the passenger seat. I slid behind the wheel, the familiar scent of worn leather and motor oil enveloping me like an old friend. As I turned the key in the ignition, the engine sputtered to life, its steady rumble a comforting constant in a world turned upside down.

We navigated the morning traffic in silence, each lost in our own thoughts. The city was just beginning to wake up, the sidewalks slowly filling with bleary-eyed commuters clutching their morning coffee like a lifeline. I watched them as we passed, wondering how many of them had any idea of the darkness lurking just below the surface of their orderly lives.

As we approached the university campus, O'Malley spoke up, breaking the silence. "I've heard about Dr. Kensington, during my college days," she said, her tone thoughtful. "I hope she can help us make sense of these runes."

I nodded, feeling a flicker of hope in my chest. "Let's hope her input can bring some clarity to this mess," I said, pulling into the parking lot outside the History Department.

We made our way inside, the hallways eerily quiet this early in the morning. Our footsteps echoed off the polished tile as we navigated the maze of offices and classrooms, following the signs to Dr. Kensington's office.

When we reached her door, I raised my hand to knock, but hesitated, suddenly unsure of what to expect. I glanced over at O'Malley, who gave me an encouraging nod, her eyes bright with anticipation.

I rapped my knuckles against the wood, the sound sharp and startling in the silence of the hallway. A moment later, the door swung open to reveal a woman in her early forties, her auburn hair pulled back in a loose bun, her green eyes sharp and inquisitive behind wire-rimmed glasses.

"Detective Black, Detective O'Malley," she said, her voice warm and welcoming. "Please, come in."

We stepped inside, taking in the cluttered office, every surface piled high with books and artifacts, the walls lined with shelves overflowing with ancient tomes and scrolls. The air was filled with the scent of old paper and dust, a testament to the countless hours Dr. Kensington must have spent immersed in her studies.

"Thank you for seeing us on such short notice, Dr. Kensington," I said, extending my hand in greeting.

Her handshake was firm and confident as she took mine. "Please, call me Laura," she insisted, motioning for us to sit down. "And it's no trouble at all. I'm always happy to help the police in any way I can."

I pulled a collection of photographs and the strange coin from my coat and arranged them on the gleaming surface of the desk. The pictures, depicting the harsh and disturbing runic symbols, stood out in sharp contrast to the varnished wood. "We were wondering if you could help us decipher these," I explained, hoping her expertise would shed some light on the perplexing case.

Laura leaned forward, her brow furrowed as she studied the symbols, her fingers tracing the intricate lines and curves. I watched her closely, searching for any flicker of recognition or understanding in her expression.

After a long moment, she looked up, her eyes meeting mine. "I've never seen anything like this before," she said, her voice tinged with a mixture of fascination and unease. "But I can tell you one thing for certain - these are no ordinary symbols. There's a meaning to them, a resonance I can almost feel emanating from the page."

A sinister feeling settled in the pit of my stomach. If Dr. Kensington, with all her knowledge and expertise, was unsettled by these runes, then we might be dealing with something far more dangerous than I had imagined.

"Can you decipher them?" O'Malley asked, leaning forward, her eyes locked on Laura's face.

Laura hesitated, her eyes flicking back to the photographs. "It will take some time," she said, her voice measured and cautious. "I'll have to consult my books, cross-reference the symbols with other ancient languages and iconography. But I'll do my best to discern their meaning. Please, have a seat."

Dr. Kensington had come highly recommended by O'Malley's academic consultant as one of the country's leading authorities on ancient languages and symbology. If anyone could decipher the meaning of the runes etched into the victims and this coin, it was her. The key to stopping this ruthless killer may very well lie in translating these arcane messages they seemed intent on leaving behind.

O'Malley and I settled into the chairs, the leather creaking under our weight. "Make yourself comfortable O'Malley, it looks like we're going to be here for a while."

I leaned forward in my seat, studying Dr. Kensington's face intently as she examined the runes and the ancient coin under her desk lamp. The warm glow cast dancing shadows across her forehead, accentuating the look of intense concentration in her piercing green eyes.

Beside me, Officer Jenna O'Malley shifted restlessly, the old leather chair creaking with her movement. I knew she was as eager as I was to hear whatever insight Dr. Kensington could provide about the strange artifact we had found inside our latest victim. The body of a young man, carved with the same cryptic runes as the others. This coin was our first real piece of tangible evidence, and possibly the key to unlocking the entire mystery.

Dr. Kensington adjusted the magnification on her desk lens, peering even closer at the coin, which she held delicately between her latex-gloved fingers. She had already spent several hours examining every minute detail of the ancient coin, but had yet to utter a word about her assessment. The only sounds that broke the heavy silence were the occasional scratch of a pen on paper as she jotted down notes, and the ticking of the antique clock on her office wall.

My eyes wandered to the rich mahogany bookshelves that lined the walls, filled to overflowing with leather-bound tomes and artifacts of antiquity. This office was a treasure trove of history and hidden knowledge, and I had no doubt that if the answers to our strange clue were to be found, they would be unearthed here.

O'Malley caught my eye, one eyebrow raised in an unspoken question. I gave a slight shake of my head. As much as we might wish otherwise, brilliance could not be rushed. We had to be patient and allow Dr. Kensington to complete her assessment thoroughly and methodically. Lives depended on it.

With a soft sigh, O'Malley settled back into her seat. She began drumming her fingers lightly on the armrest, betraying her restless energy and simmering impatience. I resisted the urge to check my watch, keeping my eyes on the doctor's gracefully bowed head. Her auburn hair cascaded over her face as she pored over the relic with a singular focus, the very picture of intense concentration.

The office was bathed in the soft glow of sunlight streaming through the windows. The light caught the dust in the air, dancing like snowflakes in December. This gentle illumination bathed the room, the atmosphere was subdued, almost reverent, befitting the priceless knowledge contained within these shelves.

Finally, after long hours that seemed to stretch into eternity, Dr. Kensington sat up. Carefully setting the coin down, she removed her gloves and glasses before turning her gaze to meet ours. Her keen intellect was evident in those piercing green eyes.

"Well, detectives, I believe I've gleaned all I can from the initial examination of the artifact," she began, her voice subdued yet authoritative. "There is still much to be deciphered, but this is certainly a significant clue."

O'Malley and I shared a charged look. This was the first real break in the case.

"What can you tell us, Doctor?" I asked, leaning intently over her desk.

Dr. Kensington folded her hands, her brow furrowed in concentration as she gathered her thoughts. "These markings," Laura began, her voice barely above a whisper, "they appear to be associated with the Zarranath culture of 25th century BC Mesopotamia."

Dr. Kensington's words set my brain on fire, my synapses firing frantically as I tried to make sense of them. Runes and symbols tied to an ancient civilization were found here on the streets of Silvergate. I exchanged a grave look with O'Malley, seeing my own grim realization echoing in her dark eyes. This case had just taken on a far more ominous tone.

"What can you tell us about the Zarranath people, Dr. Kensington?" I asked, my voice heavy with urgency. "What were their beliefs, their practices?"

Laura took a deep breath, as if bracing herself to delve into the dark history. "Well, without further research," she began slowly, "the only thing I know about the Zarranath is their chief deity, Solanar. Solanar was primarily associated with kingship, war, and punishment."

She hesitated, her gaze dropping to the ancient coin in her hand. "Again, without further research, this is what I can offer you now."

Laura paused, her fingers lightly tracing the cryptic symbols etched into the coin. "But I do know this symbol," she said, a hint of recognition flickering in her eyes. "It means balance."

A cold knot of dread settled in the pit of my stomach. Balance of what, the brutality of the murders, the runic symbols carved into their flesh... it all began to make even less sense. Beside me, O'Malley shifted forward in her seat, her gaze intent.

"So these murders, you think they're connected to the Zarranath? That the killer is somehow channeling that ancient civilization after all these centuries?"

Dr. Kensington nodded grimly. "It would appear so, though I would have to do more research to be certain. Some cultures have a way of

surviving, their beliefs and practices are passed down in secret from
generation to generation. It's also possible that someone has adopted the
Zarranath culture and is now performing their bloody rituals in the streets
of our city."

I leaned forward, my voice full of urgency. "This is the first I've heard
of the Zarranath. How many people would know about them? You had
to go through hours of research just to get a name?"

Dr. Kensington sighed, her eyes reflecting the enormity of her
discovery. "Very few, I would imagine. Zarranathism is an almost
forgotten piece of history, buried in the annals of ancient Mesopotamia. It
took me hours of poring over obscure texts and artifacts to piece together
even the basics. Whoever is behind these activities either has access to
incredibly rare knowledge or has stumbled upon something they can't
fully comprehend."

I scrubbed a hand over my face, feeling the rough scratch of stubble
against my palm. This revelation brought with it a whole new level of
darkness, of depravity. We weren't just hunting a serial killer anymore -
we might be facing retribution from ancient times.

O'Malley reached for her phone, her expression hardening with
determination. "I'm going to reach out to some of my other contacts
in academia, see if anyone has come across references to 'balance' and
the Zarranath people in their research. If this culture is back, we need to
know everything we can about their history, their methods. We need to
find a way to stop them before they kill again."

I nodded my agreement, my mind already racing with our next steps.
We'd have to dig deep into the city's underbelly, following every lead
and whispered rumor until we uncovered the truth behind these brutal
murders. The thought of the dark paths this investigation might lead us
down filled me with a grim sense of foreboding, but I pushed it aside. We
had a duty to the victims, to the people of Silvergate, to see this through
to the end.

As O'Malley began typing messages to her network of scholars and researchers, I turned back to Dr. Kensington. "We're going to need your help on this, Doctor. Your expertise in ancient languages and symbology could be the key to solving this mystery, to stopping the Rune Killer before they claim any more innocent lives."

Laura met my gaze, her green eyes shining with a fierce purpose that matched my own. "Of course, Detective. I'll do everything I can to help you with your investigation. This darkness cannot be allowed to spread. We must bring it to light and end it."

A flicker of hope ignited within me at her words, renewing my sense of determination. Together, we would find a way to stop this killer, to end their bloody reign of terror.

But even as that determination settled over me like armor, an uneasiness slithered up and coiled tightly in my chest, a sense that we were about to descend into a darkness beyond anything we had ever faced before.

As I met O'Malley's eyes across the table, I saw my own grim resolve reflected back at me. We were about to step off a cliff, into an abyss of secrets and ancient, unspeakable horrors. But we would face it together, armed with the strength of our convictions and the knowledge that we were fighting for the very soul of our city.

Taking a deep breath, I nodded to Dr. Kensington, silently signaling our readiness to begin. The hunt for the truth begins now, and may God have mercy on us all.

As O'Malley and I stepped out of Dr. Kensington's office, my mind was reeling from the revelations she had shared. An ancient civilization, possibly resurrected in the heart of Silvergate, committing brutal murders in the name of some twisted sense of divine balance? It was almost too terrifying to believe, like something out of a horror novel rather than real life.

I glanced over at O'Malley as we made our way back to the squad car, trying to gauge her reaction. She looked as shocked as I felt, her brow furrowed and her lips pressed into a thin line.

"This is... a lot to take in," she said, her voice strained. "I mean, an ancient religion? Operating right under our noses, carrying out these horrific murders?"

I nodded grimly, slid into the driver's seat, and started the engine. "I know. It sounds too bizarre to be true. But Dr. Kensington seems convinced, and she's the expert. We should take her advice seriously."

O'Malley let out a heavy sigh and rubbed her temples as if to ward off an impending headache. "I just keep thinking about the victims. The symbols carved into their skin, the inhumane ways they were killed... it's like something out of a nightmare."

I could only nod in agreement, my thoughts drifting back to the crime scene photos, the blank eyes of the dead staring back at me from the glossy prints. I had seen a lot of brutality in my years on the force, but this case was unlike anything I had ever encountered. The sheer savagery of the murders, combined with the cryptic symbols, and now the revelation of the possible involvement of an ancient civilization, made my head spin.

We rode back to the station in silence, each of us lost in our own dark thoughts. The weight of the case hung heavy in the air, a presence that seemed to fill the confines of the car. O'Malley's anger was obvious, her hands clenched tightly around the wheel, knuckles strained, jaw clenched in barely contained rage. It wasn't until we pulled into the parking lot, the familiar sight of the Silvergate Police Department looming in front of us, that she spoke again, her voice fixed with conviction.

"We have to stop them, James. Whatever it takes, we have to put an end to this." There was a steely edge to her words, a decisiveness I recognized all too well. It was the same spirit that had driven me through countless investigations, the unwavering commitment that had become the cornerstone of my life.

I met her gaze and saw the same fierce drive burning in her eyes that I felt in my own heart. At that moment, I knew we were in this together, two warriors united in a common cause. "We will," I promised her. "We're going to find the sick bastard responsible for this, and we're going to bring them to justice. No matter what it takes."

The words hung in the air between us, a solemn vow that we both knew would be tested in the days and weeks to come. As we got out of the car and made our way to the station, I felt a renewed sense of purpose, a grim determination to see this through to the end. The Rune-Killer had picked the wrong city, and the wrong detectives to mess with. And one way or another, we were going to make damn sure they paid for their crimes.

With that, we made our way into the precinct, ready to dive headfirst into the darkness that awaited us. The familiar scent of stale coffee and musty files assaulted my nostrils as we stepped through the doors, a grim reminder of the countless late nights and dead ends that littered our path. The Rune Killer's reign of terror ended here, in the hallowed halls of the Silvergate Police Department. And I'd be damned if I was going to let them slip through our fingers again.

CHAPTER FIVE

HISTORICAL REVELATIONS

The flickering fluorescent lights of the bullpen greeted us as O'Malley and I stepped off the elevator, their harsh glare a stark contrast to the warm, scholarly ambiance of Dr. Kensington's office. The air buzzed with the usual cacophony of ringing phones, clacking keyboards, and muted conversations, the soundtrack of another day in the life of a Silvergate detective.

I made my way to Chief Thompson's office, O'Malley trailing behind me. I rapped my knuckles on the frosted glass of his door, waiting for the gruff "come in" before turning the handle and stepping inside.

Thompson looked up from the stack of papers on his desk, his steely eyes narrowing as he took in the triumphant expression on my face. "Black. O'Malley. I take it you have an update on the case?"

I nodded, dropping into one of the chairs across from his desk and leaning forward. "We just got back from meeting with Dr. Laura Kensington. She's a historian who specializes in ancient civilizations and occult practices."

Thompson raised an eyebrow, his interest piqued. "So? What did she have to say?"

I couldn't keep the note of satisfaction out of my voice as I replied, "She's convinced that the symbols carved into the victims' bodies are connected to an ancient Mesopotamian civilization. One whose primary deity, Solanar, was associated with war, justice, and order."

O'Malley cut in, her tone more measured than mine. "Dr. Kensington is still working to decipher the exact meaning of the symbols, but she's confident they're authentic. Not some tribal tattoo design you'd find on a drunken frat boy downtown."

Thompson leaned back in his chair, fingers laced under his chin as he absorbed this new information. "So we're dealing with some kind of religious nutjob, is that it? A fanatic waging some kind of twisted holy jihad?"

I shrugged, a wry smile tugging at the corner of my mouth. "That's the theory, anyway. I know it sounds like a bunch of, what did you call it, hocus-pocus nonsense, but Dr. Kensington seems to know her stuff. And it's the best lead we've got so far."

Thompson grunted, his expression thoughtful. "All right. Run with it, see where it takes you. But don't get too caught up in the mumbo jumbo, Black. At the end of the day, we're dealing with a killer, plain and simple. Find them and bring them in."

I nodded and rose from my seat. "Understood, Chief. We'll keep you posted on any developments."

As O'Malley and I left Thompson's office, I couldn't help but feel a sense of satisfaction mixed with a healthy dose of apprehension. We were finally making progress on the case, but the implications of Dr. Kensington's findings were unsettling, to say the least.

As I sat back down at my desk, ready to tackle the mountain of paperwork and research that awaited me, a renewed sense of determination surged through me. No matter how dark or bizarre this case might become, I was ready to see it through to the end - to bring the killer to justice and give the victims' families the closure they deserved.

I glanced over at O'Malley, who was already typing away at her computer, her brow furrowed in concentration. Together, we would solve this mystery and end this reign of terror.

I settled into my well-worn leather chair, which fit my body like a trusty old baseball glove. I pored over the murder victims' files, searching the pages for any common characteristics that might shed light on the killer's intentions. The unfortunate souls whose lives had been cut short were a diverse bunch from all walks of life. At first glance, there was no clear link to tie them together.

With a resigned sigh, I pulled out the old yearbooks we had collected in the early stages of the investigation. Desperation had me grasping at straws, but I couldn't afford to leave any stone unturned. The smell of aging paper filled my nostrils as I opened the first yearbook and began flipping through the pages, searching for any familiar names or faces. My frustration grew with each turn of the page, the faint sound of crumpling paper echoing in my ears as I searched in vain for anything that might jump out at me.

With another heavy sigh, I pushed the first yearbook aside and reached for the second, its cover cool and smooth beneath my fingertips. My hope was fading, but I forced myself to continue, refusing to give up on even the slimmest of leads. As I carefully flipped through the pages, I focused on the student life and organization sections, hoping for a clue that would break this case wide open. And then, in a seemingly mundane list of extracurricular activities, something caught my eye: a club name that looked vaguely familiar, its letters slightly faded but still legible against the yellowed background.

I reached back for the first book, my heart pounding in my chest as I frantically flipped through the pages one more time. And there it was, staring back at me in stark black and white. I rubbed my eyes, barely daring to believe it. Could this be the thread we had been missing? The key to unraveling this whole sordid affair? I rummaged through my desk, pulling out more yearbooks and sending papers flying in my haste. I flipped through them quickly, my fingers trembling with anticipation as I scanned each page for confirmation of my suspicions.

There it was, hidden in plain sight within the pages of those old yearbooks. Each of our victims had, at some point, been a member of the same school club - the Film and Media Club. My heart raced as I cross-referenced the details, the pieces of the puzzle finally falling into place. Different schools, different years, but always the same club, like a sinister thread running through their lives, connecting them in ways none of them could have imagined.

Was someone out to get these former members? Was there some dark secret or unresolved grudge that had followed them into adulthood, a ghost of the past that refused to stay buried? This group had bound them together in a way I hadn't expected, in a school club of all things. The questions swirled in my head, each more unsettling than the last, as I struggled with the realization that this case was far more complex and twisted than I had ever imagined.

I looked up as O'Malley approached my desk, a grim expression on her face. "I just got off the phone with one of my contacts. He's never heard of the Zarranath religion before. He's assured me that he'll dig into his archives to see if he can find any information that might help us."

I nodded, feeling a flicker of hope at this potential new lead. "Good. We're going to need all the help we can get on this."

O'Malley sat on the edge of my desk, her eyes wandering over the scattered files and crime scene photos. "I keep thinking about what Dr. Kensington said, about how these cultures have a way of persisting through the centuries. It's like they're some kind of malignant growth, festering in the shadows, waiting for the right moment to resurface."

I sighed and leaned forward, resting my elbows on the desk. "And now they've chosen Silvergate as their hunting ground. But we're not going to let them turn our city into their own personal slaughterhouse.

We're going to find them and we're going to stop them. Whatever it takes."

O'Malley met my gaze, her eyes hardening with resolve. "Whatever it takes," she echoed, her voice ringing with the same fierce determination I felt in my own heart.

A sense of dread filled my stomach as we turned our attention back to the files, delving deeper into the world of the Zarranaths. I had dealt with scumbags and thugs in my time on the force, but religious zealots were a different animal altogether. The darkness we were uncovering felt overwhelming, but I knew we had no choice but to press on and follow the case wherever it led.

The faint glow of my computer screen was the only light in the bullpen as the sun dipped below the horizon, casting long shadows across the desks and filing cabinets. O'Malley and I had spent hours poring over old files and police reports, our eyes bleary and our minds racing with the implications of what we'd discovered.

It had started as a hunch, a nagging feeling in the back of my mind that there had to be some connection between the victims beyond their shared membership in a random school club. And as we dug deeper, combing through their email records and social media accounts, a pattern began to emerge.

Each of the victims had received an invitation to join a historical forum, a seemingly innocuous online community dedicated to discussing the past. But as we delved into the forum's archives, we found that it was far from a harmless hobby. The deeper we dug, the more disturbing the content became, revealing a sinister undercurrent that ran through every thread and every post.

The forum was a breeding ground for conspiracy theories and revisionist history, a place where crackpots and zealots could spout their twisted ideologies without fear of censure. Wild-eyed fanatics preached about ancient cults and forgotten gods, while pseudo-intellectuals twisted historical facts to suit their own nefarious agendas. It was a veritable snake pit of misinformation and delusion, and I felt my skin crawl as I scrolled through the endless pages of vitriol and madness.

And at the center of it all was one name that kept popping up: Ethan Ward. The name seemed to be whispered with a mixture of awe and fear, a dark figure lurking in the shadows of every conversation. I couldn't shake the feeling that this Ward character was somehow the key to unraveling the whole sordid mess, the puppet master pulling the strings behind the scenes.

I leaned back in my chair and rubbed my temples, trying to make sense of what we'd discovered. Ethan Ward was a local historian, a man with a reputation for being brilliant but troubled. He'd been involved in a number of controversial projects over the years, including a book that claimed to expose the dark secrets of Silvergate's founding families.

But what really got my attention was his personal history. Ward had lost his wife in a brutal murder some years back, a crime that was never solved, the prime suspect released after intense backlash. The case had been a media circus, with rumors of police corruption and a cover-up.

I couldn't help but wonder if there was a connection between Ward's tragedy and his obsession with the forum. Had he turned to this online community as a way to cope with his grief, to find some sense of purpose in a world that had taken everything from him?

Determined to dig deeper, I gathered my notes and made my way to O'Malley's desk. Her eyes flickered up from her own pile of paperwork as I approached.

"O'Malley, I've found something that might be worth looking into," I said, dropping a file containing everything I had on Ward.

She looked at the file, then back at me. "Ethan Ward?" she asked, raising an eyebrow.

"Yeah," I replied. "The more I dig, the more his name keeps coming up. I feel like there's something there, but I need another set of eyes on this."

O'Malley leaned forward, opened the file, and scanned its contents. "He's been involved in some shady projects, and his wife was murdered years ago... unsolved, of course." She looked up, her expression pensive. "You think his personal tragedy could be connected to what's happening now?"

"Possibly. Maybe he's been seeking some kind of twisted justice ever since," I said. "But we need more than speculation. We need to dig into Ward's history. Find out who he interacts with, who might have influenced him, and see if there's any concrete connection to our victims."

O'Malley nodded. "I'll start pulling records and see if I can find any overlaps. Maybe there's something we missed."

As we worked late into the night, the office grew quiet, except for the rustling of papers and the hum of the computer. We pieced together Ward's timeline, tracing his steps through the years.

After hours of searching, I found a record that piqued my curiosity. "O'Malley, take a look at this," I said, pointing to a document. "Ward is mentoring a young researcher named Andrew Oswald. They collaborated on several projects related to ancient rituals and justice systems."

O'Malley frowned and leaned over to examine the file. "Oswald... wasn't he connected to a recent discovery of some ancient artifacts?"

"Exactly," I said. "And these artifacts could match some of the symbols we found at the crime scenes. If Ward influenced Oswald, it could tie him to the murders."

O'Malley looked up, her eyes reflecting a mixture of determination and frustration. "It's a lead, but it's still not enough," she said, gesturing to the scattered files and printouts that littered our desks. "The connection between Ward, Oswald, and the victims is tenuous at best. We need more evidence if we're going to follow this lead."

I sighed, knowing that she was right. As much as my gut told me that Ward was involved somehow, we couldn't afford to make any mistakes. Not with a case this high profile, not with the media and the department breathing down our necks. Every move we made was being scrutinized, and one misstep could unravel the entire investigation.

"Okay," I said, pushing myself to my feet, my joints aching from hours spent hunched over the files. "Let's call it a day. We'll come back fresh in the morning, see if we can dig up anything else on Ward, Oswald, or the forum." I stretched, releasing the hours of exhaustion that had settled into my bones.

O'Malley nodded, her expression grim. "I'll reach out to some of my contacts in tech, Officer Chen has a knack for digital forensics, see if she can't help us track down the forum administrators. Maybe she can give us a better idea of who's been active on the site and when."

As we gathered our things and headed for the exit, I couldn't shake the feeling that we were on the cusp of something big. The big picture was starting to come into focus before my eyes, but there were still so many unanswered questions.

Who was behind the board, and what was their endgame? Was Ward himself a victim, caught up in something he couldn't control? Or was he the mastermind, using the forum to recruit others to his twisted cause? I didn't have the answers, but I knew one thing for certain - I would use every ounce of my hard-earned skills to uncover the truth.

As I walked into the precinct with Detective Jenna O'Malley, my thoughts swirled with the puzzling clues we'd uncovered the day before. The ancient symbols, cryptic messages, and possible connection to Ethan Ward formed a confusing web of intrigue that consumed my mind. The musty scent of old case files mixed with the bitter aroma of freshly brewed coffee, creating a familiar atmosphere that both comforted and invigorated me.

O'Malley and I exchanged a quick glance, silently acknowledging the challenging journey that lay ahead as we made our way to our desks amidst the clamor of the bullpen. Keyboards clacked and hushed conversations hummed, filling the air with a familiar buzz of activity. The ever-present lights overhead cast a harsh glow, illuminating the determined faces of our fellow officers as they worked tirelessly to bring justice to the streets of Silvergate.

Detective Theo Ramirez, a respected colleague and seasoned veteran, looked up from his desk as we entered. He had been going through a stack of case files, his brow furrowed in concentration, the lines on his face telling the story of countless late nights and hard-fought battles. When he noticed us, a flicker of concern crossed his face, his dark eyes glinting with a mixture of curiosity and apprehension.

"Morning, Detectives," Ramirez greeted us, his voice carrying a note of genuine interest. He rose from his chair, the leather squeaking beneath him, and approached us with a steady gait. "I couldn't help but overhear your discussion yesterday about the case you're working on. It sounds like it's turning into quite a mystery."

I nodded, my forehead wrinkled with worry lines, the product of weeks spent wrestling with the demands of this investigation. "It is," I admitted, my voice strained with exhaustion. "We're still trying to piece it all together. The symbols, the connection to this Ethan Ward individual... there's a lot to unravel."

Ramirez leaned against the edge of O'Malley's desk, his arms crossed over his chest, the fabric of his suit jacket stretched taut over his broad shoulders. "I've been in this game as long as you have, Black," he said, his tone contemplative. "And I've learned that sometimes the key to cracking a case lies in the smallest details, the ones that others might overlook."

O'Malley raised an eyebrow, her green eyes sparkling with intrigue. "What are you suggesting, Ramirez?"

Ramirez reached out, tapping the folder in my hand with a finger. "Do you mind if I take a look at what you've got so far? Sometimes a fresh perspective can help shed new light on things."

I hesitated for a moment, my grip on the folder tightening. It wasn't that I didn't trust Ramirez - he was one of the most respected detectives in the precinct - but the case had become deeply personal to me, and I was reluctant to let anyone else in. But as I met Ramirez's gaze, I saw a glimmer of understanding, a recognition of the burden I carried.

With a sigh, I handed him the folder and watched as Ramirez opened it and began to scan its contents. He lingered on a photograph of an ancient coin we had recently discovered, his eyes narrowing as he studied the intricate lines and curves.

"You know," he said slowly, his voice barely above a whisper, "I vaguely remember seeing something like this during a case I worked on years ago. It was a tough one, I never quite figured out the meaning behind those symbols."

O'Malley leaned forward, elbows on the desk, chin resting on interlaced fingers. "Do you think there might be a connection?" she asked, her tone hopeful.

Ramirez shrugged, his gaze still fixed on the image. "It's hard to say for certain, but it's worth looking into. The human mind has a way of drawing connections between seemingly unrelated things. But there's something familiar about these markings, an echo, like catching the scent of your grandmother's cooking".

He looked up, his eyes meeting mine, a flicker of intrigue passing between us. "Tell you what," he said, his voice stronger now, filled with intent. "Let me dig through some of my old case files and see if I can find anything that might be relevant to your investigation. If there's even a chance that my backlog of cases could shed some light, I'll pursue it."

I felt a wave of gratitude wash over me, a sense of relief that we had an ally in our corner. "That would be great, Ramirez," I said, my voice thick with emotion. "If you discover anything that might help us, let us know immediately."

Ramirez nodded, a small smile tugging at the corners of his mouth. "Of course," he assured us, his tone sincere. "I will do everything I can to help you solve this case. After all, we're all in this together. The pursuit of justice is a shared responsibility."

With that, Ramirez handed the file back to me and clapped a hand on my shoulder, a gesture of solidarity and support. "I'll get started right away," he said. "In the meantime, keep up the good work, and don't hesitate to reach out if you need anything else."

As Ramirez walked away, his footsteps echoing on the scuffed linoleum floor, O'Malley and I shared a look of appreciation, feeling a sense of renewed hope that we might be able to unravel the tangled threads of this perplexing case. Knowing that we had an experienced detective like Ramirez on our side, willing to share his expertise and insight, lifted our spirits and strengthened our resolve.

With renewed focus, O'Malley and I returned to our work, the weight of the investigation still on our shoulders, but now tempered by the knowledge that we were not alone in our pursuit of the truth. The precinct hummed with activity around us, a reminder that even in the darkest of times, there were those willing to fight for justice, to be a light in the darkness.

And as I delved back into the case files, my mind racing with theories and possibilities, I couldn't shake the feeling that somewhere, amidst the chaos and confusion, the key to unlocking this mystery lay waiting to be discovered. With Ramirez's help and the unwavering support of my fellow officers, I knew we would stop at nothing to catch this killer and restore peace to the streets of Silvergate.

CHAPTER SIX

ANOTHER MURDER

The shrill ring of my cell phone cut through the heavy silence that had settled over the evidence room like a suffocating blanket. I glanced at the screen, my heart plummeting and settling somewhere deep in my midsection as I saw the number for dispatch flashing insistently, almost mockingly. Black's piercing blue eyes met mine, a knowing look passing between us as I answered the call with a growing sense of foreboding.

"This is O'Malley," I said, my voice steady despite the fear that coiled in my gut like a venomous snake.

The dispatcher's words confirmed our worst fears, each syllable hitting me like a physical blow: another body had been found in the financial district, the scene bearing all the hallmarks of the Rune Killer's twisted handiwork. The gravity of the situation sent adrenaline coursing through my veins. I jotted down the address with trembling fingers, my hand shaking slightly as I ended the call.

"We've got another one," my announcement rang out with a numb detachment that chilled me to the core, the words tasting like ashes in my mouth.

Black nodded grimly, his jaw clenched, the muscles in his neck straining with barely contained tension. "Let's go," he said, his voice deep and determined, a steely resolve in his eyes that I clung to like a lifeline as we prepared to face the horrors that awaited us.

I hastily gathered my things, my fingers still trembling slightly as I fumbled with my notepad and keys. The oppressive silence in the room was broken only by the rustling of our movements, the very air seeming to vibrate with the grim urgency of our task. I glanced over at Black, noting the intensity etched into every line of his face, his eyes hard and flinty with determination.

His rigid posture and balled fists spoke volumes about the toll this case was taking on him. As we walked purposefully toward the door, I couldn't stop the flood of dark thoughts swirling in my head - vivid flashes of the savage cruelty we had witnessed, images seared into my brain and haunting my every waking moment. I shuddered, steeling myself for the horrors I knew we were about to face once again.

The sheer number of victims, the gruesome details of their deaths - it all added up to a horrific dream we couldn't wake from, like layers of a painting revealing nothing but blood-soaked horror. But there was no time to dwell on that now, not with another life brutally cut short and a killer still on the loose, leaving a trail of blood and runes in his wake. We had a job to do, and I'd be damned if I'd let anything get in the way of bringing this sick bastard to justice.

The crime scene was a nightmare come to life. The stench overwhelmed me as I entered the room, so strong that I could taste the sickly rot on my tongue. Bile rose in my throat as the flies swarmed overhead, their incessant buzzing filling my ears. I forced myself to look at the body lying before me.

At first glance, the man appeared to have been savagely whipped, his back a ruin of torn flesh and oozing sores. But as I approached on shaky legs, the true extent of the horror became clear. He hadn't been whipped - his skin had been methodically peeled from his living body in an intact sheet.

There it was, nailed to the ceiling above the remains. Empty flesh, dripping gore onto the grime-covered floor. I could just make out the outline of his face etched into this obscene trophy, his mouth open in a soundless scream.

I turned my eyes back to the ground, fighting the dizziness that threatened to overwhelm me. Raw muscle fibers glistened with seeping blood, nerves, and tendons exposed. Insects were already feasting on the vulnerable tissue. The stench of iron mingled with the stench of voided bowels.

It was too much. I stumbled back, bile burning my throat as I vomited helplessly in the corner. Every instinct screamed at me to leave this wretched room. But I couldn't leave. I couldn't leave my partner or this case, no matter how hellish it became.

I sensed James approaching, heard his offer to take over the scene himself. But I vehemently refused. I was no delicate flower to be shielded from the darkness – I had worked too hard to be seen as anything less than an equal. I drew a ragged breath, steadied my trembling limbs, and forced myself to return to the horror before me.

The urge to gag rose again as I gazed at the desecrated remains. But I choked it down. This was my burden to bear, my demons to face. I would not let this evil break me.

With a steady breath, I forced myself to continue examining the body, searching for any clue the killer might have left behind. That's when Black's voice cut through the oppressive silence, barking orders that snapped me back to the task at hand.

With an almost robotic focus, I fell into the familiar rhythm of documenting the scene-photographing from every angle, cataloging scraps of potential evidence, and taking samples. Black and I worked in seamless tandem, our teamwork honed by years of partnership.

The rest of the room faded away as I leaned in closer, examining every inch of ravaged flesh and glistening bone through the viewfinder.

There had to be a clue here somewhere, some microscopic breadcrumb that only my keen eye would notice. I would not leave until I found it.

As I carefully inspected the victim's head, I noticed that their lips seemed to be stuffed with some kind of cloth. Pulling on gloves, I gently removed the gag from their swollen mouth.

As the material was released, a small metal coin slipped out and hit the floor with a faint thud. I quickly retrieved it as evidence. The moment I held it up to the light, my pulse quickened - it was almost identical to the coin found at the previous crime scene.

I glanced at Black, his brow furrowed in concentration as he studied the horror before us. A silent understanding passed between us as I gathered more evidence. We would leave no stone unturned until we uncovered the truth.

"I need the victim's skin brought down for documentation," I directed the forensic team to the scene. The flayed flesh still hung obscenely from the ceiling where the killer had nailed it as a trophy.

The team sprang into action, fetching a ladder and carefully working the nails free. I watched them closely, instructing them to be careful not to tear the skin fragment as they loosened it from the wall. Dark rivulets of old blood dripped down as they handed me the evidence.

Laying it out on a plastic sheet, I leaned in with my camera, photographing the skin from every possible angle as the team held lighting equipment aloft. The cuts were efficient and precise, the work of a steady hand and a twisted mind. I couldn't help but wonder what kind of monster could inflict such horror on another human being.

When I was satisfied that we had properly documented the evidence, I instructed the team to carefully bag the skin, taking care not to compromise the integrity of the carved symbols. As it was sealed away, a sense of grim satisfaction settled over me. This crucial clue would help bring down the monster responsible for such depraved brutality.

I stood up, my legs aching from squatting for so long. The coin gleamed in the harsh light of the crime scene, its ancient markings almost mocking us. Dr. Kensington had said it was connected to the Zarranathians, whose supreme deity, Solanar, was the god of war and punishment. But what did that mean for our investigation?

I shook my head, trying to clear my mind. We needed more information, more evidence. I couldn't lose myself in speculation and guesswork.

"Did you find anything?" Black asked, his voice breaking my thoughts - a welcome interruption.

I held up the coin and watched his eyes widen in recognition. "Another one," I said. "Just like the one we found in the mouth of our impaled victim. That must mean something."

He nodded grimly, his jaw clenched. "We need to get this to Dr. Kensington, see if she can tell us more about its origin."

I slipped the coin into an evidence bag, my fingers trembling slightly. Another death, another coin. The killer seemed to be gloating, taunting us by deliberately leaving souvenirs. They must really believe they cannot be caught.

As we made our way to Dr. Kensington's office, my mind raced with unanswered questions. What was the killer's endgame? Why these specific victims? And how could we stop him before he took another life?

I thought back to my conversation with Black about the possible connections between the victims, the school club, and the historical forum. They felt like tenuous leads at best, but it was all we had to go on.

I glanced over at Black, his face illuminated by the passing streetlights, the shadows accentuating the lines of worry etched into his features. I knew he felt the same frustration and helplessness I did, the stress of this case descending on both of us like an enveloping fog.

We were the best at what we did, our partnership forged in the fires of countless investigations, but this particular case pushed us to our limits, tested our resolve and our faith in our own abilities. The air in the car was filled with unspoken doubts and fears, the silence broken only by the hum of the engine as we sped through the night, chasing leads that seemed to dissipate like wisps of smoke in the wind.

The drive to the university campus was a blur, my mind still reeling from the horror of the crime scene. The image of the victim's flayed body was seared into my brain, the cryptic symbols carved into his flesh haunting my every thought. I grasped the steering wheel firmly, my grip tightening as I maneuvered through the nearly deserted streets, the muffled sounds of the city's nightlife a distant, muted backdrop to the turmoil raging inside me.

I needed answers, some way to make sense of the madness that had descended upon Silvergate. Dr. Kensington was my best hope, her expertise in ancient civilizations and their ancient practices was the key to unlocking the mysteries of the Rune Killer. I prayed that she had uncovered something, anything, that could shed light on the darkness that had enveloped our city.

As I pulled into the parking lot, the towering buildings of the university loomed before me, their Gothic spires and ivy-covered walls a stark contrast to the modern, sleek lines of Silvergate's financial district. We made our way to Dr. Kensington's office, our footsteps echoing through the empty halls, the silence broken only by the occasional distant laughter of students enjoying the night.

The muffled thump of my knuckles against the heavy oak door sent my pulse racing, a fluttering bird caged in my ribs. Long moments stretched out, my breath held in anticipation, until finally, the door creaked open.

I was surprised at her appearance. Dr. Kensington looked exhausted, her usually immaculate auburn hair disheveled and her green eyes ringed with dark circles. With a tired gesture, she ushered us inside, the scent of old books and parchment enveloping us as we entered her office.

"O'Malley," she said, her voice strained with fatigue and worry. "I've been going through the texts, trying to find anything that might help us understand what we're up against."

I nodded, my eyes scanning the piles of ancient tomes and scrolls that littered her desk. "What did you find?" I asked, almost dreading the answer.

She let out a heavy sigh and ran her fingers through her tangled hair. "The glyphs, the ancient coins... everything points to the involvement of an ancient sect that believed in some twisted concept of divine punishment. Their origins may even predate the Zarranthians. The earliest records I've come across refer to them as the Ordo Iustitiae - the Order of Justice. They saw themselves as conduits of celestial power, delivering punishment to those who had escaped earthly justice."

I felt a shiver run down my arm as the implications of her words sank in. "So you're saying our killer sees himself as some kind of... divine enforcer?"

She nodded grimly, her eyes meeting mine. "It's a possibility we can't ignore. But there's more. I've found references to a ritual, a final act of judgment the cult would perform on those they deemed the most heinous offenders."

My blood ran cold at the thought, my mind racing with the possibilities of what such a ritual might entail. "What do we do now?" I asked.

Dr. Kensington leaned forward, her expression grave. "We keep digging. There has to be something in these texts that can help us stop this killer before they strike again."

As I left her office, I nodded, a newfound clarity settling over me. With each new detail, it felt like I was adding another brick to a mental bridge connecting the scattered pieces of the case. Each discovery strengthened my resolve, building a path to the truth one brick at a time.

The coins, the symbols, the ritualistic nature of the murders - they all pointed to a killer deeply steeped in the beliefs of an ancient civilization. But who could be so consumed by these twisted ideologies?

As I worked alongside Detective Black, poring over the evidence and witness statements for the umpteenth time, I couldn't shake the feeling that we were missing something crucial, a vital piece of the puzzle that would bring this whole picture into focus.

Black's piercing blue eyes met mine across the cluttered expanse of our shared desk, a silent understanding passing between us. We excelled at our work, our partnership forged in the fires of countless late nights and hard-won victories. But this case... it was different. It felt like we were chasing shadows, always one step behind a killer who seemed to dance just out of reach.

I rubbed my temples, trying to ease the dull throb of a headache that had been building all day. The fluorescent lights of the bullpen hummed overhead, casting a sickly glow over the sea of paperwork and empty coffee cups. We'd been at this for hours, combing through every scrap of evidence, following every lead, but it felt like we were running in circles.

"There's got to be something we're not seeing," I muttered, frustration seeping into my voice. "Some connection we're missing."

Black leaned back in his chair, his jaw clenched. "We've been over everything a dozen times, O'Malley. The victims, the crime scenes, the symbols... it's like trying to put together a puzzle with half the pieces missing."

I shook my head, unwilling to accept defeat. "We need to dig deeper. There has to be something that connects all of this to the killer, some thread we haven't found yet."

My mind raced with possibilities, each more improbable than the last. Could the killer be someone with a background in history or archaeology? Someone with access to the artifacts and knowledge of the ancient civilization? Or was it someone closer to home, hiding in plain sight?

I thought back to the strange behavior of some of our colleagues, noting how some of them seemed unusually evasive and defensive. Could one of them be involved somehow? The thought made my stomach turn, but I couldn't rule out any possibility, no matter how disturbing.

"Let's go over this again," I said, reaching for the nearest case file. "There's got to be something we've missed, some clue that will lead us to the killer."

The pressure grew with each passing day, the force of the city's expectations pushing us further into sleepless nights and waking nightmares. I could feel it in the taut set of Black's shoulders, in the grim determination etched into the lines of his face. This case was pushing us far beyond our limits.

Chief Thompson had called us into his office that morning, his usually stoic demeanor cracking under the strain. "The mayor's all over me and this department," he'd said, his voice cracking with barely contained frustration. "The media's all over it, and the public is starting to lose faith in our ability to keep them safe."

I'd nodded, my jaw tightening as Chief Thompson's words sank in. I knew he was right - we were on a slippery slope, and the media wasn't making it any easier. Isabel Reyes, the ambitious young journalist who had been hounding us every step of the way, had been particularly relentless in her coverage of the case.

Her articles painted a bleak picture of our department, portraying us as a police force in over our heads, unable to stop a killer who seemed to strike at will and with impunity. Each headline felt like a personal jab, a reminder of how far we still had to go to bring this psychopath to justice. But I refused to let it shake my resolve. If anything, it only fueled the fire within me, the determination to prove them all wrong and show the city that we were more than capable of ending this horror.

But I also knew that rushing this investigation would only lead to more bloodshed. We had to be methodical, to follow every lead, no matter how small. It was the only way to solve this mystery and bring the killer to justice.

Black and I had spent hours sifting through the evidence, our eyes bleary from lack of sleep and too much caffeine. We'd followed every lead, interviewed every witness, but it still felt like we were missing something crucial.

"We need to go back to the beginning," I said, my voice hoarse with exhaustion. "There's got to be something we missed, some connection we haven't made."

We dove back into the files, our minds racing with possibilities. I only hoped we could find the missing piece before the Rune Killer struck again. The thought of another body, another family torn apart by grief, made my stomach churn. I would see this through to the end, even if it meant sacrificing everything else in my life.

CHAPTER SEVEN

LAYERS UNPEELED

I received the positive ID on the latest victim along with a box of his case files and school yearbooks as requested. With a mixture of hope and dread, I immediately began going through the yearbooks, starting with the freshman year and working my way up. As I quickly flipped through page after page, growing anxiety washed over me.

With each yearbook I tossed aside, I became more desperate in my search. I was looking for a connection, some thread that would tie all the victims together. I had been so sure that the killer was targeting people connected by their membership in the Film and Media Club. But now this latest victim seemed to completely unravel that theory.

I grabbed the senior yearbook and flipped through it quickly, scanning each page with laser-like focus. My eyes darted manically over the photos and names, desperate to find anything that would connect this victim to the others. As I neared the end, a nervous sweat broke out on my forehead. I could feel the answer slipping away.

And then I saw it. Or rather, I didn't see it. This victim wasn't in any of the same clubs, sports, or academic groups that had connected the other victims. The realization struck me like a blow to the kidneys. The yearbook slipped from my fingers and fell to the floor with a thud.

A hollow, disturbing laugh, devoid of any humor, erupted from my throat. It was the chilling laugh of a man coming unhinged. I ran a hand through my hair as I laughed, teetering on the edge of sanity.

As quickly as it started, the laughter died on my lips. My face twisted into a mask of rage and frustration. With a guttural scream, I lashed out, sweeping the contents of my desk in one violent motion. Case files and notebooks went flying. The meticulously assembled evidence board crashed to the floor, pictures and documents scattered across the worn linoleum.

Breathing heavily, I surveyed the destruction I had wrought. One of the few solid leads I thought I had, gone. Just like that. I had been so convinced that the killer was targeting former club members, punishing them for some long-held grudge or injustice from their school days.

But this latest victim had no discernible connection to the others. No shared classes, clubs, nothing. It had all been a coincidence, a fluke. I had seen patterns where there were none, like finding shapes in the clouds.

A knock on the door pulled me out of my spiraling thoughts. Officer Jenna O'Malley stepped cautiously into the wrecked office, taking in the scene with wide eyes.

"Rough day, I take it?" she said softly, glancing at the wreckage surrounding my feet.

I ran a hand over my face, trying to collect myself. "You could say that. I was wrong about the victims being connected by their school days. This last one breaks the pattern."

O'Malley nodded thoughtfully and knelt down to help me gather the scattered documents and reassemble the evidence board.

"Well, it was a long shot anyway," she said reasonably. "We never had definitive proof that it was the connection. But at least now we can refocus the investigation, look at other angles."

Her calm response helped deflate my swirling anger and frustration. She was right - it had only been a working theory, not a certainty. I took a deep, calming breath, then joined O'Malley on the floor to reassemble the evidence board.

"You're right, of course," I admitted ruefully. "I just had such a strong feeling that I was on the right track. Now it feels like we're back to square one, grasping at straws. And the public is clamoring for answers. The Chief is ready to have my badge if we don't catch this guy soon."

O'Malley gave me a reassuring smile. "Hey, we've cracked tougher cases with less. We'll figure this out. Why don't we go over the case files again with fresh eyes? Maybe there's something we missed."

Together, we finished reassembling the board and resumed our review of the evidence. As frustrating as it was to hit another dead end, I felt the familiar thrill of the hunt take over. The killer had made a mistake somewhere, and I would find it.

As if on cue, the phone on my desk rang, its shrill tone cutting through the tense silence. I grabbed it, my heart pounding away the last of my anger. "Black!"

The voice that crackled through the receiver was familiar, but the message it carried reignited my simmering anger. "We've got another one, Detective. Same M.O. as the others."

I slammed the phone back into its cradle with more force than necessary, the plastic creaking in protest. My jaw clenched tight, muscles knotting under my skin as I fought to control the flood of frustration and anger that threatened to overwhelm me once again.

"Gear up, O'Malley," I growled, my voice raw with barely contained emotion. "We have work to do." We both knew that horrors awaited us at our destination, but we also knew that it was a chance to gather more clues. And in this case, every clue would mean the difference between life and death for the killer's next target.

As I navigated the bustling streets of Silvergate, the neon signs and glittering storefronts casting a medley of colors across my windshield, I couldn't help but marvel at the city's resilience. Even in the face of the

Rune Killer's reign of terror, life went on, the people of this metropolis seemingly indifferent to the darkness that lurked in its shadows.

I watched as couples strolled hand in hand, their laughter mingling with the distant wail of sirens, a jarring reminder of the harsh reality that lay beneath the surface. Families hurried past, their faces aglow with the promise of a night on the town, blissfully unaware of the savagery unfolding just blocks away.

It was a strange dichotomy, this juxtaposition of light and dark, of joy and sorrow. How could the world go on, how could people live their lives with such unspeakable evil walking among us? The thought gnawed at me, a nagging and persisting pain that no amount of distraction could ease.

Beside me, O'Malley sat in silence, her gaze fixed on the passing scenery, her thoughts no doubt as troubled as my own. We had seen so much, witnessed the depths of human depravity, and yet we were expected to move on, to put on a brave face and pretend that all was well.

But it wasn't all right. Not by a long shot. With each new victim, each twisted spectacle left in the killer's wake, I could feel a piece of myself slipping away, consumed by the darkness that threatened to engulf us all.

As we approached the crime scene, the flashing lights of patrol cars and the somber faces of uniformed officers a stark reminder of the grave task ahead, I couldn't help but wonder how much more I could take. How many more lives would be lost, how many more families would be shattered before this ordeal finally came to an end?

The car rolled to a stop, the sudden silence deafening in the confined space. I took a deep breath, steeling myself for what lay ahead, knowing that the horrors I was about to witness would be forever seared into my memory, another scar on my already battered psyche.

Beside me, O'Malley reached out, her hand finding mine in the darkness, a silent gesture of support and understanding. In that moment, I was grateful for her presence, for the knowledge that I wasn't alone in this fight, that there was still someone who understood the toll this case was taking on both of us.

Together we stepped out into the night, the cool air a welcome respite from the stifling confines of the car. The crime scene loomed before us, a twisted spectacle of flashing lights and yellow tape, a haunting stage upon which the killer's latest act had unfolded.

As we ducked under the police tape and made our way to the waiting officers, I couldn't shake the feeling that we were walking into something far more sinister than anything we'd encountered before. The Rune Killer was escalating, their methods growing bolder and more depraved with each passing day, and I feared we were running out of time to stop them.

With one last look at the glittering cityscape behind us, a world that seemed so far removed from the horror that awaited us, I squared my shoulders and stepped forward, ready to face whatever lay ahead.

The scene was a haunting hellscape come to life. The victim had been chained by the neck to the center of the room like an animal, the collar dug into his flesh. Dark pools of blood spread outward from their tortured body.

My eyes were drawn to the gruesome metal instruments that were ripping the victim from the inside out. One had been inserted into the mouth - its central screw-like shaft leading to four curved spoon-shaped petals.

Blood and drool dripped from where the flared metal segments had torn the skin at the corners of the mouth, ripping open the victim's cheeks in a horrific rictus grin. The flesh hung in ragged strips from the grotesque wound, completely mutilating the area that surrounded the lips.

Another identical device had been embedded in the victim's anus, the four petal-shaped blades blooming from the opening like some hideous mechanical flower. The delicate tissue was shredded by the relentless metal, which continued to push until the sphincter tore and the rectum prolapsed.

It was clear that both devices had been designed to penetrate the orifices and then gradually expand to maximize the damage to the soft tissue trapped inside. No doubt they had screamed and thrashed against the relentless metal ripping them open from within before shock and blood loss finally took their lives. What twisted mind could conceive of such deliberate, clinical cruelty?

O'Malley was already kneeling beside the body, her gloved hands gently probing the wounds. "Same symbols carved into the flesh," she said, her voice tight with anger. "And another coin, just like the others."

I nodded, my mind racing as I tried to put the puzzle together. "We need to find out what these symbols mean, and quickly. Call Dr. Kensington, see if she's made any progress in deciphering them."

As O'Malley made the call, I turned my attention to the rest of the scene, my eyes searching for anything out of place. The room was a mess of overturned furniture and shattered glass, the signs of a desperate struggle.

Amidst the chaos, a glint of metal caught my eye, and I crouched down to get a closer look. It was a small, intricately carved knife, its blade stained with dark, dried blood. The handle was wrapped in worn leather, and strange symbols were etched into the metal.

I carefully bagged the knife, my heart pounding with a mixture of excitement and trepidation. This was the first real lead we'd had in days, a tangible clue that might help us unravel the mystery of these brutal murders.

We spent hours combing the crime scene, our eyes scanning every inch of the blood-soaked room for any other clues that might lead us to the killer. I watched as O'Malley meticulously cataloged each piece of evidence, her brow furrowed in concentration as she worked. The responding officers hovered nearby, their faces etched with a mixture of awe and unease as they watched us work.

I pulled one of the officers aside, a young rookie with a face that still held the untouched innocence of youth. "What can you tell me about the victim?" I asked.

The rookie swallowed hard, his eyes darting nervously to the body on the ground. "Not much, sir. We got the call about an hour ago, the neighbor reported hearing muffled screams. By the time we got here, it was too late."

I nodded, my jaw clenching in frustration. It was the same story every time, a life snuffed out in a moment of senseless violence, leaving us with more questions than answers. I turned back to the scene, my eyes scanning the room again, looking for anything we might have missed.

Weary but determined, we gathered our evidence and headed back to the car. The crisp morning air contrasted sharply with the stifling confines of the crime scene, and I took a deep breath, trying to clear my mind. O'Malley walked silently beside me, her expression pensive as we secured the evidence and slid into the car.

I glanced over at O'Malley, her face drawn and pale in the faint light of the rising sun. "We need to get that knife to forensics as soon as possible," I said, my voice catching with exhaustion. "Maybe they can find something on it that will give us a lead."

O'Malley nodded, her eyes distant and unfocused. "I hope so," she murmured, her voice barely audible over the hum of the engine. "We're running out of time."

I glanced down at the knife, tucked securely in an evidence bag on the seat beside me. It was a small thing, a shard of metal that seemed almost insignificant in the grand scheme of things. But I knew it might hold the key to solving this case, to finally ending the killer's reign of terror.

Back at the station, I paced my office, my mind racing with theories and possibilities. O'Malley burst through the door, her face flushed with excitement.

"I just got off the phone with Dr. Kensington," O'Malley announced breathlessly. "She deciphered the meaning of the runes, and she says they represent various sins and crimes. The Ordo Iustitiae would carve the symbols into the flesh of those they killed. Marks of divine judgment, forcing their target to carry the stains of their misdeeds into the grave for all to see."

I nodded, "Sins and crimes, did we miss something? The coins, did she mention what their purpose is?"

I took the file from O'Malley, my eyes quickly absorbing the details she had discovered. "According to this, the coins are engraved with the symbol of Malthor - the deity of retribution and balance. His role was to judge the spirits impartially as they passed into the afterlife."

I felt a rush of adrenaline coursing through my veins, the thrill of the hunt taking hold. "So we're dealing with a modern version of that cult, someone who believes they're dispensing some kind of twisted justice."

O'Malley nodded, her face grim. "And they won't stop until they've punished everyone they deem deserving."

I slammed my fist down on the desk, my frustration boiling over. "We need to find out who's behind this, and fast. Start digging into the victims' backgrounds, see if there's any connection we missed. And get me everything you can on this cult, I want to know everything about their beliefs and practices."

As O'Malley hurried off to carry out my orders, I sank into my chair, barely able to process the whole ordeal. What the hell kind of monstrosity was stalking our city?

I went through the victim's history again, this time with a redirected focus. My previous efforts had only scratched the surface, uncovering the usual minor infractions - a drug bust here, a parking ticket there. But armed with a deeper understanding of the killer's twisted motives, I knew I had to dig deeper, to peel back the layers of the victim's past until I found what I was looking for.

I searched every inch of their records, looking for the slightest hint of wrongdoing that might have slipped through the cracks. I looked for the charges that didn't stick, the accusations that never made it into an official report. Something that might have painted a target on the victim's back in the eyes of our deranged killer.

That's when the pattern began to emerge, it had been staring me in the face all along. Each of the victims had a history of crimes that had gone unpunished. Amanda Myers, a jilted lover who drove her ex to his death, but was let go for lack of evidence. Christopher Booth, a former gang member suspected of multiple murders, but never charged. Tyler Walsh, a wealthy businessman rumored to have ties to human trafficking, but with enough money and influence to avoid prosecution.

The most recent victims continued the trend. Ryan Foster, a security guard accused of using excessive force that led to the death of a suspect, but was cleared after an internal review. Javier Torres, a doctor who faced multiple malpractice lawsuits after patients died under his care, but managed to avoid any criminal liability or loss of his medical license. Derek Collins, a high school teacher who was accused of sexually assaulting several students but was never charged due to a lack of physical evidence.

"It's like the killer is trying to right the wrongs of the system." O'Malley nods, her mind racing with the implications of this discovery. "But who has the knowledge and motive to carry out such a twisted form of vigilante justice?" she wonders aloud.

I lean back in my chair, my eyes glued to the evidence board. "We're looking for someone who has intimate knowledge of these cases and a deep-seated belief that the system has failed to deliver an impartial verdict."

My mind wanders to Ethan Ward, the local historian whose name keeps popping up in our investigation. Could he be the one behind these gruesome murders? Or is he just one more piece of the puzzle?

I push myself up from my desk, my body thrumming with nervous energy. "We need to dig deeper into Ward's background, his wife's unsolved murder fits the Rune Killer's selection criteria. And we need to do it quickly."

O'Malley nods, her face set with determination. "I'll reach out to my contacts in the academic world, see if anyone knows anything about Ward's research into ancient cults. Maybe there's a clue we've missed."

I grab my jacket from the back of my chair, my mind already racing with thoughts of our next move. "I'll hit the streets, see if any of my informants have heard anything about someone with a grudge against the justice system. If we can find a connection between the victims and their cases, it might lead us right to the killer."

As the morning sun crept through the blinds of my office, casting a faint light across my cluttered desk, I rubbed my eyes, trying to shake off the exhaustion that seemed to cling to my bones. Another day, another chance to unravel the twisted web of the rune-killer's crimes.

O'Malley was already there, her face drawn and pale as she pored over the files spread out before her. "I don't get it," she muttered, her voice hoarse with exhaustion. "Why would the killer target these particular victims? Why them? There are so many people who have abused the system."

I shook my head, my own frustration mirroring hers. "I don't know, but we need to find out. And fast. Every minute we spend chasing down dead ends is another minute the killer could be stalking their next victim."

Just then, the door swung open and Detective Marcus Jones strode into the room, a fierce intensity etched into his face. "I heard about the latest victim," he said, his voice hushed and urgent. "What can I do to help?"

I felt a surge of gratitude at his words, a reminder that we weren't alone in this fight. "We need to find a connection between the victims," I said, my voice tense. "Something that links them to the killer's twisted sense of justice."

Jones nodded, his eyes scanning the files on his desk. "I'll start digging into their backgrounds with fresh eyes, see if I can find anything that might have put them on the killer's radar."

As he settled into the chair next to O'Malley, his presence a welcome respite from the darkness that surrounded us, I felt a flicker of hope in my chest. With Jones on our side, we might just have a chance to crack this case.

But even as I drew strength from his words, from the fierce determination that seemed to emanate from him like a primal force, I could sense O'Malley's unease. This case was really starting to take its toll on her.

As the hours ticked by, we worked in silence, our eyes scanning the files for any clue that might lead us to the killer. O'Malley's brow was furrowed in concentration, her pen flying across the page as she jotted down notes and theories.

Marcus, too, seemed lost in thought, his gaze distant as he pored over the victim's background. Every now and then he would mutter something to himself, some half-formed idea he couldn't quite bring himself to say.

As the sun began to set outside the precinct windows, casting long shadows across the room, I pushed myself up from my desk, my body aching with fatigue. "Let's call it a night," I said, my voice raspy with exhaustion. "We'll start fresh in the morning, see if we can find anything we missed."

O'Malley nodded, her own weariness evident in the slump of her shoulders. But Jones hesitated, his eyes darting to the files on the desk. "You two go ahead," he said, his voice carefully neutral. "I think I'll stay a little longer, maybe I can find something."

I noticed the weariness etched into Marcus's face and decided to cut him some slack. "Take it easy, Marcus," I said, forcing a smile. "Don't work yourself too hard. We're going to need your help in the upcoming nights."

CHAPTER EIGHT

THE HISTORIAN'S LAIR

A s O'Malley and I made our way through the labyrinthine corridors of the university, our footsteps echoed off the walls, the sound reverberating through the empty hallways. The air grew thicker with each step, a feeling of apprehension settling in my stomach as we approached Dr. Ward's office.

We finally reached the door to Ethan Ward's office, a solid oak barrier standing between us and the answers we sought. I raised my hand to knock, but hesitated, a sudden uneasiness washing over me. O'Malley gave me a questioning look, but I just shook my head and rapped my knuckles against the wood.

The door creaked open to reveal two young men with charming demeanors and polite smiles. "Detective Black, Officer O'Malley, please come in," the first said, stepping aside to let us in. "I'm Andrew Oswald, and this is my colleague, Lucas Parker. We're Dr. Ward's assistants."

Upon entering, we were greeted by the sight of shelves overflowing with ancient texts and artifacts. The room was a testament to Ward's obsession, every surface covered with relics from civilizations long gone. The very air was alive with history, the significance of centuries gathered around us.

Lucas led us deeper into the office, weaving between towering stacks of books and display cases of intricate stone carvings. "Detective Black,

Officer O'Malley, it's a pleasure to meet you. Dr. Ward will be here shortly. Please make yourselves comfortable."

O'Malley, ever the professional, began the questioning. "Mr. Parker, Mr. Oswald, how long have you both worked with Dr. Ward?"

Lucas leaned against a display case containing an intricate stone sculpture. "I joined the team about six years ago, but Andrew's been here a lot longer."

Andrew nodded, his posture relaxed and open. "About eight years now. I started as his research assistant when I was still a graduate student."

I studied the couple closely. "And what exactly do you assist with?" I asked, my tone measured and even.

"Mostly cataloging artifacts and translating ancient texts. Dr. Ward's research is quite extensive." Andrew's brown eyes met mine, reminding me of my brother's.

O'Malley began again. "Mr. Oswald, I read in the paper that you were part of a recent discovery of relics," she said. "Would you care to elaborate?"

Andrew's eyes widened slightly and he glanced at Lucas before answering with a confident smile. "Yes, I recently stumbled upon a cache of ancient artifacts during one of my research expeditions. It was quite a find, really."

O'Malley nodded and reached into her pocket. "And did any of those artifacts resemble this?" She pulled out a small evidence bag containing a tarnished copper coin, its surface etched with intricate runic symbols.

Andrew and Lucas both leaned forward and squinted at the coin. Andrew's brow furrowed as he studied the markings, a flicker of recognition crossing his features. "You know, now that you mention it, there were a few pieces that bore a striking resemblance to this coin. Same runic script, same worn patina..."

Suddenly, the office door swung open with a bang, instantly stopping all conversation. Standing in the doorway was the disheveled figure of

Dr. Ethan Ward. His dark hair was unkempt, and his piercing blue eyes were wild and intense. "Detectives! I apologize for my tardiness. I have been immersed in some new translations."

I stood and held out my hand. "Dr. Ward, thank you for agreeing to meet with us."

Ward shook my hand, his grip firm and slightly clammy. "Of course, anything to help with the investigation. I must say, I find these murders quite fascinating from an academic standpoint."

O'Malley raised an eyebrow, her tone sharp. "Fascinating? People are dying, Dr. Ward."

Ward had the decency to look flustered. "I'm sorry, I didn't mean to sound insensitive. It's just that these symbols, the archaic style of the murders, all point to a level of knowledge and devotion that is quite rare."

I leaned forward, my elbows on my knees. "And what can you tell us about that knowledge, Dr. Ward? Our investigation has led us to believe that the killer may be connected to your area of expertise."

Ward's eyes lit up, a spark of excitement that sent a shiver down my spine. "Well, Detective, the symbols you showed me do indeed seem to be connected to an ancient civilization I've been studying for years. A society obsessed with the concept of divine justice and retribution."

As Ward launched into a detailed explanation of the cult's practices, the room seemed to close in around me, the ancient artifacts taking on a menacing air.

I glanced at O'Malley and saw my own unease reflected in her eyes. We were entering dangerous territory, and I had a sinking suspicion that the true horror of this case was only just beginning to reveal itself.

As I settled into the worn leather chair across from Dr. Ward, the musty scent of ancient texts and artifacts filled my nostrils. The room was dimly lit, the flickering glow of antique lamps casting eerie shadows on the walls. Lucas excused himself, muttering something about cataloging new arrivals, and disappeared into the depths of the office, leaving us alone with Andrew and the eccentric historian.

Ward leaned forward, his eyes glowing with a manic fervor that sent shivers down my spine. He began to speak, his voice deep and intense, weaving tales of ancient rituals and forgotten gods. The words poured out of him like a dam bursting, his passion for the subject evident in every syllable.

"You see, Detective, these symbols represent a complex system of beliefs, a code of justice that transcends the boundaries of time and culture," he said, gesturing wildly with his hands as he spoke. "The ancients believed in a higher power, a divine force that would mete out punishment to those who escaped earthly castigation."

I glanced at O'Malley, who was furiously scribbling notes in her pad, her brow furrowed in concentration. I turned back to Ward, trying to steer the conversation to more relevant topics.

"Dr. Ward, while this is all very fascinating from a historical perspective, we're more interested in any possible connections to modern cult activity," I said, my tone firm but polite. "Have you come across any groups or individuals who might be taking these ancient practices to a dangerous extreme?"

Ward's eyes darted from mine, his fingers drumming nervously on the arm of his chair. "Well, Detective, as I'm sure you're aware, there are always those who seek to twist the teachings of the past for their own base purposes," he said, his voice taking on a slightly defensive edge. "But I can assure you that my research is purely academic in nature."

I leaned back in my chair and studied Ward's face closely. There was something about his demeanor that didn't sit right with me, a sense of evasiveness that set off alarm bells in my head. I glanced around the room, taking in the towering shelves of books and the glass cases.

As my eyes wandered over the statues and figurines, I felt a sudden shudder run down my spine. The carved stone faces seemed to stare into my very being, their eyes filled with an intensity that made my skin crawl. I shook my head, trying to dispel the unsettling sensation, and focused back on Ward.

"Dr. Ward, I understand your reluctance to speculate, but we're dealing with a very real threat here," I said, my voice taking on a harder edge. "If you have any information that could help us catch this killer, it's your duty to share it with us."

Ward shifted uncomfortably in his seat, his eyes darting to the shadowy corners of the room. "I wish I could be more helpful, Detective, but I'm afraid I don't have any concrete leads to offer you," he said, his voice shaking slightly. "These murders, while undeniably connected to the ancient practices I study, are the work of a twisted mind, someone who has taken those beliefs to a dark and dangerous place."

I leaned forward and fixed him with a piercing stare.

"Dr. Ward, I couldn't help but notice the parallels between your research and the recent murders," I said, my voice dour and measured. "The killer seems to be targeting individuals who have escaped requital, much like the ancient practices you described."

Ward's eyes narrowed, a flicker of something dark and dangerous crossing his features. "Detective, are you suggesting that I have some connection to these heinous crimes?"

I held up my hands in a calming gesture. "Not at all, Dr. Ward. But I do find it curious that someone with your expertise would be so fascinated by a case that seems to embody the very principles you've dedicated your life to studying."

Ward's jaw clenched, his knuckles turning white as he gripped the arms of his chair. "Once again, Detective, I can assure you that my interest in this case is purely academic."

I nodded, but the uneasy feeling in my gut only intensified. I glanced at O'Malley, who was watching the exchange with a wary expression, her hand hovering near her service weapon.

"Dr. Ward, I couldn't help but notice the photos on your desk," I said, gesturing to the framed pictures of a smiling woman. "Is that your wife?"

Ward's face softened, a flicker of grief crossing his features. "Yes, that is my beloved Amelia. She passed away a few years ago."

I hesitated, knowing I was treading on delicate ground. But further probing on such a sensitive subject might throw him off guard and cause him to admit something he normally wouldn't. "I'm sorry for your loss, Dr. Ward. If you don't mind me asking, how did she die?"

Ward's eyes flashed with anger, his voice rising to a shout. "She was murdered, Detective. Brutally murdered by a man who should have spent the rest of his life rotting behind bars. But instead, he walked free, protected by a system that values technicalities over true justice."

I could feel the anger radiating from him in waves that seemed to suck the oxygen out of the room.

"I'm sorry, Dr. Ward," I said, my voice soft and sincere. "I can't imagine the pain you've been through. But surely you don't condone the actions of the Rune Killer, no matter how much they might agree with your personal beliefs?"

Ward's face contorted, a twisted smile spreading across his features. "Don't I, Detective? The Rune Killer is doing what the Silvergate PD should have been doing all along. Putting the fear of God back into the hearts of the wicked. Making sure that those who escape guilt face a reckoning beyond the grave. I was overjoyed to learn that Amelia's killer had met his fate in a hit-and-run. I only regret now that it was not at the hands of the Rune Killer.

I felt a tingling down my spine, the hairs on the back of my neck stood on end. There was a manic gleam in Ward's eyes, a fervor that bordered on madness.

"Dr. Ward, I think you need to think very carefully about what you say next," I warned. "Endorsing vigilante justice is a dangerous road to go down."

Ward let out a bark of laughter, the sound harsh and grating. "You think I care about your warnings, Detective? I've spent my entire life studying the ways of the ancients, learning the true nature of justice. And now, finally, someone is putting that knowledge into practice. The Rune Killer is a true believer, a warrior of the divine."

Before I could respond, Andrew stood up, his expression worried as he observed Ward's agitated state. "Dr. Ward, I think we should take a break," he said calmly, placing a hand on Ward's shoulder. "Detective Black is just doing his job, and this conversation is getting a little heated."

Ward shrugged off Andrew's hand, his face contorted with anger. "I don't need a break, Andrew. I need these so-called detectives to open their eyes and see the truth."

Andrew's voice remained calm."I understand your frustration, Dr. Ward, but this isn't the way to handle it.

Let's step away for a moment and clear our heads."

Turning to me, Andrew offered an apologetic smile. "Detective Black, I apologize for the interruption. If you don't mind, I think it's best if we finish this interview here. I'll make sure Dr. Ward gets the rest he needs."

I nodded, recognizing the wisdom in Andrew's words. "I appreciate your cooperation, Mr. Oswald. We'll be in touch if we have any further questions."

I stood abruptly, my chair scraping the hardwood floor. "Dr. Ward, I think we've heard enough. We'll be in touch if we have any more questions."

Ward's face twisted into a sneer, his eyes burning with a feverish intensity. "Get out of my office, Detective. And take your lapdog with you. You're not welcome here anymore."

I nodded to O'Malley and we made our way to the door, the oppressive atmosphere of the room clinging to us like a second skin. As I reached for the handle, Ward's voice rang out behind me, threatening.

"You're on the wrong side of history, Detective. The Rune Killer is just the beginning. Soon the streets of Silvergate will be bathed in the blood of the unrighteous, and there's nothing you or your precious department can do to stop it."

I paused, my hand hovering over the doorknob, and turned back to face Ward. "We'll see, Dr. Ward. We'll see."

As we walked out of Dr. Ward's office, I couldn't shake the feeling of unease that had settled deep in my bones. The historian's tirade had been disturbing, to say the least, and his eyes burned with a fervor that bordered on madness. I glanced back over my shoulder and caught a glimpse of Andrew at Ward's side, his hands raised in a soothing gesture as he tried to calm his mentor's agitation.

I turned to O'Malley, my brow furrowed in concern. "Did you see the way he snapped?" I asked, my voice troubled.

"It was like he was possessed, like something had taken over him."

O'Malley nodded, her own expression reflecting my unease. "I've never seen anything like it," she said, shaking her head. "One minute he was all academic passion, the next he was ranting about divine punishment and bathing the city in blood."

We made our way down the dimly lit hallway, our footsteps echoing off the polished wood floors. As we rounded the corner, we nearly collided with a familiar figure – Lucas Parker, Ward's protege.

"Mr. Parker," O'Malley greeted him, her eyes widening slightly in surprise. "We were just leaving."

Lucas nodded, his eyes flickering between us. "I heard raised voices. Is everything okay?"

I exchanged a look with O'Malley before answering. "Just a disagreement with Dr. Ward. Nothing to worry about."

O'Malley wasn't about to let the opportunity pass. "Actually, Mr. Parker, I was hoping to ask you something." She reached into her pocket and pulled out the coin we had found earlier. "Andrew commented that it bore a striking resemblance to some of the relics he acquired during a recent expedition. Do you know anything about them?"

Lucas frowned, took the coin from O'Malley, and examined it closely. "I've seen this before," he murmured, his brow furrowed in concentration. "It bears a definite resemblance to the ancient relics Dr. Ward recently acquired. But I don't know much about their origin or significance."

Before O'Malley could continue, the sound of approaching footsteps echoed through the corridor. Dr. Ward rounded the corner, his face contorted with anger as he spotted us.

"Detectives!" he snapped, his voice sharp and accusatory.

"I thought I made it clear you were no longer welcome here. And now I find you harassing my assistants?"

I stepped forward and placed myself between Ward and O'Malley. "Dr. Ward, we were just leaving. But we couldn't help but notice the similarities between the artifacts in your possession and the evidence from our crime scenes."

Ward's face contorted into a sneer, his eyes blazing with barely contained rage. "You have no right to question me or my staff, Detective. I've already told you all I know. Now I suggest you leave before I call campus security and have you escorted off the premises."

O'Malley put the coin back in her pocket, her jaw tightening. "This isn't over, Dr. Ward. We'll be back with a warrant if necessary."

Ward let out a harsh burst of laughter. "You do that, Detective."As we exited the building, the cool evening air was a welcome respite from the suffocating tension inside.

I turned to O'Malley, my mind racing with the implications of our recent encounter.

"We need to keep an eye on this guy," I said. "Whether he's connected to the murders or he's the Rune Killer, we can't risk him slipping through our fingers."

O'Malley murmured her agreement, her hand resting lightly on the butt of her service weapon. "I'll put in a request for surveillance," she said, her tone all business. "See if we can dig up anything on his background, any red flags that might indicate deeper involvement."

I nodded, my mind already racing with possibilities. Ward's obsession with ancient justice, the circumstances surrounding his wife's death, and her killer's eventual demise, all added up to a disturbing picture.

As we stepped out into the bright afternoon sunlight, my thoughts drifted back to my brother Samuel. The look in Andrew's eyes stirred old memories, painful reminders of the tragedy that had shattered my world so many years ago.

I could still see Samuel's face, his eyes wide with terror as he fell into the darkness. His incoherent babbling, his words tumbling over each other in a frantic rush. I had tried to calm him down, to make sense of what he was saying, but it was no use.

He was too far gone, lost in a world of his own making.

The doctors had called it a psychotic break, a complete disconnect from reality brought on by the trauma of the impact. They had pumped him full of drugs, tried to stabilize him, but nothing seemed to work. He had withdrawn into himself, his once lucid mind shattered into a million pieces.

I had visited him every day, sat by his bedside, and held his hand, trying to coax him back into the world of the living. But he remained lost, trapped in a maze of his own shattered thoughts. Eventually, I had to accept that the brother I knew was gone, replaced by a hollow shell of a man.

The memory hit me like a freight train, a wave of grief and guilt washing over me. I had failed Samuel, just as I had failed so many others over the years. The cost of my failures grew heavier with each passing day.

I shook my head, trying to clear my thoughts. This was no time for self-pity. I had a job to do, a killer to catch. I couldn't afford to let my personal demons distract me from the task at hand, I had to clear my head.

I turned to O'Malley, who was already buckling her seat belt in the passenger seat. "I need to go see Samuel," I said, feeling myself getting emotional. "After everything we just learned, I need to process it all, and try to make sense of it for myself."

O'Malley nodded, her eyes filled with understanding. "Take all the time you need, James," she said, placing a comforting hand on my arm.

"I'm going back to the station and start digging into Ward's background. If there's anything there, I'll find it."

I managed a grateful smile, feeling a surge of affection for my partner. O'Malley had been by my side through thick and thin, a constant source of support and encouragement in a job that could often feel like an uphill battle.

As I pulled out of the parking lot and onto the main road, my thoughts turned to Samuel. It had been months since my last visit, and the guilt gnawed at me like a festering wound. I knew my brother's condition wasn't entirely my fault, but I couldn't shake the feeling that I had failed him. I shouldn't have pushed him so hard.

The drive to the care facility was a somber one, each mile taking me further from the bustling heart of Silvergate and deeper into the quiet outskirts of the city. As I turned onto the winding road leading to the facility, I felt a sense of unease settle over me, a weight that grew heavier with each passing moment.

The care facility came into view, a sprawling Victorian mansion that had been converted into a home for those who had lost their way. The once grand structure now looked tired and worn, its paint peeling and its windows clouded with age. The grounds were overgrown, the gardens wild and untamed, as if nature itself had begun to reclaim what man had long since abandoned.

I parked my car in the nearly empty lot and sat in the car for a long moment, my hands gripping the steering wheel as I tried to collect my thoughts. I knew that seeing Samuel would be difficult, that it would bring up all the old wounds and painful memories that I had tried so hard to bury.

Taking a deep breath, I got out of the car, the gravel crunching under my feet as I stepped out into the cool fall air. The wind whispered through the trees, carrying with it the faint scent of decay and neglect. I shivered and pulled my coat tighter around me as I made my way towards the entrance.

In the dimly lit confines of the apartment, the figure's face was bathed in the sickly glow of the laptop screen, casting an eerie glow over their features. Fingers moved quickly across the keyboard, urgency evident in each keystroke, a bead of sweat glistening on a furrowed brow as they navigated a complex digital landscape. The quiet of the room was broken only by the relentless clacking of keys and the occasional groan of the office chair, sounds that echoed through the heavy air, thick with concentration and an undercurrent of tension.

Navigating a maze of encrypted files and hidden folders, their eyes darted back and forth, meticulously erasing any digital breadcrumbs that might lead back to them.

One misstep, one overlooked connection could bring down their carefully constructed house of cards around them, exposing their deceitful activities to the world.

With a final, decisive keystroke, a slow exhale of relief followed, the figure allowing themselves a brief moment of respite. The evidence was gone, buried so deep in the digital abyss that even the most skilled digital forensics team would be hard-pressed to recover it. A moment of satisfaction was allowed, a smirk tugging at the corners of their mouths as they rejoiced in their handiwork.

But the work was far from done, and the figure knew they could not rest on their laurels.

A pile of case files was pulled from the closet, its contents spilling across the bed in a haphazard mess of papers and photographs. These were the cases that had haunted the figure for years, where the guilty had walked free, mocking the very system sworn to uphold justice and protect the innocent. Their purpose clear, they sifted through the files, the memories of each injustice like a dull knife twisting deeper and deeper, fueling the burning desire for retribution that consumed them.

With a methodical eye, the details of each case were scanned, searching for those that best fit the criteria of the Rune Killer.

The killer's message was clear – divine retribution for those who had escaped justice, a brutal reckoning for the sins of the past. There was a disturbing sense of twisted kinship with the killer's mission, a dark part of the character's psyche that had festered over the years, fueled by personal failures and the system's shortcomings.

One by one, the files that fit the pattern were separated and placed in a neat pile, each one representing a potential target for the killer's next strike. These were the chosen ones, the cases that would fuel the killer's brutal acts of vengeance against a world too complacent, too willing to let the wicked slip through the cracks and escape the consequences of their actions.

Eyes were drawn back to the computer, the screen casting an eerie radiance into the dimly lit room, bathing the figure's face in a ghostly light. Logging into the message board of a nondescript historical forum, fingers danced across the keyboard with practiced ease, manipulating the virtual space that had become their domain, a playground to manipulate narrative and sow seeds of chaos and misdirection.

Fingers flew over the keys, crafting an email invitation with the same precision and care given to the case files. The individuals who had avoided consequences by navigating legal loopholes would no longer escape justice; their time had come. An invitation would be extended, a summons to their own inner hell, where they would finally face the consequences of their actions.

As the cursor blinked steadily on the screen, there was a pause, the figure's mind racing with the implications of these actions.

Once this invitation was sent, there would be no turning back, no way to undo what had been set in motion.

A chain of events would unfold that could tear the city apart, exposing its darkest secrets and challenging the very foundations of law and order. But in that moment, there was a strange sense of clarity, a conviction that what was being done was necessary, a brutal but necessary step toward a higher form of justice that transcended the limitations of the system.

With a deep breath, the send button was pressed, the message disappearing into the digital ether, a silent siren call to the one who dared to embrace the shadows.

CHAPTER NINE

DISCOVERY

As I approached the front door, I couldn't shake the feeling that I was entering a world far removed from the one I knew. The care facility was a place for lost souls, for those who had been broken by the cruelties of life and left to drift in the shadows of their own minds. It was a place where hope went to die, where the forgotten and the abandoned were left to wither in silence.

I hesitated for a moment, my hand hovering over the door handle. I knew that what awaited me inside would be difficult, that seeing Samuel in his current state would be a painful reminder of all that he had lost. But I also knew that I had to face it, confront the ghosts of my past, if I was ever going to find a way to move forward.

Steadying myself, I pushed open the door and stepped inside, the stale scent of disinfectant and despair washing over me like a wave. The lobby was dimly lit, the once ornate chandelier now covered in cobwebs and dust. The floors creaked beneath my feet, the sound echoing through the empty halls like a mournful sigh.

I made my way to the reception desk, where a tired looking woman was hunched over a stack of papers. She looked up as I approached, her eyes dull and lifeless. "Can I help you?" she asked, her voice flat and monotonous.

"I'm here to see my brother," I said, my voice sounding strange and distant to my own ears. "Samuel Black."

The woman nodded, shuffling through her papers until she found what she was looking for. "Room 217," she said, handing me a visitor's pass. "Down the hall to the left."

I took the pass with a nod of thanks, my heart pounding in my chest as I made my way down the narrow hallway. The walls were lined with faded photographs and peeling wallpaper. As I ran my hands along the walls, I felt the rough texture of neglect beneath my fingertips, each bump and crack echoing a sense of lost hope.

As I approached room 217, I felt a sense of dread wash over me, a cold sweat break out on my brow. With a trembling hand, I reached out and turned the knob, and the door swung open with a soft creak.

And there he was, my brother, surrounded by a sea of paintings, each one a chaotic mess of colors and shapes that seemed to twist and turn before my eyes. I recognized the style immediately - it was the same one that had haunted Samuel's work since the incident, a window into the fractured landscape of his mind.

I approached slowly, my footsteps echoing loudly in the silence of the room. Samuel didn't look up, his gaze fixed on the painting in front of him, his hand moving feverishly across the canvas.

"Samuel," my voice barely above a whisper. "It's me, James."

For a moment there was no response, and I felt a familiar pang of disappointment wash over me. But then, slowly, Samuel turned to face me, his eyes wide and unfocused.

"James," he said, his voice hoarse and tense. "You came."

I nodded, swallowing down the lump in my throat. "Of course I did," I said, forcing a smile. "I'll always come for you, Samuel."

He stared at me for a long moment, his gaze boring into me with an intensity that made my skin crawl. And then, without warning, he reached out and took my hand, his fingers digging into my flesh with surprising strength.

"It's coming, James," he whispered, his voice barely audible over the pounding of my heart. "The hollow soul. They're coming for all of us."

I felt a tingle run down my spine, and my breath caught in my throat. "What are you talking about, Samuel?" I asked, my voice shaking slightly."Who's coming?"

But Samuel just shook his head, his eyes filling with tears. "I can see them, James," he said, his voice rising. "They're here, in the shadows, waiting. Waiting for the right time to strike."

I tried to pull my hand away, but Samuel held on, his grip like a vise. "You have to stop them, James," he pleaded, his voice cracking with emotion. "You're the only one who can. The only one who understands."

I stared at my brother, my mind reeling with confusion and fear. I had never seen him like this, so lucid and yet so terrified. And in that moment, I knew that whatever he was seeing, whatever haunting vision had taken hold of his mind, was real to him in a way that I could never fully comprehend.

I took a deep breath and realized that I had to approach this delicately. I gently placed my free hand on Samuel's shoulder, hoping that the physical contact would help anchor him in the present moment. I knew I couldn't just dismiss his claims, but I couldn't feed into his delusions either. I had to find a way to navigate this conversation carefully, gathering all the information I could while making sure my brother felt heard and supported.

"Samuel, I hear you," I said, keeping my tone even and reassuring. "I know that what you're experiencing feels very real to you. But I need you to help me understand. Can you describe these 'hollow souls' to me? What do they look like?"

Samuel's eyes darted around the room as if searching for some unseen threat. "The coins," he whispered, his voice barely audible. "Malthor's tokens are the key. Find them and you'll find him."

A wave of excitement mixed with dread washed over me. The coins – the same ones left at the crime scenes, the ones that seemed to hold the key to unlocking the mystery of the Rune Killer. Could it be that Samuel, in his shattered state, had stumbled upon a vital clue?

"What about the coins, Samuel?" I pressed, my heart hammering in my chest. "What do they mean? Where did you hear the name Malthor?"

But Samuel just shook his head, his eyes filling with a fresh wave of tears. "I can't," he mouthed. "It's all shattered, like broken glass on the sidewalk."

I felt a wave of frustration wash over me, but I pushed it down, forcing myself to remain calm. Samuel's grip on reality was tenuous at best, and getting angry would only make things worse. Patience was the key, and if I was going to get anywhere with him, understanding was essential.

"Try to remember, Sam," I urged gently, leaning closer. "Where did the name Malthor come from? Anything might help us."

Samuel's eyes grew distant, and he began to mutter to himself, words that made no sense, fragments of thought that spun out of control. "Malthor... shadows... the coins... the endless wheel..."

"Sam, focus," I tried again, squeezing his shoulder for reassurance. But it was no use. His moment of clarity began to dissipate like mist in the morning sun.

"I can't remember!" he cried, pulling away from me. His eyes grew wild, darting around the room as if he saw horrors only he could perceive."Broken... shattered... fractured... splintered..."

He collapsed into himself, rocking back and forth, lost in his own tortured world. I could see the storm of confusion and terror engulfing his mind, taking him further away from the fleeting moment of awareness he had just shared.

"It's okay," I said, trying to calm him as I reached out again. "We'll get through this together. Just take your time."

But even as I spoke, an uneasiness settled over me like a dark cloud. The figure with the hollow soul. The coins. The missing pieces of the puzzle that seemed scattered across the city like breadcrumbs leading to some final, terrible truth. And as Samuel slipped away, I feared we might never gather all those pieces in time. I left the facility with a heavy heart, my mind reeling from the cryptic warnings Samuel had given me.

As I walked to my car, I pulled out my phone and dialed O'Malley's number, my fingers trembling slightly as I keyed in the digits. She answered on the second ring, her voice crisp and alert despite the late hour.

"Black," she said, her tone tinged with concern. "What's going on?"

I hesitated for a moment, unsure how to put into words the feeling of unease that had taken hold of me. "I need you to come over," my voice sounded strained even to my own ears. "Something's happened to Samuel, and I... I don't know what to make of it."

There was a brief pause on the other end of the line as O'Malley processed my words. "I'll be there on the hour," she said, her voice firm and resolute. "Hang in there, Black. We'll figure this out together."

I felt a wave of relief wash over me at her words, a small spark of hope igniting in the darkness that had threatened to consume me. O'Malley had always been there for me, a steadfast partner and friend in a world that often felt cold and unforgiving. If anyone could help me make sense of the tangled web of secrets and lies that seemed to be closing in around us, it was her.

I heard a knock at my door and opened it to find O'Malley standing there, her face etched with concern. "You look like shit, Black," she said bluntly, stepping inside and shrugging off her coat. "What's going on?"

I led her to the rooftop terrace, the cool night air a welcome respite from the stuffy confines of my apartment. The city stretched out before us, a glittering expanse of lights and shadows that seemed to pulse with a life of its own.

I took a deep breath, the cool night air filling my lungs as I tried to gather my thoughts. O'Malley stood beside me, her brow furrowed in concern as she waited for me to speak.

"Samuel said something about the coins and Malthor," I began. "He said they were the key to finding the Hollow Soul, whatever that means."

O'Malley's eyes widened and her lips parted in surprise. "The coins?" she repeated, her voice tinged with disbelief. "How does he know about the coins or that name? That information was never made public."

I shook my head, "I don't know," I admitted, running a hand through my hair in frustration. "But he seemed so sure, so... clear. Like he had seen something or someone that had left a permanent mark on his psyche."

O'Malley was silent for a moment, her gaze fixed on the glittering city below. "There is something greater at work here, Black," she said. "Something beyond the scope of any ordinary investigation."

I nodded, "I know," I said, my voice breaking slightly. "But what are we to do? How are we supposed to make sense of any of this?"

O'Malley turned to face me, her eyes blazing with a fierce determination I had come to know all too well. "We do what we always do," her hand came to rest on my shoulder.

"We follow the evidence, we trust our instincts, and we don't stop until we find the truth."

I felt a wave of gratitude wash over me at her words. "You're right," I said, my voice growing stronger with each passing moment. "We can't let this break us. We have to keep going, no matter what."

O'Malley nodded, a small smile tugging at the corners of her lips. "Damn right," she said, a fierce determination in her voice. "And we'll start by seeing if Dr. Kensington's research uncovered any evidence of a Hollow Soul. There must be some connection, some clue we're missing."

"I'll contact Dr. Kensington first thing in the morning," I said, my voice filled with a newfound determination. "If anyone can shed some light on the meaning of this Hollow Soul or the coins, it's her."

O'Malley nodded, "And I'll see if I can dig up any more information on Ethan Ward," she said, her voice laced with a hint of suspicion. "I'll check his past schedule, see if it matches up with the previous murders."

A flash of unease hit me at the mention of Ward's name, the memory of our disturbing encounter still fresh in my mind. "Sounds good," I said, my voice softening. "If we can tie him to the places and times of the previous murders, we'll have a solid lead."

O'Malley placed a comforting hand on my arm, her touch a welcome reminder that I wasn't alone in this fight. "We'll figure it out, Black," her voice filled with a quiet strength that never ceased to amaze me. "Together."

I've never really told anyone about my brother. It's not something I like to talk about, the memories still raw and painful after all these years. But as O'Malley and I stood on that rooftop, the city stretched out before us like a glittering tapestry, I felt a sudden, overwhelming need to unburden myself, to share the weight of my past with someone I trusted.

"My brother Samuel wasn't always handicapped," I began. "He was a bright kid, always curious, always exploring. We used to have this secret hideout, an old abandoned warehouse on the outskirts of town. It was our own little world, a place where we could escape the troubles of the real one."

I paused, my throat tightening with emotion as the memories flooded back. "One day I insisted that we go out and play, even though Samuel wanted to stay home. I was bored, restless, and wouldn't take no for an answer. So we went to the warehouse, just like we always did."

I could feel O'Malley's eyes on me, her gaze filled with a quiet understanding that gave me the strength to continue. "We climbed around on the old machines, pretending to be adventurers in some faraway land. And then... then it happened."

My voice cracked, the words catching in my throat as I struggled to get them out. "Samuel walked over this old wooden beam, high up in the rafters. I remember the look on his face, the way his eyes widened in fear as the wood gave way beneath his feet. There was this sickening crack, like a gunshot, and then he fell, his scream cutting through the air like a knife."

I closed my eyes, the memory of that moment still vivid in my thoughts. "He hit the ground hard, his body crumpled like a rag doll. I remember running to him, my heart pounding in my chest as I prayed to every god I could think of that he would be okay. But when I got to him, when I saw his head twisted at an unnatural angle, the blood pooling beneath him... I knew that nothing would ever be the same."

O'Malley reached out, her hand coming to rest on my arm in a gesture of silent support. I took a shuddering breath, the tears I had held back for so long finally streaming down my cheeks.

"The impact broke more than his skull. It broke him as a person, shattering his mind into a million pieces that no one could put back together. He was never the same, never the bright, curious boy I had known and loved."

I felt O'Malley's arms wrap around me, her embrace a welcome comfort in the face of the pain that threatened to consume me. "I'm so sorry, James," she whispered, her voice thick with emotion. "I had no idea."

I nodded, my throat too tight to speak. For a long moment, we just stood there, two souls clinging to each other in the darkness, the weight of our shared pain a bond that could never be broken.

Finally, I pulled away, wiping the tears from my eyes with the back of my hand. "Samuel's warning, about the figure with the hollow soul... I think, no, I know it's connected to all of this, to the Rune Killer and the coins and everything else that's happened. We need to find out what it means, O'Malley. We have to uncover the truth, no matter where it takes us."

O'Malley nodded, her lips curving into a small, determined smile. "Consider it done," she said, her voice calm and reassuring. "I'll start pulling strings first thing in the morning, see what I can dig up on our mysterious professor."

"Thank you, O'Malley," my voice filled with heartfelt sincerity. "For everything. I don't know what I'd do without you."

O'Malley's smile widened, her eyes sparkling with a warmth that seemed to chase away the chill of the night air. "That's what partners are for, Black," she said, her voice filled with a quiet strength that never ceased to amaze me. "Through thick and thin, always."

And as we stood on that rooftop, the city stretched out before us like a shining tapestry, I knew she was right. Together, we would find the truth, no matter where it took us. For Samuel, for the victims, and for the city we had both sworn to protect.

The bullpen hums with frenetic energy as the investigation into the Rune Killer case ramps up. Cluttered desks overflow with case files, the air thick with the biting taste of mounting desperation. The weight of my secrets bears down like an oppressive shroud, threatening to crush me under its relentless pressure.

Ethan Ward's name has surfaced, the ghosts of my past inextricably tying me to this bloody affair. I glanced across the sea of desks to where

Black and O'Malley were poring over the evidence, their brows furrowed in concentration. If only I could confide in them, make them see that I'm not the enemy here. But their minds are too rigid, too bound by the brittle confines of law and order, to ever grasp the necessity of my actions.

Black has been a constant presence in my life, his steely resolve and unbending moral code acting as guideposts that have kept me grounded even in my darkest moments. And then there's O'Malley, the naive spark of youthful idealism still burning defiantly within her. Part of me envies the blind certainty she clings to, even though I know it is a dream as fleeting as a desert mirage.

If only they could have witnessed firsthand the impotent rage and soul-crushing despair that contorted Ethan Ward's features as he watched the last shreds of possible justice for his murdered wife disintegrate before his eyes. In that moment, I saw the system I had put all my faith in exposed for the hollow sham it truly was.

When I looked into Ethan's eyes after that travesty and saw the hatred burning there, the all-consuming obsession that would ultimately lead him down the path to the ritualistic savagery of the ancient dogma of the Ordo Iustitiae, it was like staring into a funhouse mirror's distorted reflection of my own soul.

There was a brutal elegance to their doctrine, one that eschewed the niceties of due process and legal bureaucracy in favor of a system far more primal and merciless. I understood the intoxicating appeal of such a worldview, the seductive fantasy of a realm where the guilty could never again escape the consequences they so richly deserved.

But the further down that road I went, the harder it became to discern my true motivations. Was I still acting as a shepherd, directing his zealotry toward those who deserved it? Or had I simply become so mired in my own cynicism that I was now using him as a smokescreen to channel my own repressed resentments?

So that's where I am now - seemingly assisting in the hunt for this depraved killer, while covertly misdirecting the efforts of the investigation, throwing them off the trail whenever they get too close to the awful truth. Perverting the course of justice to facilitate its most unrestrained deliverance.

Part of me longs to reach out to Black and O'Malley, to lay myself bare and explain the painful path that has brought me to this crossroads. But I know in my heart it would be in vain. They could never look into the abyss and move forward as I have. They would simply recoil in horror at what stares back.

So I will continue to walk this lonely path, doing what I must to keep this clash of values on its present course. Not out of malice, but out of the same weary pragmatism that allowed me to peel back the rotting scales that covered my eyes so long ago. I am simply the harbinger, clearing the way for the cataclysm that must be allowed to run its course before anything can be rebuilt upon the rubble.

CHAPTER TEN

ETHICAL QUAGMIRE

The moment I crossed the threshold of the department's conference room, the suffocating tension wrapped around me like a vice. Our unsolved case cast a pall over the assembled officers, an oppressive veil that suffocated the room. Chief Thompson commanded the bullpen, his forehead wrinkled with deep furrows and his jaw muscles twitching. Frustration etched itself into the jagged lines of his weathered face, the relentless pressure to produce results increasing with each passing day.

"Black, Ramirez," he barked, his voice cutting through the silence like a knife. "Tell me you've got something, anything that can help us catch this asshole."

I looked over at Ramirez and saw the same weariness in his eyes that I felt in my own. We'd been working around the clock, chasing down leads and questioning witnesses, but the Rune Killer always seemed to be one step ahead of us.

"Chief, we're doing everything we can," I said, my voice steady despite the frustration simmering beneath the surface. "But this case, it's not like anything we've seen before. The killer's methods, the shocking lack of physical evidence..."

Ramirez leaned forward, his elbows resting on the table as he fixed the Chief with a hard stare. "What Detective Black is trying to say, Chief, is that we need to be more aggressive. We can't just sit back and wait for the next body to drop. We need to take the fight to the killer, hit the streets, and shake things up until we get the break we need."

I felt my jaw tighten at Ramirez's words, a spark of anger igniting in my chest. "And what exactly are you suggesting we do, Ramirez?" I snapped, my voice harsher than I'd intended. "Start kicking in doors and roughing up suspects? We have to do this legitimately, or any evidence we find will be thrown out in court."

Ramirez's eyes narrowed and his lips curled into a sneer. "Wake up, Black. This killer doesn't play by the rules, and neither should we. We need to do whatever it takes to stop them, even if it means bending a few rules along the way."

The room erupted into chaos, voices rising and tempers flaring as the other officers took sides. Some nodded in agreement with Ramirez, while others looked at me, their eyes pleading for reason and restraint.

The Chief slammed his hands down on the table, the sharp crack of flesh on wood silencing the room. "Enough!" he shouted, his voice ringing with authority. "We are not vigilantes, and we are not above the law. We are officers of the Silvergate Police Department, and we will conduct this investigation with the integrity and professionalism that our badges demand."

Chief Thompson turned to Ramirez, their eyes locked. "Ramirez, I understand the pressure you're under, we all feel it. Don't think for a second that I don't want to crack skulls all over this city until we find this guy - believe me, I do. But I know what happens when you do, and we can't afford that right now. We have to be thorough, follow every lead, and examine every piece of evidence until we have an airtight case. Anything less and we risk letting this killer slip through our fingers."

The Chief's eyes bored into Ramirez, his expression unreadable. For a long moment, Ramirez said nothing, the silence stretching between them like a taut wire. Finally, he nodded, a grudging respect in his eyes.

"All right, Chief," he said, his voice gruff but not unkind. "I'll do it your way for now. But if the body count continues to rise, drastic measures will have to be taken, and I'm sure the mayor would agree."

The Chief nodded, and the tension in the room began to ease. "That may be, but we'll cross that bridge when we come to it."

As the meeting broke up and the officers filed out of the room with renewed purpose, I caught Ramirez's eye. There was a flicker of something, a darkness that seemed to go on forever. But before I could dwell on it, he turned away, his shoulders square as he stalked out of the room.

As I watched Ramirez a feeling of unease settled in the pit of my stomach. His words, his insistence on a more aggressive approach, had struck a chord with some of the officers, and I knew it would take more than a few impassioned speeches to keep everyone in line.

I turned to O'Malley, my partner and one of the few people in the department I trusted implicitly. "We need to talk," I said, my voice controlled and urgent. "Somewhere private."

She nodded, her eyes darting around the room before settling back on me. "Lead the way."

We made our way to one of the empty interrogation rooms, the heavy metal door swinging shut behind us with a resounding clang. I leaned against the wall, my arms crossed over my chest, trying to collect my thoughts.

"What Ramirez said in there," I began, my voice tight with tension, "about bending the rules, about doing whatever it takes... I can't let that happen, O'Malley. We have to do this the right way, or we're no better than the criminals we're trying to catch."

O'Malley sighed, her shoulders slumping as she sank into one of the hard plastic chairs. "I know, James. But sooner or later, this case is going to be taken out of our hands..."

She trailed off, the implication hanging heavy in the air between us. We both knew what was at stake - not just our careers, but the safety of the entire city. If we failed to stop the Rune Killer, more people would die, and their blood would be on our hands.

"I get it," I said, my voice softening as I moved to sit beside her. "But we can't let the pressure push us into making mistakes, into crossing lines we can't come back from. We have to be better than that, O'Malley. We have to be the ones who stand on principle, no matter how dim it gets."

She looked up at me, her eyes searching mine for a long moment before she nodded. "You're right. We'll do it your way, James. But we have to be smart about it. We can't let the killer stay one step ahead of us forever."

I reached out and squeezed her shoulder in a gesture of solidarity. "We won't. We'll find them, O'Malley. I promise you that."

As I stepped out of the interrogation room, I found myself face-to-face with Chief Thompson. His expression was a mixture of weariness and determination, the weight of the world seemed to rest on his broad shoulders.

"Black," he said, his voice gruff but not unkind. "A word in my office, if you don't mind."

I nodded and fell into step beside him as we walked through the busy corridors of the precinct. The air was thick with the smell of stale coffee and the hum of fluorescent lights, a familiar backdrop from the countless hours I'd spent within these walls.

As we entered the Chief's office, he motioned for me to take a seat behind the large oak desk that dominated the room. He leaned back in his chair as he fixed me with a steady gaze.

"I know you're under a lot of pressure, Black," he began, his voice measured and even. "We all feel it. The mayor is constantly on my case, the media is running wild with stories about this killer, and the community is beginning to doubt our ability to protect them."

I nodded, my jaw clenching as I thought of the headlines splashed across the front pages of every newspaper in the city. "The Rune Killer Strikes Again," they screamed, each new victim a fresh wound on the soul of Silvergate.

"I understand, Chief," I said, my voice hoarse with exhaustion. "We can't let the mindset of Ramirez pressure us into making mistakes. Like you said, we have to do this the right way, or we risk losing everything we've worked for."

The Chief sighed and closed his eyes before speaking again. "I hear you, Black. And I agree, to a point. We can't afford to cut corners, not when the stakes are this high. But we also can't afford to let this case drag on forever. The longer this killer is out there, the more lives will be lost."

I leaned forward to meet his gaze directly. "I know that, Chief. And I promise you, I'm doing everything in my power to bring this bastard to justice. But I need you to trust me, to give me the time and resources I need to do it right."

The Chief was silent for a long moment, his eyes searching mine as if looking for any sign of weakness or doubt. Finally, he nodded, a grudging respect in his eyes.

"All right, Black," he said. "You have my support, for now. But you must understand the gravity of the situation. The brass is putting a lot of pressure on me, and if we don't show some progress soon, they'll be looking for someone to blame."

I felt a flicker of anger at the implication, but I pushed it down and focused on the task at hand. "I understand, Chief. And I appreciate your confidence in me. I won't let you down."

The Chief leaned forward, his expression serious. "Make sure you don't, Black. I'm giving you two weeks to get a real lead on this case. If you can't deliver by then, I'll have no choice but to call in the feds. The story of our Rune Killer has spread far beyond Silvergate and has caught the attention of the Department of Justice."

I shuddered at the prospect of the feds swooping in and commandeering the case. Their love of bureaucracy and protocol would surely spell disaster when pitted against the unpredictable madness of our prey. But I bit my tongue, knowing that protesting to the Chief would only make matters worse. I settled for a solemn nod, my face a mask of determination tinged with unease.

"I understand, Chief. I'll do everything in my power to get us a lead before then. You have my word."

As I left the Chief's office, I felt the weight and responsibility of the badge on my chest. I knew that the next two weeks would be crucial, that every moment would count if we were to stop the Rune Killer before they struck again or the feds were called in.

As I walked out of the station, the cool evening air hit my face, a welcome respite from the overwhelming tension that had permeated every corner of the building. My mind was still reeling from my conversations with O'Malley and Chief Thompson, their words echoing in my ears like a relentless drumbeat.

I was so lost in thought that I didn't notice the figure approaching me until they were practically on top of me. I looked up, my hand instinctively reaching for my gun, only to be confronted by a familiar blonde ponytail and a pair of piercing hazel eyes.

"Detective Black," Isabel Reyes said, her voice dripping with false sweetness. "Just the man I was hoping to see."

I felt my jaw clench, my patience already wearing thin. Isabel Reyes was a reporter for the Silvergate Gazette, and she had been hounding us for weeks, looking for any scrap of information she could use to sell papers.

"Ms. Reyes," I said, my voice tight with barely contained annoyance. "I'm afraid I don't have time for your questions right now. I have work to do."

But Isabel was not so easily deterred. She stepped in front of me, blocking my path with her slender frame. "Come on, Detective," she purred, her eyes narrowing. "Surely you can spare a few minutes for the press. The people of Silvergate have a right to know what's going on with this case."

I felt my temper flare, my hands balling into fists at my sides. "The people of Silvergate have a right to be safe," I snapped, my voice rising despite my best efforts to control it. "And that's exactly what I'm trying to do - keep them safe from a killer who's still out there."

Isabel scoffed, her pretty face twisting into a sneer. "Is that so? Because from where I'm standing, it doesn't look like you're doing a very good job. How many people have to die before you catch this guy, Detective? How many bodies will it take before you admit you're in over your head?"

I felt my blood begin to boil, my vision turning red at the edges. "You have no idea what you're talking about," I growled, my voice deep and dangerous. "You think this is some kind of game, some way to sell papers and further your career? Well, let me tell you something, Ms. Reyes. This is real life, and real people are dying out there. And I will not rest until I bring their killer to justice."

I felt my anger continue to rise, Isabel's words cutting deep, her accusation that I was letting the people of Silvergate down hitting way too close to home.

"You want to know what we're up against?" I said sharply, my voice carrying a bitter edge. "This killer? As if their use of runes wasn't enough of a calling card. Now they've started leaving ancient coins behind, a twisted token to commemorate their deeds. They fancy themselves some kind of vigilante, taking justice into their own hands."

The moment the words left my mouth, I knew I'd made a mistake. Isabel's eyes widened, a gleam of triumph flashing in their hazel depths.

"Ancient coins?" she repeated, her voice eager and hungry. "What kind of coins? Where did they come from?"

I cursed under my breath, my hand running through my hair in agitation. "That's confidential information," I said, my voice tight with barely contained anger. "I shouldn't have said anything."

But it was too late. I could see the wheels turning in Isabel's head, her reporter's instincts kicking into high gear. "This is big, Detective," she said, her voice cracking with excitement. "The public needs to know. They have a right to know what kind of monster is stalking their streets."

I shook my head, my jaw tensing in frustration. "No, they don't," I said, my voice clear and intense. "Not yet. Not until we have something solid. If we release this information now, it could jeopardize the entire investigation."

Isabel scoffed, "Or maybe you just don't want to admit you're in over your head," she said, her voice dripping with contempt. "Maybe you're afraid that if the public knew the truth, they'd lose what little faith they have left in the Silvergate Police Department."

I took a deep breath, trying to regain my composure. "I can't discuss the details of an ongoing investigation," I said, seething. "And if you print anything about those coins, Ms. Reyes, I swear to God I will have you arrested for obstruction of justice."

Isabel's eyes narrowed and her lips curled into a mocking grin. "Is that a threat, Detective?"

"No," I said, my voice cold and hard. "It's a promise."

With that, I pushed past her, my shoulder brushing roughly against hers as I stalked down the street. I could feel her eyes boring into my back, but I refused to look back, refused to give her the satisfaction of seeing how much she had gotten under my skin.

As I walked, I could feel the anger and frustration boiling inside me, threatening to erupt at any moment. I knew I had to pull myself together, focus on the task at hand, and not be distracted by the likes of Isabel Reyes.

But as I made my way back to my apartment, my mind kept drifting back to those coins, to the strange symbols etched into their surface and the secrets they held.

I thought back to my visit with Samuel, to the cryptic warning he had given me about the "hollow soul figure". Could Samuel have been referring to Ethan Ward? The man's evasive answers during our interview, the sense of unease that had settled over me as we left his office... it all seemed to indicate something sinister lurking beneath the surface.

But what if I was wrong? What if my own biases, my own desperate need for answers, were leading me down the wrong path? I had seen it happen before, good cops so consumed with closing a case that they lost sight of the truth.

I couldn't let that happen to me. I had to stay focused, follow the evidence wherever it led, even if it meant facing uncomfortable truths about myself and the people I trusted.

As I sat there, staring into the darkness, I felt the weight of my own mortality bearing down on me. I had seen too much death in my time on the force, too many lives cut short by the cruelty and callousness of others. And now, with the Rune Killer on the loose, that darkness seemed closer than ever.

But I knew I couldn't let it get to me. I had to keep fighting, keep pushing forward, no matter how hard it got. Because if I didn't, if I let the darkness win... then what was the point?

With a heavy sigh, I pushed myself to my feet, my bones aching with the weight of the day. Tomorrow would bring new challenges, new obstacles to overcome. But for now, all I could do was try to get some rest and gather my strength for the battles ahead.

As I lay on my narrow bed, my thoughts drifted to Ramirez, to the darkness I had seen in his eyes during the meeting. I couldn't shake the feeling that there was more to his story than he was letting on, that his obsession with the case ran deeper than mere professional pride.

But that was a puzzle for another day. For now, all I could do was close my eyes and pray for dreamless sleep, for a few precious hours of respite from the horrors that awaited us in the waking world.

Miles away, in a nondescript apartment on the outskirts of the city, a figure hunched over a computer screen. The room was shrouded in darkness, the only illumination coming from the eerie glow of the monitor. The figure's face was obscured by shadows, but their eyes shone with a cold, calculating intensity.

They scanned the message board with a practiced eye, their gaze settling on the invitation from their contact. A slow, sinister smile spread across their face as they read the words, a sense of anticipation building in their chests. They reached into their pockets and pulled out a small, ancient coin, its surface etched with intricate runes that seemed to writhe and dance in the dim light.

The calling card of the Rune Killer.

They turned the coin in their fingers, feeling its weight, the power it held. This was more than a symbol of their dark deeds. It was a promise, a vow to bring the full force of their uncompromising retribution upon those who had escaped judgment for too long.

The figure's eyes flicked back to the screen, their smile widening as they began to gather information on their next target. The poor soul had no idea what was coming, no idea of the suffering that was about to befall them. The figure's fingers danced across the keyboard with practiced ease, pulling up records and personal details, weaving a tapestry of the target's life. Each piece of information was another thread in the grand design, a new vulnerability to exploit, a new pressure point to manipulate.

The target's mundane existence played out on the screen, blissfully unaware of the unyielding force that now dissected their every move. The figure leaned back, a sense of power and anticipation coursing through their veins as they contemplated the delicious terror they were about to unleash. This was more than just a hunt – it was an art form, a sacred ritual of pain and suffering that few could truly appreciate. But the figure understood.

The Rune Killer leaned forward in their chair, a sense of calm washing over them as they prepared for the next phase of their meticulous plan. The world saw them as a monster, a twisted killer driven by some dark, unknowable force that compelled them to commit unspeakable acts of violence and depravity. The authorities and the media portrayed them as a soulless creature, devoid of humanity or conscience, a boogeyman to be feared and reviled by all who valued peace and order.

But the Rune Killer knew the truth. They relished their role as an agent of order, an agent of an older form of justice that the world so desperately needed. A tool of divine retribution for those wronged by a system that had failed them time and again. The corrupt, the powerful, the untouchable – they had all escaped the consequences of their actions for far too long, shielded by wealth and influence from the righteous hand of punishment. The Rune Killer had taken it upon themselves to balance the scales, to mete out the justice that the courts and the law had been too weak or too compromised to deliver.

And they would not rest until every last one of the guilty had paid the price for their sins. Each meticulously planned murder was a sacred act of purification, a way to cleanse the world of the rot and filth that had been allowed to fester for far too long. The work of the Rune Killer was not done, and they would continue their crusade until the streets ran red with the blood of the wicked and unjust.

CHAPTER ELEVEN

DEVELOPMENTAL CLUES

I leaned back in my chair and rubbed my tired eyes behind my blue-tinted glasses. The glow of the computer screens illuminated my face in the dimly lit office. O'Malley's words echoed in my mind as I recalled our conversation a few days ago.

"Emily, I need you to dig into this historical forum," O'Malley had said, her voice urgent. "Any information you can find on the users, their interactions, anything that might give us a lead on the Rune Killer."

I nodded, understanding the gravity of the situation. "I'll do my best, O'Malley. You know you can count on me."

O'Malley had smiled and put a hand on my shoulder. "I know, Em. I have complete faith in you. If anyone can uncover something, it's you."

Now, as I sat hunched over my keyboard, I couldn't help but feel the importance of this assignment. My fingers flew over the keys, lines of code, and data streaming across the screens. I had been at it for days, barely stopping to eat or sleep. The historical forum was a maze of coded messages and hidden identities, each clue leading me down another twisted path.

I sighed and pushed my glasses up the bridge of my nose. My attempts to contact or locate a web administrator to simplify this undertaking had all failed. The more I dug, the more frustrated I became. It seemed that every time I got close to something substantial, the trail went cold. Usernames led to dead ends, IP addresses bounced through multiple proxies, and encrypted messages defied even my most advanced decryption algorithms.

The office was quiet, save for the hum of the computers and the occasional creak of my chair. The rest of the department had long since gone home, but I couldn't bring myself to leave. Not with O'Malley and the others counting on me. Not when the Rune Killer was still out there, waiting to strike again.

I glanced at the clock, the glowing numbers telling me it was well past midnight. My eyes burned from staring at the screens for so long, and my neck ached from being hunched over. But I couldn't stop. Not now.

I took a sip of my now cold coffee, grimacing at the bitter taste. I had lost count of how many cups I had consumed in the past few days. It was the only thing keeping me going, the caffeine coursing through my veins like a lifeline.

As I continued to work, I thought of O'Malley and Detective Black, out there on the front lines, working tirelessly to catch the killer. And here I was, hidden away in my office, trying to piece together the digital puzzle.

But I knew my work was just as important. The Historical Forum held the key to unlocking the identity of the Rune Killer, I was sure of it. And I wouldn't rest until I found it.

The hours ticked by, the night giving way to the first hints of dawn. My eyes grew heavy and my fingers slowed on the keys. Still, I pressed on, determined to find something, anything, that would help me crack the case.

Finally, I leaned back in my chair, a triumphant grin spreading across my face as I stared at the list of IP addresses on my screen. It had taken days of relentless work and countless hours of sifting through encrypted data and chasing down digital dead ends, but I had finally done it. I had compiled a list of users accessing the historical forums, the very same forums that held the key to unlocking the Rune Killer's identity.

I quickly printed out the list, my heart racing with excitement as I collected the pages. I couldn't wait to share this breakthrough with O'Malley and Detective Black. I could clearly see the toll their relentless pursuit of the killer had taken on their faces. And now I finally had something concrete to contribute to the investigation.

I hurried out of my office, the printouts clutched tightly in my hand. The hallways of the department were still quiet, most of my colleagues were not yet in for the day. But I knew O'Malley and Black would already be here, poring over case files and chasing down leads.

I found them in the conference room, hunched over a table strewn with papers and photographs. They looked up as I burst in, their eyes widening at the sight of the printouts in my hand.

"I've got something," I announced, unable to keep the excitement out of my voice. "I've compiled a list of IP addresses accessing the historical forums. We can use this to narrow down our list of potential suspects."

O'Malley's face lit up, a grin spreading across her features. "Emily, that's fantastic! I knew you could do it."

I handed over the printouts and watched as O'Malley and Black pored over the information.

"This is a huge break," Black said, his voice gruff with exhaustion. "We can cross-reference these IP addresses with our existing list of suspects, see if any names jump out."

I nodded, feeling a surge of pride at being able to help move the investigation forward. "I'll keep digging into the forums, see if I can uncover any more information about the users' interactions or communications."

O'Malley placed a hand on my shoulder, her eyes bright with gratitude. "Thank you, Emily. This is exactly what we needed to keep the investigation moving forward."

I smiled, basking in the glow of her appreciation. It felt good to be a part of something so important, to know that my skills and expertise were making a real difference in the fight against the Rune Killer.

But even as we celebrated this small victory, I could see the caution in Black's eyes. He had been on the force long enough to know that any misstep could set them back, that the killer was always one step ahead.

"We have to be careful," he warned, his voice serious. "We can't afford to tip our hand too soon. If the killer catches wind of our progress, they could go underground or change tactics."

I nodded, understanding the seriousness of the situation. "I'll be discreet in my inquiries, making sure not to raise any red flags."

Black gave a curt nod, his eyes already back on the printouts. "Good. And keep us informed of any new developments. The sooner we can identify the killer, the sooner we can put an end to this nightmare."

I left the conference room with a renewed sense of purpose, my mind already racing with ideas on how to dig deeper into the forums. I knew it wouldn't be easy, that the killer was cunning and elusive. But I also knew that I had the skills and determination to uncover the truth, no matter how deep it was buried.

As I walked back to my office, I couldn't help but feel a sense of pride and accomplishment. I had always been the quiet one, the technical expert hidden behind computer screens and lines of code. But now I was a vital part of the team, my work just as important as the detectives on the front lines.

I settled back into my chair, my fingers already flying across the keyboard as I dove back into the forums. I had a killer to catch, and I wouldn't rest until I had uncovered every last bit of digital evidence.

The hours ticked by, the glow of the computer screens my only companion as I worked. But I didn't mind the solitude or the long hours. I knew that every minute I spent with my hands on the keyboard was a minute closer to ending the Rune Killer's bloody reign.

And with O'Malley and Black by my side, I knew we would succeed. We were a team, each of us bringing our own unique skills and strengths to the table. Together, we would unravel the mystery of the Rune Killer.

The news from Officer Chen filled me with a renewed sense of purpose, a spark of hope igniting within me. We were finally making real progress on this twisted case, getting closer to the truth with each new lead. I turned to O'Malley, a smile tugging at the corners of my mouth, the anticipation of our impending breakthrough palpable in the air between us. "I think it's time we paid Laura a visit, see if she's uncovered anything useful," I said, my voice steady despite the excitement coursing through my veins.

O'Malley looked up, her dark eyes sparkling with the same anticipation I felt. "Let's go," she said, grabbing her jacket from the back of her chair, the leather creaking softly as she pulled it on.

The city blurred past, a streak of gray and harsh neon, as I weaved through the streets toward the university, my mind hungry for new discoveries. A tingle of certainty crept up my spine, a bone-deep conviction that we were teetering on the knife's edge of revelation, the truth straining to break free from its shackles.

But as we approached Dr. Kensington's office, that feeling evaporated, replaced by a growing unease that settled like a lead weight in the pit of my stomach. The door was ajar, and I could see papers strewn across the floor, fluttering in the breeze from the open window.

I exchanged a glance with O'Malley, my hand instinctively reaching for my gun, the cool metal a reassuring presence against my palm as I pushed the door open, the hinges creaking ominously in the silence.

The scene that greeted us was one of utter chaos, a stark contrast to the orderly sanctuary I had come to associate with Dr. Kensington. Her usually immaculate office had been ransacked, artifacts and papers strewn about as if someone had been searching for something in a desperate frenzy. Bookshelves had been overturned, their contents spilled across the floor in a tangle of leather and parchment.

I stepped cautiously into the room, my eyes scanning the debris for any sign of Dr. Kensington, my heart pounding in my ears. O'Malley followed close behind, her own gun drawn, the soft click of the safety a reminder of the danger lurking in the shadows. "Laura?" I called, my voice sounding unnaturally loud in the eerie silence, echoing off the walls like a ghostly howl.

There was no response, only the faint rustle of papers in the breeze. I moved cautiously further into the office. Someone had gone to great lengths to disrupt our investigation, to suppress the findings that Dr. Kensington had come so close to uncovering. But who? And why? The questions burned in my mind, fueling my determination to solve this mystery once and for all.

As I surveyed the chaotic scene, a sudden banging sound from the back of the office made me freeze, my breath catching in my throat. O'Malley and I exchanged a tense look, our weapons raised as we crept toward the source of the noise, our footsteps muffled by the debris littering the floor. My heart pounded in my chest, adrenaline coursing through my veins as I prepared myself for what lay ahead, the unknown danger lurking just beyond our line of sight.

With bated breath, I lifted the heavy wooden lid, a tempest of anticipation and apprehension raging within me. My pounding heart stopped as my gaze fell on the trembling form of Dr. Laura Kensington, her once poised facade shattered. Wide, haunted eyes stared back at me from a ghostly pale face, her normally styled hair now tangled in disarray. She looked like a cornered animal, cowering in the shadows of her makeshift prison.

"Laura, it's okay. You're safe now," I said softly, reaching out to help her from the confines of the chest.

O'Malley holstered her gun and knelt beside me, her voice soft as she tried to calm the frightened historian. "Dr. Kensington, can you tell us what happened?"

Laura took a deep, shuddering breath, her hands still shaking as she accepted our help. "I... I was working late, researching the coins and their connection to the ancient cult. Suddenly there was this loud, aggressive banging on the door. It was so violent, I thought it was going to come off its hinges."

She paused, her eyes distant as she relived the terrifying moment. "I heard someone shouting, their voice filled with a desperate, almost inhuman energy. They were speaking in an ancient tongue, one I couldn't quite place, but it sounded like a dark incantation."

"And then what?" I asked, my voice full of urgency.

"I hid," Laura admitted. "I couldn't face whoever was out there. I heard them stalking through the office, rifling through my books and artifacts as if they were looking for something. It felt like an eternity before they finally left."

As Laura gradually regained her composure, I helped her to a nearby chair, clearing a space amidst the chaos of her once-tidy office. "You mentioned that you were researching the coins. Have you discovered anything new?"

Laura nodded, her eyes glowing with a flicker of her usual passion. "I had just discovered an ancient tome that dealt with the origins and purpose of the coins. It spoke of how each coin was a way for the cult members to leave a final mark, a binding signature that tied them to the dark deeds they carried out."

She paused, her brow furrowed as she collected her thoughts. "The coins were more than just a calling card; they were a symbol of ownership, a way for the cultists to claim responsibility for their actions. By leaving a coin at the scene, they were essentially signing their work, declaring to the world that they were the architects of the horrors that had been wrought."

Laura's voice softened, almost reverent. "In a twisted way, the coins were a form of devotion, a physical manifestation of the cultists' commitment to their dark purpose. Each coin left behind held a piece of their essence, a fragment of their souls, forever bound to the atrocities they had committed in devotion to Malthor."

She looked up at me, her eyes haunted. "The Rune Killer is following in their footsteps, Detective. By leaving these coins at the crime scenes, they're not just taunting us; they're proclaiming their allegiance to the cult's legacy. They're declaring themselves the rightful heirs to the cult's dark power."

A shudder ran through me as she spoke, her haunting words sinking in. The implications were profound. If the Rune Killer truly saw themselves as upholding the cult's hideous mission, then their atrocities went beyond mere acts of brutality; they were ritualistic offerings, twisted tributes to some malevolent, unholy force.

"So you're saying that the Rune Killer isn't just some random psychopath," I said slowly, trying to wrap my head around the concept. "They're a true believer, a disciple of this ancient cult."

Laura nodded grimly. "Exactly. And if that's the case, then their actions are driven by something far more powerful than mere human impulses. They're guided by a higher purpose, a divine mandate to bring about the cult's dark vision of justice."

She looked around the room, her brow furrowed. "But the book... it's gone. Whoever ransacked my office must have taken it. I fear that with its loss, we may have lost a vital piece of the puzzle."

"We'll find it," I assured her, my voice filled with a conviction I didn't quite feel. "In the meantime, we need to ensure your safety. I'm placing you under police protection for the time being."

I placed a reassuring hand on Laura's shoulder and met her gaze with a steady stare. "I promise you, we will get to the bottom of this. The Rune Killer won't get away with their crimes, not while I'm on the case."

Laura looked like she wanted to protest, but the lingering fear in her eyes told me she understood the importance of having someone watching her back. She nodded, accepting the offer of protection with a grateful, if somewhat strained, smile. "Thank you, James. I know you and O'Malley will do everything in your power to keep me safe and solve this mystery."

As O'Malley made the necessary arrangements, calling in a protective detail and coordinating with the university's security team, I couldn't shake the feeling that we were running out of time. The Rune Killer was growing bolder, more desperate, and now they had struck at the heart of our investigation, targeting the very person who had helped us decipher their twisted motives.

If the killer was willing to go after Dr. Kensington, it meant they were getting closer to their endgame, whatever that might be. We had to act quickly, and put an end to this madness before anyone else got hurt.

I glanced over at Laura and noticed the fear and uncertainty in her eyes. It was a look I had seen far too often in my line of work, the look of someone whose world had been turned upside down by the actions of a depraved criminal.

As I stepped into my dimly lit apartment, the weight of the day's events felt like cement shoes dragging me beneath the waves. I shrugged off my coat, tossing it carelessly onto the nearest chair, and made my way to the kitchen, my footsteps heavy on the hardwood floor.

I poured myself a generous glass of whiskey, the amber liquid glittering in the dim light filtering through the blinds. The first sip burned as it went down, but I welcomed the sensation, a reminder that I was still alive, still fighting. I carried the glass to my desk and sank into the worn leather chair with a weary sigh.

The events of the day played out in my mind like a twisted highlight reel. The discovery of Dr. Kensington's ransacked office, the fear in her eyes as we found her huddled in that chest, the sinking realization that the Rune Killer was growing bolder, more desperate. The thoughts simmered inside me, detonating a thunderhead of rage in my head.

I reached for the file on my desk, the one that had consumed my every waking thought for the past few months. The Rune Killer case. I flipped through the pages, my eyes scanning the gruesome crime scene photos. The cryptic symbols that seemed to mock us took on greater meaning as their secrets were revealed. We were so close, I could feel it in my bones, but every time we seemed to be gaining ground, another obstacle threw us back.

The attack on Dr. Kensington was a turning point, a sign that the stakes had been raised. If the killer was willing to go after one of our lead investigators, what else were they capable of? The thought sent a rush of anger through my veins and I took another sip of whiskey, savoring the burn as it slid down my throat.

We had to be more careful, more vigilant than ever. It was clear now that the hunters had become the hunted, that the Rune Killer was after us as well. This knowledge burrowed into my depths, a constant reminder of the danger that lurked in every shadow.

I leaned back in my chair, my eyes drifting to the window, to the city stretching before me. Somewhere out there, the Rune Killer was planning their next move, choosing their next victim. And it was up to us to stop them, to bring them to justice before they could strike again.

The thought of failure, of another life lost to this madman, was almost too much to bear. I closed my eyes, my grip on the glass in my hand tightening. We had to succeed, there was no other way. I had made a promise to myself, to the people of this city. I would not rest until the Rune Killer was behind bars, until their reign of terror was finally over.

But a small, insidious voice in the back of my mind whispered doubts. The targets weren't completely blameless, they all had their share of horrible misdeeds. It was a heavy burden to carry, knowing that the people whose deaths I was investigating were not blameless themselves.

But that was the point, wasn't it? Regardless of their transgressions, it was not the Rune Killer's place to assume the role of judge, jury, and executioner. That was the job of the judiciary, the courts, and the law. By taking matters into their own hands, the Rune Killer had crossed a line, a line that separated the civilized from the barbaric.

I shook my head, trying to clear the conflicting thoughts from my mind. It was a slippery slope, one I couldn't afford to tread. My job was to uphold the law, to ensure that those who broke it faced the consequences of their actions. The Rune Killer, no matter how much they believed in their twisted cause, was no exception.

I set my glass down on the table, my resolve hardening. I would see this through to the end. The Rune Killer would face justice, true justice, not the perverted version they had chosen for themself. And I would be the one to bring it, to ensure that the victims, flawed as they may have been, received the closure and peace they deserved.

Chapter Twelve

Ominous Portents

The call came as the first light of dawn began to creep across the city, a thin ray of hope in an otherwise bleak and unforgiving landscape. I was already awake, hunched over my desk with a steaming cup of coffee, its rich aroma wafting through the air, when the familiar chirp of my phone pierced the silence. The shrill sound reverberated through my cramped office, bouncing off the walls lined with case files and faded photographs of happier times.

I answered on the second ring, "Black."

The voice on the other end was tense, urgent. "Detective, we have another one. Abandoned warehouse at 5th and Main. It's... it's bad."

White-hot anger boiled in the pit of my stomach. Another life cut short by the twisted game of this depraved monster. I clenched my jaw, hands curled into fists as fury coursed through my veins. "I'm on my way," I growled.

I grabbed my coat and keys, the movements automatic, mechanical. How many times had I done this? How many crime scenes had I entered? Too many to count, and yet each one felt like ripping off a scab, exposing a fresh wound on an already battered soul. The weight of countless unsolved cases pressed down on me, a crushing burden that never seemed to lift.

The drive to the warehouse was a blur, my mind racing with the possibilities of what I might find. The killer had escalated, their methods growing more brutal, more calculated with each passing day. What new horrors would they have in store for us this time? The thought made my stomach churn, acid burning at the back of my throat.

As I pulled up to the scene, the flashing lights of the patrol cars casting an eerie red and blue glow over the dilapidated building, I felt a sudden sense of familiarity wash over me. At first, I couldn't quite place it, my anger and frustration clouding my perception. But as I stepped out of the car and took in the surroundings, the realization hit me like a wrecking ball.

This was the warehouse where my brother's accident had happened all those years ago. The place where our lives had been irreparably shattered, where the course of our futures had been changed forever. I hadn't recognized the address at first, too consumed by the urgency of the call and the adrenaline pumping through my veins. But now, standing here in the harsh glare of the floodlights, it was all too clear.

The gritty asphalt beneath my feet, the stench of decay and neglect that permeated the air - it all came back to me in a tidal wave of memories. I could almost hear the echoes of that fateful day, the scream, and the sickening crunch of bones. It was as if time had folded back on itself, taking me back to that moment of horror and helplessness.

I shook my head, trying to clear the ghosts of the past from my mind. I couldn't afford to get lost in memories, not now. There was a job to do, a killer to catch. I had to focus on the present, on the task at hand. But even as I steeled myself and made my way to the warehouse entrance, I could feel the stress of the tragedy bearing down on me, threatening to drag me back into the depths of despair.

It was a kind of twisted homecoming, a return to the place where my life had been shattered beyond repair. But I couldn't let it break me, not again. I had to be stronger than this. I pushed forward, jaw clenched and heart heavy, ready to face whatever horrors awaited me within the walls of the warehouse.

I ducked under the police tape, my pulse quickening as I made my way inside. The stench of death surrounded me, thick and cloying in the stagnant air. I breathed through my mouth, trying to block out the smell as I moved deeper into the warehouse.

The pungent stench broke through all my defenses, leaving me gagging as I entered the kill room. There, under the harsh glow of the halogen lights, was a sight that would be seared into my subconscious for years to come.

The victim had been encased in a makeshift cube of thick acrylic panels, bolted together to form an inescapable, transparent prison. Only her head, hands, and feet were exposed to the elements.

Through the scratched acrylic, I could see her bloated, discolored body. She appeared to be a black woman in her early 40s, her face gaunt and her eyes sunken from prolonged suffering. Camera flashes highlighted her sallow skin in gruesome detail, accentuating every lesion and blemish on her ravaged flesh.

Scattered around the scene were empty bottles of honey and cases of milk - weeks' worth of containers left to pile up. A crude IV system had been inserted, presumably to provide just enough hydration to prolong the torture.

The victim's body showed signs of severe diarrhea. Her torso and the enclosure were soiled with semi-solid feces that had been expelled uncontrollably from her bowels. A gruesome result of being force-fed copious amounts of milk and honey, as evidenced by the empty containers scattered around the room. The putrid secretions pooled at the bottom of the cube with nowhere to drain.

The IV tubing and injection site itself appeared clear and free of contamination. But the victim's exposed head and limbs were covered in weeping sores, the skin ravaged by the voracious insects that had swarmed over the defenseless flesh...

This slow, sadistic torture was designed to punish, not kill. The arcane runes, meticulously carved into the face, ensured prolonged suffering while keeping fatal infection at bay. The murderer would not allow the sweet release of death until the ritual was complete.

Revulsion rose in my throat at the methodical, clinical cruelty of what had been inflicted here. That a human mind could coldly devise such sadistic suffering was beyond my comprehension. But one thing was clear - this was no ordinary man we were hunting. This was evil in its purest incarnation.

I knelt beside the body, my eyes tracing the lines of the runes, searching for some clue, some hint of the killer's identity. But there was nothing, only the cold and lifeless stare of the victim, her eyes fixed on some distant point beyond the veil.

I stood, my legs shaking beneath me. The warehouse seemed to be bearing down on me from all sides, the walls closing in like the jaws of some great beast. I felt a sudden urge to run, to escape this place and the horrors it held. But I knew I couldn't, I knew I had a duty to the victim, to the people of this city.

I turned to the officers behind me, my voice steady despite the turmoil raging inside me. "Secure the scene. I want every inch of this place gone over with a fine-toothed comb. If there's a shred of evidence, I want it found." My words carried the force of my conviction and echoed through the cavernous warehouse. The atmosphere around me hummed with a lingering malevolence, an almost tangible force that made my teeth grind.

They nodded, their faces etched with purpose. I noticed the same haunted look in their eyes that resided in my own, a testament to the endless horrors of this case. The air was thick with unspoken fears and doubts, but we pushed them aside and focused on the task at hand. There was no room for weakness, no moment for doubt. We had a job to do, and we were determined to see it through.

As I stepped back out into the cold morning air, the first rays of sunlight breaking through the clouds, a nagging thought gnawed at the back of my mind. The place where the body was found, a place that held such deep meaning for me, seemed like more than just a coincidence. Did the Rune Killer know about my connection to this place? Were they trying to send me a message, to show that they had intimate knowledge of my past and could use it to get to me?

The biting wind whipped at my coat, but I barely felt it, my mind consumed by the ramifications of this idea. If the killer had deliberately chosen this place, it meant he had been watching me, studying my life and my history. The thought made my skin crawl, the idea that someone was lurking in the shadows, privy to my most personal moments and memories.

As I left the scene, a renewed sense of purpose settled over me, tinged with a hint of unease. The killer had made this personal, had brought the fight to my own backyard. They wanted to rattle me, to throw me off balance by digging up the ghosts of my past.

I refused to let them win. I would use this newfound clarity to fuel my hunt, to push myself harder than ever before. The Rune Killer may have thought they could break me, but they had only succeeded in strengthening my resolve. I would find them, and I would make them pay for every life they had taken, for every scar they had left on this city and on my soul.

Detective Black leaned back in his chair, glancing around the crowded briefing room as he discussed the latest developments in the Rune Killer case. Most of the other officers were dutifully taking notes or flipping through the case files in front of them. One officer, however, seemed less engaged; he already knew everything there was to know about this investigation, perhaps even more than Black realized.

As Black continued the briefing, the officer instead subtly observed the reactions of their colleagues. Their gaze quickly focused on O'Malley, who scribbled away, and asked pointed questions, her dark eyes missing nothing.

O'Malley's instincts were sharp, almost as sharp as Black's. Almost.

"The last victim, Destiny Jackson, was on trial last year," Black said. "The defense attorney managed to discredit the witness's testimony on a technicality, even though Ms. Jackson was clearly guilty."

Murmurs rippled through the room. The officer maintained a stoic facade, giving no indication that this revelation was anything but new information.

"So the pattern holds," O'Malley said. "Each victim was central to a case where the proceedings collapsed and they were released back into society."

Black nodded, "It's clear now that the Rune Killer is taking matters into their own hands. They've lost faith in the legal system and have appointed themselves judge, jury, and executioner. But it's more than that."

He gestured to the evidence board, where photos of the ancient coins and runic markings were pinned next to the victims' faces. "The symbols, the ritualistic nature of the killings... this isn't just a vigilante with a grudge. The Rune Killer believes they're fulfilling some kind of sacred duty."

He paused, his brow furrowed as another realization hit him. "But there's something else that bothers me. How does the killer know about these people and their involvement in these cases? It took me days to dig up some of these records, to uncover the connections between the victims and the failed prosecutions."

O'Malley leaned forward, her eyes narrowing. "You're right. It's not like this information is just floating around out there. Someone would have to have pretty high-level access to even know where to start looking."

Black nodded, "Which means we have to consider the possibility that the Rune Killer is someone with intimate knowledge of the legal system. Someone who knows how to navigate the bureaucracy to find the skeletons in the closet."

Reynolds added, "That, or more worrisome, they have someone on the inside feeding them information" Reynolds's comment caused a sudden commotion in the bullpen. Voices rose and desks creaked as detectives leaned in to exchange whispers and worried glances.

The thought turned his stomach as a nagging doubt began to fester. A mole, leaking case details to aid this depraved killer's twisted game? Who among his colleagues could be capable of such unforgivable treachery? The paranoia threatened to crush him before he violently cast it aside.

He turned to O'Malley, his expression grave. "We need to start looking at everyone involved in these cases who might have had access to this kind of information. Witnesses, defendants, lawyers... even officers and judges. Anyone with a personal stake in these failures."

O'Malley's face paled at the thought. "Are you really suggesting that it could be someone inside the system? Someone we've trusted? You can't seriously be considering Reynolds' idea of an insider?"

Black's gaze was unwavering. "It's a possibility we can't ignore. The Rune Killer's knowledge, their access... it all points to someone with deep ties to the legal world. And if that's the case, we have to be prepared for the call to come from inside the house."

Reynolds scoffed. "Who in this town hasn't been failed by the system? Could be half the population for all we know."

"Then you better get started," Black replied evenly. Always so cool under pressure. One of the many things to admire about him over the years. Too bad the admiration had to be repaid with deception.

"Chen, keep digging into those IP addresses. Someone is using this forum to leak information, we need to know who." Black instructed. "Jones, re-interview everyone involved in the related cases. See if they know of anyone who might have had a vendetta."

Jones agreed and hurriedly made some notes. Black turned his piercing gaze on Ramirez. "Ramirez, you and I are going to take another look at the physical evidence, see if forensics missed anything."

Ramirez gave a curt nod. "You got it."

When the briefing was over, Jones stayed behind, waiting until the others had filtered out before approaching Black.

"That researcher you brought in, Dr. Kensington," Jones said casually. "You really think she's onto something with those coins and runic symbols?"

Black's expression was guarded. "I'm positive. Her original assessment seems to be holding up, and the deeper we dig, the more her theory is validated."

A skeptical snort escaped Jones' lips. "Seems a little far-fetched, if you ask me."

"Right now it's the only lead we have," Black said firmly. "Unless you have a better angle?"

Jones held up his hands in mock surrender. "Hey, just making conversation. You know I'll follow wherever the evidence leads."

Black studied Jones for a moment before nodding slowly. "Hey Ramirez, let's see what forensics has."

Black and Ramirez found Reynolds already in the lab, poring over the case files with one of the technicians. He looked up listlessly as they entered.

"Detective Black, I think I found something! Remember the knife recovered from the fifth crime scene, the flayed victim?"

"The one with no prints or DNA?" Black asked. Reynolds nodded.

"I checked the evidence log, and there's no record of it being checked out. But when I went to examine it just now, the knife was gone."

Black frowned. "What do you mean, gone?"

"As in missing," Reynolds said. "Not in the evidence locker where it should be."

Ramirez stepped forward, a look of grave concern on his face. "Are you saying we have compromised evidence? A break in the chain of custody?"

Reynolds scowled. "It looks that way."

"That's unacceptable," Ramirez said sharply. "We need that evidence secured. Our whole case could be in jeopardy now."

Black held up a hand. "Let's not jump to conclusions just yet. I'll talk to the evidence clerk and find out what happened."

The furrow in Black's brow and the worried glint in his eyes showed that the magnitude of the situation was sinking in. One missing knife wouldn't derail the entire investigation, but it was enough to raise questions about their handling of the case.

Questions that could only benefit certain interests.

Over the next few days, the team's efforts seemed to shift away from Dr. Ward, with some conveniently misplaced evidence and witness statements that were dubious at best. It was just enough to muddy the waters and deflect any scrutiny away from Ward.

They had also planned for the possible re-questioning of Dr. Ward.

When Black sent Jones and Ramirez to the university for an informal check on Dr. Ward and his staff, they gave Ward advance warning through their usual line of communication, giving him enough time to vacate the premises. However, it was only a matter of time before O'Malley caught on to their machinations.

The receptionist led them to Dr. Ward's office, but they found Andrew instead of the professor himself.

"I'm afraid Dr. Ward and Lucas aren't here right now," Andrew explained. "They went on a research trip to the Southwest to study some newly discovered archaeological sites."

Andrew's expression became apologetic. "Dr. Ward wanted me to convey his sincere apologies for the way he acted during the previous questioning. He was in a sorry state after that incident and asked me to express his remorse for his brusque behavior toward you and Detective O'Malley."

Ramirez nodded in understanding. "I get it, we can rub people the wrong way sometimes in this job, especially when it's personal stuff like what happened with Dr. Ward's wife. A little back and forth is par for the course, no need to dwell on it."

Jones cut to the chase. "We've received tips that someone in this department may be connected to the Rune Killer murders. Anything you'd like to share?"

Andrew's eyes widened. "Absolutely not! I'm appalled that anyone would think we were capable of such brutality. Dr. Ward and the others are dedicated academics."

He shook his head vehemently. "I understand your need to investigate thoroughly, but the idea that any of us could be involved in these murders is borderline absurd. We're soft-spoken academics, barely able to hold a lengthy conversation in an intimate setting, let alone commit some of the barbaric acts reported in the news. Yes, we may dig up the dead, but we certainly don't bury them."

"Well, if you notice anything strange, let us know," Jones said, handing Andrew his card. "Especially any breakthroughs on the Ordo Iustitiae cult that might be relevant."

As they left, Ramirez glanced back at the photos on Ward's desk, one in particular caught his eye, one of Dr. Ward smiling next to his late wife. "You know, between Ward's family photos and the kind of people he surrounds himself with here, I'm having a hard time picturing him as a killer."

"Appearances can be deceiving," Jones replied evenly. "But you may be right, he doesn't fit the usual profile. Still, we should look into his background more thoroughly, just to be sure."

Ramirez grunted in agreement as they stepped outside into the sweltering afternoon air.

Unfortunately for the officer, Jones and Ramirez's report did little to dissuade O'Malley from her suspicions about Ward. She urged Black to bring the professor in for formal questioning.

Black, to his credit, refused to act on speculation alone. But O'Malley's persistence began to affect Black's actions.

It seemed that they would have to escalate their interference. As much as they hated to betray their trusted colleague, protecting Dr. Ward had to take priority. This was about much more than one man. It was about flaws in the system, about true justice.

Black would understand one day. They had to believe that.

The next day, Black sent an officer to interview a witness from an old case linked to a recent victim. But when they arrived at the witness's house, they found the place deserted, the door wide open. They called for backup and searched the house, but found no sign of a struggle or forced entry.

Back at the precinct, the officer spun a tale of a panicked witness who apparently fled the city in fear after learning his name was linked to the Rune Killer.

"Said they didn't feel safe with this maniac targeting people connected to unsolved cases," the officer told Black with a serious shake of his head.

Black's expression was grim. "It doesn't make sense that they would just disappear without contacting us first. Are you sure there were no signs of kidnapping?"

"None," they insisted. "They probably took off when they realized we couldn't guarantee their safety. Can't say I blame them."

They left out the part about slipping a sizable "relocation stipend" under their door to finance their impromptu trip out of state. Amazing what people are willing to do when properly motivated.

Black clearly wasn't happy about losing a potential lead, but with no evidence to work with, he had no choice but to move on.

But O'Malley seemed to grow more suspicious with each passing day, watching her fellow officers' every move with those piercing eyes that missed nothing. Even Black began to give his fellow officers deliberate, thoughtful looks when he thought they weren't paying attention.

Looks that told them their time as Ward's silent protector was running out.

CHAPTER THIRTEEN

TURNING POINT

Harsh lights buzzed overhead as I walked into the conference room, my heart beating laboriously against my ribs. I clutched a stack of files and evidence reports, the fruit of countless late nights and endless cups of coffee. With every step I took toward the front of the room, I could feel every scrutinizing eye piercing through me.

I took a deep breath and turned to face my colleagues, their faces a mix of curiosity, skepticism, and anticipation. I cleared my throat and began, "Thank you all for coming. I know we're all under a lot of pressure to solve this case, and I think I've uncovered some crucial evidence that could help us do just that."

I clicked the remote, and the projection screen flickered to life, displaying a web of links and photographs. "As you can see, there are clear links between our victims and cases where they walked free on technicalities or dismissal of evidence."

"And working with our consultant, Dr. Kensington, we've been able to decipher the runes carved into each victim," O'Malley added. "The runes themselves appear to represent crimes and sins. When we cross-referenced them with the cases in which each victim had previously been released, they matched exactly."

I paused, letting the information sink in. After a moment's silence, I continued, "In addition, my investigation revealed that all of the victims had received invitations to join an online historical forum prior to their deaths.

I shuffled through the stack of papers and pulled out a printout. "On the surface, this forum appears innocuous - a simple discussion board for history buffs. However..." I locked eyes with each person around the table, "It also serves as a haven for individuals with radical views on ancient civilizations and their brutal methods of retributive justice."

"That's not all," I continued earnestly. "And guess who else was an active member and frequent poster on this very forum? Ethan Ward - a local historian who frequently posted about the failings of our modern justice system. He went on and on about how ancient civilizations had it right, with their brutal, unyielding codes of honor and retribution."

I paused to catch my breath. "He also became erratic and unhinged during questioning by Detective Black and myself, ranting about how the killer was doing God's work. He practically glorified the killer's actions, portraying him as an avatar waging a righteous crusade. This level of obsession is deeply disturbing."

Letting that sink in, I revealed the final piece of the puzzle. "Ward and his colleagues recently acquired a cache of ancient coins during a recent expedition. His research assistants noted that the coins were eerily familiar to those left at the murder scenes as a sort of calling card."

The room erupted in murmurs and whispers. I could see Detective Black leaning forward, his brow furrowed in concentration. But before I could continue, a voice cut through the noise.

"Wait a minute, O'Malley." It was Detective Ramirez, his tone calm and measured. "I think you're jumping to conclusions."

I felt a flash of irritation, but kept my voice calm. "How so, Detective Ramirez?"

Ramirez stood, his eyes locked with mine. "Just because these people may have visited the same forum as Ward doesn't mean he's involved in the murders. It's a public site, after all. And as for the victims' histories, well, it's not exactly uncommon for criminals to slip through the cracks of the justice system. It doesn't necessarily indicate a pattern."

He paused, then continued, "When Jones and I talked to Andrew the other day, he mentioned that Ward and Lucas were on a research trip in the Southwest for a few days. I checked on that - they've been gone almost a week now. According to the latest autopsy report on the victim, the contents of her stomach were far too recent for Ward to have committed this murder before leaving town."

I could feel the energy in the room shift as doubt began to creep in. My grip on the remote tightened as I argued, "But the striking similarities between the victims' cases can't be ignored. And Ward's obsession with ancient punishment practices can't be mere coincidence."

Jones shook his head, a condescending note in his voice. "Coincidences happen all the time in this line of work, O'Malley. The guy's a history professor specializing in ancient civilizations. With his wife's murder, it's no surprise that his professional and personal life would bleed together. You've got some solid leads, but you can't let speculation and gut feelings cloud your judgment and derail the case."

Ramirez nodded in agreement. "He's right. We need to follow the evidence, not get hung up on theories that may or may not pan out. For all we know, Ward could be another dead end like the others."

I opened my mouth to protest, but before I could speak Chief Thompson interjected. "All right, let's all take a step back here. O'Malley, you've obviously put a lot of work into this, and you raise valid concerns, but Ramirez and Jones make valid points as well. For now, we'll continue to pursue all angles, but we can't bring Ward in without solid evidence linking him to the murders. Are we clear?"

I could feel my cheeks burning, a mixture of frustration and embarrassment. "I understand, Chief. But I really think we're on to something here. If we could just -"

"I've made myself clear," Chief Thompson interrupted, his voice rising. "We need to focus on hard evidence, not gut feelings. Until you have something solid, this discussion is over."

The room fell silent, the tension palpable. I could see the doubt and uncertainty etched into the faces of my colleagues, despair running like ice water through my veins. I had been so sure of my findings, so convinced that I was on to something big. But now, with Ramirez's words ringing in my ears, I felt that certainty erode slightly.

Detective Black cleared his throat, breaking the silence. "The Chief may be right, but while O'Malley's findings may not be conclusive, they're certainly worth investigating further."

I gave him a grateful look, but the damage was done. The team was divided, the trust and unity we had worked so hard to build were now fractured and strained.

As the meeting adjourned, I gathered my files and evidence, my mind racing with doubts and questions. I had been so sure of myself, so convinced that I was on the right track. But now, with Ramirez's challenge fresh in my mind, I couldn't help but wonder if I had been chasing shadows all along.

I made my way back to my desk, my steps heavy and my heart even heavier. I knew I couldn't give up, not with so many unanswered questions and so much at stake. But as I sat down and stared at the piles of paperwork and evidence in front of me, I couldn't shake the feeling that I was climbing a mountain that I might never see the summit of.

I sat alone in the darkness of my office, the glow of my desk lamp barely penetrating the shadows gathered in the corners of the cramped room. The evidence files were spread out before me, crime scene photos, lab reports, O'Malley's research on Ethan Ward – a damning mosaic of clues pointing to a connection between Ward and the sadistic killer we were hunting.

And yet, earlier today, Ramirez had effortlessly cast doubt on it all, his deep voice calmly dismantling each shred of evidence with practiced ease. I rubbed my eyes, fatigue creeping into my bones. The long nights and the constant dead ends were taking their toll. This case had burrowed its way into my psyche, haunting my dreams with glimpses of arcane symbols and the anguished faces of the deceased. I needed clarity, but the path ahead was obscured by doubt.

My fingers traced over a crime scene photo, lingering on the intricate markings carved into the flesh. O'Malley was convinced of Ward's involvement, I could see it in her eyes, feel it in the urgency of her voice as she presented her findings. She had spent countless hours researching Ward's background, uncovering his obsession with punishment and archaic justice. And her instincts were rarely wrong.

But Ramirez had been quick to point out the lack of physical evidence actually linking Ward to the murders. No fingerprints, no DNA, no eyewitnesses. As much as I wanted to believe that O'Malley was right, I couldn't deny that Ramirez had raised legitimate concerns. He wasn't one to dismiss a lead lightly, not with his decade of homicide experience.

Perhaps I had let my own doubts and frustrations cloud my judgment. This case had taken a toll on all of us, worn away our objectivity. Ramirez was just being pragmatic, stepping back when the rest of us were too close to see clearly. He had always been the voice of reason, keeping us focused during the most difficult investigation of my career. I trusted him completely.

But now, for the first time, I felt the faintest flicker of uncertainty. Why had Ramirez been so quick to dismiss O'Malley's findings? As I replayed his rebuttal in my mind, he had offered solid evidence to counter her theories. Ramirez made a compelling case for Ward's alibi-he was out of town during the last murder, based on the victim's time of death. His reluctance to pursue Ward further was understandable in light of this evidence, even if it contrasted with his usual open-minded approach.

I thought back to previous cases we had worked on, trying to quell the doubts that were swirling inside of me. A memory surfaced that I had buried long ago - a shooting from my early days as a detective. Ramirez and I had responded to a late-night call - a known drug dealer shot dead outside a crowded nightclub. Dozens of witnesses, but none had gotten a clear look at the shooter in the chaos.

All the evidence pointed to a ruthless rival gang leader who had been slowly taking over new territory. But before we could apprehend him, the suspect turned up dead, an apparent overdose. After that, the trail went cold, and the brass insisted that we close the case for lack of evidence. It never sat right with me, too many loose ends. I wanted to dig deeper, but Ramirez warned me not to.

"Sometimes you have to leave the past in the past, Black," he had said. "Chasing ghosts will only drive you crazy. We need to keep our eyes forward."

His words had comforted me at the time, but now they took on a more ominous tone. Was he trying to distract me from a truth that he didn't want to be revealed? The thought left a sour taste in my mouth. There had to be some explanation, some context I was missing. Detective Ramirez was one of the few souls in this world that I trusted. I refused to accept that he could be complicit in obstruction of justice, no matter how murky the waters seemed.

Still, I couldn't ignore the small voice in the back of my mind telling me to keep digging, not to accept easy answers. Something didn't add up in this case. Too many strange coincidences, too many dead ends that seemed almost intentional. I had to follow this maze to the heart of the labyrinth.

I swept the case files back into a pile, determined to keep my doubts at bay until I had more solid evidence. For now, they were just shadows, illusions conjured up by my own exhaustion and paranoia. Revealing them to O'Malley would only cause more dissension in an already fractured team.

No, for now, I would keep quiet, stay the course. But I vowed to keep my eyes open, not to let loyalty blind me to uncomfortable truths. I owed that to the troubled victims, to their families.

A heavy sigh escaped my lips as I rose from my desk, my joints creaking in protest. I needed to clear my head before I could review the evidence with fresh eyes. As I stepped out into the empty hallway, the fluorescent lights seemed overly grating, reflecting off the scuffed tile floors and faded paint peeling from the walls. This place wore its history plainly, decades upon decades of trying to find order in chaos. Most days it felt like trying to empty the ocean with a bucket. But it was the only job I had ever known.

I made my way to my brother's care facility. My footsteps echoed down the hall as I made my way to the front desk. Visiting hours were long past, but the night shift orderly owed me a favor or two. I slipped into the patient quarter and navigated the maze of shadowy rooms that were as familiar to me as the streets I had walked as a child. The air was saturated with the unique scent of sterility and tragic lives, that unmistakable asylum aroma. It clung to my clothes long after each visit.

I paused outside room 217, gazing through the small window at the hunched form sitting on the edge of the bed. My brother Samuel was staring straight ahead, his eyes distant, trapped in whatever vivid dreamscape was living in his mind. The orderly nodded silently as he let me in, not a glimmer of judgment in his tired eyes. My brother's demons were no secret within these walls.

"Hey, Sammy," I said softly as I pulled up a chair. His eyes drifted to mine, and for a moment I thought I saw a glimmer of recognition. But then it faded back into nothingness. I studied his face, looking for traces of the bright, kind child he had once been, before the darkness had taken hold. He had endured so much pain, so much that I had failed to protect him from it. I would give anything to take it all back, to spare him this emptiness.

I sat in silence for several minutes, holding Samuel's hand, wishing I could anchor him here with me, wishing my touch would bring a moment of clarity. "I'm trying, Samuel," I whispered. "I'm trying to find the Hollow Soul. But sometimes the path is hard to see. I just have to stay the course." I hoped that saying the words aloud would solidify my wavering resolve. I had to stay on mission, not lose sight of why I had chosen this path so long ago-to be a light against the darkness. No matter where this case led, I could not abandon that purpose. I would find the truth, even if it shattered everything I thought I knew.

I rose slowly and placed a gentle hand on Samuel's shoulder. "Get some rest, little brother. I'll visit you soon." He made no response as I slipped out into the hallway. The shadows seemed to close in on me from all sides as I navigated the maze back toward the distant light of the exit. I quickened my pace, suddenly desperate for fresh air to clear the stale hopelessness that lingered in my lungs.

As I stepped out into the cool night air, I took a deep breath and let the fresh breeze wash over me. My mind kept drifting back to my brother, whose mental state never seemed to improve no matter how much time passed. I walked slowly to my car, the distant sounds of the city a muted backdrop to the tumult of my thoughts.

The drive back to my apartment was foggy, the familiar streets and landmarks barely registering as I navigated on autopilot. Before I knew it, I was standing in my darkened living room, the silence broken only by the soft ticking of the clock on the wall.

I went through the motions of putting away my coat and keys, each action mechanical, devoid of conscious thought. My mind was still back in my brother's room, replaying the vacant look in Samuel's eyes, the way his hand had lain limply in mine. No matter how many times I visited, it never got easier to see him like that, a shell of the vibrant boy I had known.

I made my way to the bathroom, stripped off my clothes, and stepped into the shower. The hot water cascaded over me, the steam rising in tendrils that curled and danced in the air. I stood there for a long while, letting the heat soak into my aching muscles, wishing it could reach the deeper pain within.

When I finally emerged, toweling off and pulling on a clean t-shirt and sweatpants, I caught sight of my reflection in the mirror. The face staring back at me was haggard, the eyes shadowed with exhaustion and the weight of too many sleepless nights. Some days I barely recognized myself, the toll of this job etched into the lines of my face.

I stumbled into the hallway, my gaze drawn to the glint of metal on the small table by the door. My detective's badge lay there, the insignia catching the faint light filtering in from the window. I picked it up and ran my thumb over the cool surface, tracing the familiar contours.

How many times had I pinned this shield to my chest, setting out to serve and protect, to be a force for good in a world so often consumed by darkness? It had been a source of pride, a symbol of the oath I had taken, the duty I had sworn to uphold. But now, as I stared at it, I couldn't help but wonder how much longer I could go on like this.

This case was pushing me to the brink, the cracks in my team widening with each passing day. O'Malley's relentless pursuit of the truth, Ramirez's growing resistance, the Chief's increasing pressure for results - it was all building to a breaking point. And at the center of it all was the specter of Dr. Ethan Ward, his shadow looming over every piece of evidence, every new lead.

I thought of the doubts that had begun to take root in my mind, the sinking feeling that something wasn't right within our own ranks. Could

I trust my instincts, or were they just the product of a mind pushed to its limits? I didn't know anymore. All I knew was that I couldn't stop, couldn't rest until we found the answers, no matter how painful they might be.

I put the badge down, my fingers lingering on the metal for a moment. I had to believe that we could weather this storm, that our shared commitment to justice would see us through. But as I stood in the hallway, the weight of all the unknowns pressing down on me, I couldn't shake the feeling that we were standing on the edge of an abyss, one misstep away from shattering.

I turned away with a sigh and made my way to the bedroom. I needed to sleep, needed to clear my head before I faced another day of dead ends and mounting pressure. As I lay down, staring up at the shadowed ceiling, I sent a silent prayer into the void – for strength, for guidance, for the wisdom to see the truth through all the lies and darkness.

The mattress creaked as I shifted in search of a comfortable position, my body overflowing with exhaustion. I closed my eyes and let the fatigue wash over me, my last conscious thought a vow to keep going, not to let this case break me, break us. We had sworn an oath, and I would see it through to the end, regardless. With that final resolve, I surrendered to the waiting embrace of sleep, the badge in the hallway glinting softly in the darkness, a stalwart guardian standing vigil over the troubled dreams of those who bore its weight.

Chapter Fourteen

Taken

The warehouse door groaned in protest as I forced it open, its rusted hinges screeching like a banshee into the cavernous void. Heart pounding, I hesitated at the entrance, every nerve ending crackling with anticipation of what might lurk in the shadows. The wind whistled through the jagged panes of broken glass, a ghostly sigh echoing throughout. I swung my flashlight in a wide arc, kicking up clouds of dust that swirled and shifted in the stark glare. As I crossed the threshold, my footsteps echoed through the eerie silence, each one a deafening reminder of how alone I was.

The informant's tip led me here, to this abandoned relic of the industrial age. Strange occult markings on the interior walls, they claimed, similar to the Rune Killer's grisly crime scenes. A tenuous lead, but my gut told me to follow it, even as a sense of trepidation set in.

I moved cautiously, my free hand resting on my holstered weapon as the flashlight's beam cut through the darkness. The place seemed utterly deserted - abandoned machinery, rusted chains hanging like skeletal fingers, cobwebs thick as curtains, layers of dust and debris. The musty stench of decay hung in the air. Nothing outwardly sinister caught my eye, but the oppressive atmosphere pressed in from all sides.

Then I saw it - a crude runic symbol etched into a support column, accompanied by what looked like dried blood. My pulse quickened as

I hurried over. It matched the killer's markings exactly. Three harsh intersecting lines formed a disturbing glyph that seemed to shift before my eyes. I blinked hard. There could be no doubt now - this was the confirmation I'd been looking for, no matter how much I wished otherwise.

The undisturbed warehouse mocked my unease as I pushed forward, fear rising in my throat with each step. Rusty stairs beckoned, a questionable path to the catwalk ringing the upper level. I wrapped my fingers around the railing, rust flakes biting into my skin, and found it solid. Taking a steady breath, I climbed. Each step produced a groan of protest from the aged metal, an unsettling creak that echoed through the cavernous space and kept my nerves on edge.

Nervously, I shone my light into every dark corner, trying to ignore the shadows that stretched out like grasping fingers. More decaying machinery and cobwebs were my only companions until a faint glimmer caught my eye - a small alcove hidden by a moldering tarp. I pulled it aside with a shaking hand, and beneath it lay an ancient wooden chest.

Kneeling down, I examined the chest, my breath coming in short, sharp gasps. Strange symbols were carved into the aged wood. Their edges had worn smooth with time, but they still radiated an aura of malevolence. The lid was sealed tightly with an old, rusted padlock that seemed to stare at me in the dancing light. I pulled my lock-picking kit from my pocket and went to work with trembling hands. The tumblers clicked quietly as I maneuvered the delicate instruments. Moments later, the padlock popped open, clattering to the floor with a satisfying thud. I lifted the lid and braced myself.

Inside were piles of tarnished coins. I recognized them instantly - just like those left at the Rune Killer's murder scenes, their surfaces etched with the same disturbing symbols. My pulse thundered - concrete evidence linking this place to the killer. I quickly snapped photos with my phone, my hands shaking uncontrollably.

I had to let Black know right away, even though every instinct screamed at me to flee this place and never look back. Keeping one hand on my gun, I pulled his name from my contacts, my finger hovering over the call button as I fought to control my ragged breathing.

Suddenly, a floorboard creaked behind me, the sound dull and hollow through my adrenaline-soaked state. I spun around, pointing my gun in the direction of the sound, just as a dark figure lunged out of the shadows, a deeper blackness against the darkness.

Something hard cracked against my temple, an explosion of blinding pain as I crumpled to the catwalk. Shadows crept in as I fought to stay conscious, to reach for my dropped weapon, but my limbs wouldn't respond. The silhouette of the killer loomed over me, their features obscured in the darkness, a specter of pure malevolence.

I tried to scream, but could only manage a choked gasp before a chemical-soaked rag was pressed against my face. The sweet fumes of chloroform filled my nose and mouth, seeping into my reeling mind like tendrils of corruption. The flashlight rolled from my limp fingers, its beam illuminating a symbol etched into the wall just before it flickered out, plunging me into nebulous darkness. The mark of the Rune Killer taunted me with its sinister promise. They'd been here all along, watching me, toying with me like a mouse in a cat's claws.

I drifted in and out of murky oblivion as I was dragged away, my last coherent thought a desperate plea for Black to find me. When my senses finally cleared, I found myself suspended by chains in an unfamiliar place, completely at the mercy of the killer...

They stood before me, watching me with clinical interest as I hung suspended and immobilized, a specimen pinned down for their twisted pleasure. Fear coursed through my veins like ice water, chilling me to the core. I was in another place, that much was certain. The killer must have transported me while I was unconscious, realizing that their lair had been compromised.

I had to get free, find a way to contact Black and the others before it was too late. I struggled weakly against my bonds, the rough fibers biting into my wrists, but I could only flail helplessly.

The killers stood still and silent, their face shrouded in shadow, a figure of pure nightmare. They seemed content to watch me struggle, drinking in my fear and helplessness like a fine wine. Savoring my despair with a kind of detached amusement that was somehow more terrifying than enraging.

I forced myself to meet their gaze, summoning what little defiance I could. "Why are you doing this?" I demanded, my voice ragged and raw. "Let me go, you bastard!"

The killer tilted their head, as if intrigued by my audacity, like a scientist observing a fascinating specimen. Even with such an advantage, the killer left nothing to chance, their distorted artificial voice a chilling rasp that raised the hair on my arms and sent shivers down my spine, the voice of the damned.

"You should not have come, Officer O'Malley. I do not take kindly to those who interfere with my work." They took a step closer, the shadows clinging to them like a shroud. I recoiled instinctively, my chains rattling. "But perhaps fate has brought us together for a purpose."

Fear clawed at my insides, threatening to devour me from within. "What purpose?" I whispered, my voice shaking.

Their hand shot out and caught my jaw in an iron grip that bruised my flesh. I cried out as they forced me to look into their eyes, twin pits of darkness that seemed to swallow the light. They were cold and empty, without humanity or mercy. The eyes of a monster that had lost its soul long ago.

"In time you will understand." Their grip tightened painfully, their fingers digging into my skin hard enough to leave marks. "For now, sleep."

I barely had time to catch my breath to scream before the rag was pressed against my face again, the chemical stench overwhelming. I struggled and choked against the overpowering fumes, but it was like fighting against the tide. Quickly, without pause, everything was swallowed by darkness once more, my struggles growing weaker and weaker until I went limp in my bonds, my last thought a desperate prayer that Black would find me before it was too late.

This time the shadows did not retreat, but wrapped me in their cold embrace as I sank into oblivion.

The call came in just as I was packing up for the day, the jarring tone cutting through the usual din of the precinct. O'Malley's name flashed across the screen of my phone, and I answered with my usual gruff greeting, a sense of unease already beginning to prickle at the back of my neck.

"Black here. What's up, O'Malley?"

Silence greeted me on the other end, an eerie, unnatural silence that made my skin crawl. I frowned and pulled the phone away briefly to check the connection, a sinking feeling settling in my gut.

"O'Malley? You there?"

I put the phone back to my ear, straining for any sign of life, and that's when I heard it - the faint sound of scuffling in the background, like a struggle muffled by distance. My instincts immediately kicked in, every nerve in my body screaming that something was very, very wrong.

"Jenna? Talk to me, what's going on?" I demanded, grabbing my keys and heading for the door. More silence, followed by what sounded like a muffled scream, a sound that made my blood run cold. My partner was in trouble, and every second counted.

"Jenna! Where are you?"

The line went dead, the sudden absence of sound more terrifying than any scream could be. I broke into a run, sprinting for my car as I tried O'Malley's cell again, each unanswered ring intensifying the dread that tightened in my chest. No answer. I jumped in and sped out of the parking lot, tires screeching as I raced through the streets of downtown, weaving through traffic with reckless abandon.

My mind raced just as fast, running through possible scenarios, each more grim than the last. Had she stumbled upon something related to the case? Was the Rune Killer behind this? My blood began to boil at the thought as my hands tightened on the wheel.

I dialed Chen back at the station and barked orders before she even had a chance to speak. "Chen, it's Black. I need you to ping O'Malley's cell phone now!" She replied without hesitation, the panic in my voice enough to convey the urgency of the request. A minute later, she sent me her last known location - an old warehouse in the industrial area on the outskirts of town, a place that had been abandoned for years.

Adrenaline surged through my veins, igniting every nerve ending as I weaved through the congested streets. The city passed in a haze of dirty streets and neon signs. I stomped on the accelerator, trying to push the car beyond its limits, milking every ounce of available horsepower. Ominous storm clouds brewed overhead, a palpable echo of the cold knot of panic and anger roiling in my stomach. Hang in there, Jenna. I'm coming.

I screeched to a halt outside the chain link fence surrounding the vacant industrial lot, the screech of metal on metal echoing through the empty streets. This area had been abandoned for years, the perfect place for illegal activity to go unnoticed. Like a serial killer's lair. I drew my Beretta, the weight of the gun in my hand a small comfort against the unknown horrors that awaited me.

I slipped into the nearest warehouse, the massive sliding door partially open like a gaping maw waiting to swallow me whole. The interior was vast and empty, the air heavy with the smell of rust and damp concrete, a pungent reminder of the building's age and disuse. My eyes quickly adjusted to the darkness, scanning the shadows for any sign of movement, any hint of where my partner might be.

"Jenna!" I called, my voice echoing eerily in the vast room, bouncing off the concrete walls and ringing back at me like a mocking chorus. No response except my own ragged breathing and the pounding of my heart in my ears. Moving deeper inside, I swept my flashlight in wide arcs, the beam cutting through the darkness like a knife, searching for any sign of disturbance, any clue that might lead me to O'Malley.

As I ventured further into the warehouse, the signs of a struggle became more apparent. Scratches marred the floor, and a trail of debris led to the far end of the building. My heart raced as I followed the path of destruction, dreading what I might find at its end.

I pulled out my phone and dialed O'Malley's number, hoping against hope that she would answer. Instead, the sound of her ringtone rippled through the cavernous room, directing me to the upper catwalk. I raced up the stairs, my footsteps clanging against the metal grating, the ringtone growing louder with each step.

There, at the base of a broken railing, its sharp, rusted teeth bared in a silent snarl, lay O'Malley's phone. The purple casing was unmistakable even in the darkness, a spiderweb of cracks marring the screen. As my fingers closed around the device, the implications of what I'd found sent my thoughts into a sickening spiral.

The stench of blood and neglect assaulted my nostrils as I examined the area, my pulse pounding in my temples. Bright red stains marred the concrete floor, the unmistakable sight of fresh blood. It was clear that O'Malley had struggled here, fighting for her life against an unknown assailant.

I followed the trail of destruction back to the warehouse floor. A growing sense of dread formed like a knot in my stomach, twisting my insides until I thought I might be sick. Where was she? What had that psycho done to her? The questions raced through my mind, each more terrifying than the last, fueling the rage and desperation building inside me.

A flicker of light from outside caught my eye and drew me to the open door like a moth to a flame. I moved to the threshold, sweeping my flashlight beam across the gravel lot, searching for any sign of life, any hint of where O'Malley might have been taken. And there, near the chain-link fence, something reflective glinted in the darkness, drawing my attention. I approached slowly, afraid of what I might find.

My light glinted off a silver badge lying in the dirt, tossed carelessly to the ground like a piece of trash. O'Malley's shield, the symbol of her devotion and bravery, was discarded as if it meant nothing. I picked it up with a shaking hand, the metal cold and heavy in my palm, and clung to it as if it could somehow bring her back to me. They'd taken her. That sick bastard had my partner, and God only knew what they were doing to her.

I began to search the area, looking for any other clues, any indication of where they might have taken her. About 20 yards away, a strange mark on the pavement drew me closer, the beam of my flashlight illuminating the crude etching. There, carved into the concrete, was a now-familiar symbol. The same runic design found at the other crime scenes, the calling card of a deranged killer. O'Malley had been on the right track. This was the Rune Killer's lair, and she had walked right into their clutches.

Hot rage boiled inside me as I stared down at the arcane imagery, my free hand clenching into a fist so tight my knuckles turned white. This was a message... a taunt. The killer was operating right under our noses, growing bolder with each murder, reveling in their twisted game. And now they had my partner, the one person I trusted most in the world, the one person I couldn't bear to lose.

I rose slowly, every muscle in my body coiled with tension, ready to explode into action at a moment's notice. The storm rumbled overhead, the sound of thunder echoing my own raging anger. The cold raindrops that began to fall mingled with the blood stain on the unforgiving pavement, swallowing all traces of the haunting abduction. But I knew better. There was no way I was going to let that psychopath take O'Malley from me. I was going to find her, no matter what it took, no matter how far I had to go or what lines I had to cross. I didn't care if I had to tear this whole town apart brick by brick.

Thunder cracked loudly, taught muscles instinctively recoiled, while my nerves stretched to the breaking point. A second later, my radio came to life, the static-filled voice of the dispatcher cutting through the white noise in my head.

"Detective Black, this is dispatch. Please respond."

I unbuckled the radio from my belt with shaking hands, pressing the transmit button so hard I thought it might break. "This is Black." My voice sounded alien to my own ears, cold and hard as steel. I let my hand fall to my side in defeat before raising the radio again, my voice barely more than a murmur. "That sick bastard has Officer O'Malley."

"Say again, Detective," the dispatcher's voice was laced with uncertainty.

The radio crackled in my hand as I struggled to form the words. "The Rune Killer has O'Malley," I said, each syllable burning like cinders in my throat. There was an agonizing silence as dispatch fully processed my statement.

"Copy that, Detective," they finally replied in a hollow voice.

Clipping the radio back onto my belt, I took another look at the runic symbol etched into the ground. My expression hardened with cold resolve, a resolve born of desperation and anger. I was going to find O'Malley even if I had to burn this entire city to the ground, even if I had to wade through an ocean of blood and face the devil himself. There was no turning back now.

I turned and walked back to my car, the engine roaring like a beast awakening from its slumber, ready to hunt. Tires spraying gravel, I roared off into the stormy night, sirens blaring, a banshee's wail announcing my approach. The game was about to change, the rules thrown out the window in the face of unimaginable horror. No more playing nice, no more playing by the book. If that's what it took to get O'Malley back, to stop this psychopath once and for all, then so be it. I was willing to do whatever it took, to cross any line, to sacrifice anything and everything.

The Rune-Killers had just made the biggest mistake of their lives, and I was going to make sure it was their last.

Chapter Fifteen

Deep Waters

Heavy raindrops pelted the windshield as I steered the car through the deserted city streets. My hands gripped the steering wheel tightly, knuckles straining against the taut skin. My mind raced through a thousand scenarios, each one worse than the last. I couldn't shake the image of the runic symbol etched into the floor, a taunting reminder of my failure to protect my partner. The intricate lines and curves seemed to dance before my eyes, taunting me.

I pounded my fist against the dashboard, the pain barely registering through the haze of rage and despair that consumed me. How could I let this happen? O'Malley was my responsibility, my partner, my friend. I should have been there, I shouldn't have let her go alone. But I was too caught up in my own demons, too busy chasing ghosts from my past to see the danger right in front of me. The guilt gnawed at my insides, a relentless beast threatening to devour me whole.

The radio crackled with information about the ongoing search for O'Malley. I barely heard them, their voices drowned out by the downpour and my own muddled haze. I knew that every second counted, that the longer she was in the hands of this psychopath, the less chance we had of finding her alive. The thought of what she might be going through right now sent a new wave of nausea through me. Visions of her bound and bloodied, screaming for help that never came, flashed through my mind, each more vivid and horrifying than the last.

I took a sharp turn, tires screeching as I pushed the car to its limits. I had to think, I had to concentrate. The Rune Killer had left clues before, taunting us with their twisted game. There had to be something, some clue as to where they had taken her. I racked my brain, trying to remember every detail of the previous crime scenes, every scrap of evidence we'd managed to collect.

My mind flashed back to the historical forum, to the invitations that preceded their deaths at the hands of the Rune Killer? Or was it just another dead end, another pointless detour that would lead me nowhere? The uncertainty was maddening, a constant whisper in the back of my mind that refused to be silenced. I began to wring the steering wheel, the frustration and helplessness threatening to overwhelm me.

I needed answers, I needed something to hold on to, a glimmer of hope in the darkness that was engulfing me. But the more I grasped at straws, the more they seemed to slip through my fingers, leaving me with nothing but a growing sense of dread.

I slammed on the brakes and the car skidded to a stop in front of a familiar building. The Blue Lantern. My subconscious drew me to the one place where I could always find some measure of peace. Exhaustion clawed at every inch of my being, the grueling chase wearing me down to the bone. My muscles ached, a dull throb pulsing through my body with every heartbeat.

I needed this momentary escape in the endless storm that was this case, a brief moment to collect my battered thoughts before I threw myself back into the fray. A mountain of doubt tugged at me, every dead end a boulder threatening to grind me to dust. The weight of unsolved mysteries pressed down on my shoulders, threatening to crush me under its weight.

With a heavy sigh, I turned off the engine and stepped out into the downpour. The rain soaked through my coat in seconds, pinning my hair to my forehead as I made my way to the entrance. Each step felt like a struggle, as if the air around me had thickened and was resisting my progress. The cold droplets stung my face, a stark contrast to the numbness spreading through my chest.

I pushed through the heavy wooden door, the familiar smell of cigarettes and spilled whiskey embracing me like an old friend. The bar was nearly empty, save for a few regulars nursing their drinks in the shadows. Feeling all but dead inside, I made my way to the bar in a slow, lifeless shuffle. The floorboards creaked beneath my feet, each step echoing in the hushed atmosphere.

"The usual, Detective?" Sully asked, his voice gruff but full of concern. I nodded, afraid to speak, afraid my voice would crack and betray the turmoil inside me. He poured a generous amount of whiskey into a glass and slid it across the polished mahogany. The amber liquid glinted in the dim light, promising a temporary respite from the demons that haunted me.

I wrapped my fingers around the shot glass, the chill of it a stark contrast to the heat of my skin. I brought it to my lips, the first sip searing a path down my throat. I welcomed the pain, the momentary distraction from the chaos raging inside me. For a brief moment, the world seemed to fall away, and all that existed was the burn of the whiskey and the steady throb of my own heartbeat.

Sully leaned against the bar, his eyes studying me with a knowing intensity. "Rough night?" he asked, though it was more of a statement than a question.

I slammed the glass down on the bar, whiskey sloshing over the rim and onto my trembling hand. A choked sob tore from my throat as months of sleepless nights and my own failures metastasized.

"O'Malley..." I choked out, my voice cracking under the strain. "The Rune Killer took her. Right from under our noses."

I buried my face in my hands, hot tears stinging my eyes as the image of her empty car, the driver's side door still ajar, flashed through my mind. The sickening realization that I had failed her, that I hadn't been there when she needed me most, twisted like a knife in my heart.

"I should have been there," I whispered, the words tasting of impotence on my tongue. "I should have protected her." The thought of O'Malley in the hands of that psychopath, suffering unimaginable horrors even now, made the bile rise in the back of my throat.

I clenched my fists, my nails digging into my palms hard enough to draw blood, as a white-hot rage began to build in my chest. All the frustration, the helplessness, the guilt - it all came together in a single, burning desire for vengeance. I wanted to hunt down the Rune Killer, to make them pay for what they'd done. To tear them apart with my bare hands if I had to.

Sully's eyes widened, a flicker of surprise quickly replaced by grim understanding. He poured himself a drink and downed it in one swift motion. "I'm sorry, Black. I know how much she means to you."

My grip on my glass tightened, the sturdy glass threatening to shatter. "How can I even call myself a detective?" The words came out with self-loathing.

Sully shook his head, his weathered face softening with sympathy. "You can't blame yourself, Black. You're not responsible for the actions of a madman."

"But I am responsible for her safety. She's my partner, my friend. I let her down." My voice cracked at the last word, the weight of my failure crushing me from within. The guilt was a physical thing, a lead weight pressing down on my chest, making it hard to breathe.

Sully was silent for a moment, his gaze distant as if lost in memory. When he spoke again, his voice was low and measured. "I've been where you are, Black. More times than I care to admit." He refilled my glass, the amber liquid sloshing against the sides. "When you're in this line of work, you're bound to face some hard choices. Decisions that keep you up at night wondering if you did the right thing."

I met his gaze, the understanding in his eyes a lifeline in the storm of my emotions. "How do you live with that?" I asked, my voice barely audible. How did he carry this weight day after day without being crushed under it?

Sully sighed, the sound bearing the brunt of his own demons. "You don't, not really. It becomes a part of you, a scar that never quite heals." He poured himself another drink and took a sip, his eyes growing distant again. "But you learn to carry it, to use it as a reminder of why you do what you do. Of the people you fight for."

I nodded slowly, the lump in my throat making it hard to swallow. His words rang true, striking a chord deep within me.

"I just... I can't shake the feeling that my time is running out. That every second I spend here is another second she's in danger." My stomach knotted at the thought, and a cold sweat broke out on my forehead.

Sully leaned forward, his palms resting on the bar as he fixed me with an intense stare. "Listen to me, Black. I've seen a lot of good cops lose themselves in cases like this. They get so caught up in the chase and the what-ifs that they forget they're just as human as anyone else." He tapped his finger on the bar for emphasis. "You can't let that consume you. You have to remember who you are, what you stand for."

I met Sully's piercing gaze, knowing that his words held wisdom forged over decades on the force. He had seen officers far more experienced than me fall into the abyss, the darkness of the job swallowing them whole. I thought of the burning rage that gripped me as I reviewed countless horrific crime scene photos, the unbridled anger at the injustice of it all. For a moment, the world had gone black, and I could feel the darkness beckoning, whispering seductively of the power that lay in embracing it fully.

I closed my eyes, the truth of his words cutting through me like a razor. He was right. I couldn't let my desire for revenge cloud my judgment, couldn't let it turn me into something I wasn't. But the thought of O'Malley out there, alone and afraid, was a gut-wrenching agony.

"I don't know if I'm strong enough, Sully." The confession humbled me, the words caught in my throat. "I don't know if I can do this without her."

Sully's hand came to rest on my shoulder, the understanding clasp a comforting presence in the midst of my turmoil. "You're stronger than you know, Black. And you're not alone. You have a whole department behind you, a whole city counting on you to bring this bastard down."

I nodded, the knot in my chest loosening slightly. He was right. I wasn't alone in this fight. I had my colleagues, my friends. People who believed in me, who were counting on me to see this through to the end. And I had Sully, the one constant in a world that seemed to shift beneath my feet with each passing moment.

I took another sip of my drink, savoring the way the alcohol made its way down my throat and settled in my stomach. It was a familiar sensation, one that had become all too common over the past few weeks as I struggled to deal with the weight of my failures. O'Malley's disappearance was another dark cloud, another reminder of the many promises I had broken and the partner I had failed.

But Sully's words echoed in my mind, a ray of light in the darkness that threatened to consume me. He spoke of principles, of the ideals that had driven both of us to become cops in the first place. To serve and protect, to stand up for those who couldn't stand up for themselves. It was a noble calling, one I had once believed in with every fiber of my soul.

But now, faced with the harsh reality of my own limitations, I found myself questioning everything I had once held dear. How could I protect others when I couldn't even protect my own partner? How could I serve a community that seemed to be crumbling around me? Torn apart by the very evil I had sworn to fight?

Sully leaned forward, his weathered face etched with lines of understanding and compassion. He had been there before, faced the same doubts and fears that now plagued my every waking moment. And yet he had persevered, found a way to carry on even when all hope seemed lost.

As he spoke of his old partner Mack and the missing persons case that had nearly broken them both, I felt a flicker of recognition deep in my soul. I knew the pain, the gnawing sense of helplessness that comes with knowing that someone you are responsible for is out there somewhere, lost and alone. The endless nights spent poring over case files, chasing down every lead, no matter how tenuous, only to come up empty-handed.

But Sully's words also carried a message of hope, a reminder that even in the darkest of times, there was still a chance for redemption. He had never given up on that missing girl, had never stopped searching until he had brought her home safe and sound. And now he was telling me to do the same for O'Malley.

I nodded slowly, he was right.

I couldn't give up, couldn't let the darkness win. I had to keep fighting, keep searching, until I found my partner and brought her back to where she belonged. No matter how long it took, no matter what obstacles stood in my way.

Because that is what good cops do.

We kept going, we kept pushing until justice was served and the innocent were protected. It was a heavy burden to carry, but one I was ready to shoulder once again.

With a newfound sense of purpose burning in my veins, I finished my drink and rose from the bar. I had work to do, leads to follow, and clues to uncover.

"Thank you, Sully. For everything."

He waved away my gratitude, his eyes twinkling with warmth. "Anytime, Black. You know where to find me if you need me."

I nodded, a small smile tugging at my lips. I knew where to find him, and that knowledge was a comfort, a reminder that I wasn't alone in this fight. Sully had been there from the beginning, a gruff but steady presence in the madness that often consumed this job. He understood the burden we carried, the sacrifices we made, in a way few others could.

I made my way to the door, my steps firm with renewed determination. Sully watched me go with a proud smile on his face, his eyes shining with the knowledge that he had given me a piece of his own strength. As I stepped out into the rain-soaked night, I felt a flicker of hope in my chest, a glimmer of light in the darkness.

The cool rain was a shock to my overheated skin, but I welcomed it, letting the drops wash over me like a baptism. I took a deep breath, filling my lungs with the crisp night air, and for a moment, the weight on my shoulders seemed to lighten slightly.

I was going to find O'Malley and bring her home. No matter what it took, no matter what I had to do. Because that was my duty, my calling. To serve and protect, even in the face of impossible odds. The oath I had sworn years ago echoed in my mind, taking on new weight, new meaning in the wake of recent events.

As I walked away from the Lantern, the neon sign casting a soft glow on the wet pavement, I made a silent promise to myself and to Sully. I would stay true to my principles, to the values that had brought me to this point. I would seek justice, real justice, not the kind that could be bought or traded for with favors and compromises.

But I also knew that the world was rarely black and white, that sometimes hard choices had to be made, lines had to be blurred in pursuit of a greater good. It was a lesson Sully had taught me, one I would carry with me as I navigated the treacherous waters ahead. There would be times when I would have to get my hands dirty, do things that made my stomach turn, all in the name of upholding the law.

The pounding rain followed me back to my unmarked sedan, each raindrop a pattering note in the dark symphony of the night. But beneath the relentless deluge, a fire burned in my chest. I knew the path ahead was twisted through shadows and hard choices that would test everything I believed in. But I drew strength from knowing I wasn't walking alone - I had the support of the few who still believed in me and the tarnished badge I wore. Their trust was a hidden well from which I could draw deep in the dark days to come.

And so I stepped back into the fray, my eyes fixed on the horizon. I would find the Rune Killer and bring them to justice. For O'Malley, for the victims, and for the city I had sworn to protect.

The Rune Killer was out there, a vicious shadow haunting the streets I'd walked most of my life. O'Malley's blood still visible under my fingernails, the faces of his victims forever etched in my memory.

They fueled every step as I pushed through the downpour toward the uncertain horizon. This went beyond duty now, I would drag this twisted soul into the light and make them face the scales of justice. For everyone they had wronged, and for the city I had bled to defend, I would see this through to the bitter end.

I was Detective James Black, and I would not rest until justice was served, until the Rune Killer was behind bars where they belonged.

The rain continued to fall as I slid behind the wheel, but I barely noticed. My mind was already racing, formulating plans, running through scenarios. The hunt was on, and this time I would be the one doing the hunting.

CHAPTER SIXTEEN

FRACTURED ALLIANCE

A sudden knock on my window jolted me from my thoughts. I looked up to see Detective Marcus Jones staring at me, his face unreadable in the dim glow of the streetlights. I slowly rolled down the window.

"Thought I'd find you here," he said, his voice soft and gravelly.

I just nodded, not sure what to say. We shared a somber silence for a moment, the patter of the rain filling the space between us.

Finally, Jones broke the stalemate. "O'Malley's abduction is all over the wire."

I clenched my jaw, anger rising in my chest at the mention of her name. "Yeah, I know."

Jones let out a long sigh and ran his hand over his face. I could see how exhausted he looked now, his eyes bloodshot and ringed with dark circles. This case was taking its toll on all of us.

"We will find her James," he said after another pause. "I swear to you, we'll bring her home."

Jones shuffled his feet, glancing around the empty street before meeting my gaze again. "James, I have something to tell you. Something... hard to hear."

My pulse quickened. "What is it?"

He hesitated, fighting with himself. When he finally spoke, his voice was laced with deep regret. "You were right about Ward. About all of it. I should have listened to you and O'Malley in the first place. I just..."

He trailed off, shame etched on his face. I waited, bracing myself for whatever revelation he was about to make.

"The truth is," he began again, "I have been helping the Rune Killer. Feeding them information, sabotaging the investigation."

The words hit me like a sledgehammer, knocking the air out of my lungs. I stared at Jones, my mind reeling, refusing to accept the devastating confession. His words carved deep wounds of betrayal that left me raw and bleeding.

I wanted to believe it was all some sick, twisted joke. But the look in his eyes, that unmasked despair, told me this was no joke. My partner, a man I trusted with my life, had conspired with the same sadistic monster who had taken O'Malley.

I stared at Jones, I wanted to lash out, to demand answers, but I forced myself to remain calm. I needed to hear him out, to understand why he'd done this.

"Why, Marcus?" I asked, my voice shaking with disbelief. "Why would you help that monster?"

Marcus closed his eyes, his shoulders slumping under the weight of his guilt. When he spoke, his voice was thick with solemn emotion. "You remember my sister Keisha?"

I nodded, the memory of Marcus' little sister Keisha flashing through my mind. She'd been a ball of energy, always following behind us with a toothy grin, before Marcus and I had earned our badges. Then that senseless shooting ripped her away, an innocent life lost in a city that devours its young.

"I was there when she died, James," Marcus said, his words burdened with old heartbreak. "Cradled her on that blood-stained sidewalk as the life drained from her eyes. And the bastard who shot her? He melted back into the street like a ghost, untouchable."

I remembered poring over Keisha's case file after I became a detective. It had been a dead end from the beginning. No witnesses were willing to come forward, no evidence linking anyone to the crime. In a city where death was commonplace, Keisha's murder was just another file gathering dust in the archives of forgotten tragedies.

Jones opened his eyes and fixed me with a haunted stare. "I saw him, James. A few years ago. He was working in that auto shop on 7th, a wolf among sheep. Carefree, laughing with his co-workers, a slap in the face to the torment he put my broken family through."

I could hear the raw pain in his voice, the anger that had been festering for years. I understood all too well. How many times had I seen the guilty walk free, protected by the very system I'd sworn to uphold?

"I couldn't let it go," Jones continued, his hands clenching into fists. "I started digging, trying to find something, anything that would put him away. But there was nothing. No evidence, no witnesses. Just... nothing."

He took a shuddering breath, his eyes glistening with unshed tears. "I watched him closely, waiting for him to slip up, but he never did. Then the Rune Killer contacted me, explaining how they were going to punish those who had escaped retribution. And I thought... maybe this was the answer. Maybe this was how I could finally put Keisha's soul to rest.

Icy tendrils snaked down my back as his confession continued. Someone I once trusted, a man I called a friend, had fallen under the Rune Killer's spell, seduced by their warped view of righteousness. The betrayal cut deep, a jagged slash across my soul... almost too much to bear.

"So you sent him Booth's name," I said, my voice flat and unemotional. "You helped hand him his first kill on a silver platter."

Jones nodded, his expression a mixture of shame and defiance. "I did. And when I saw Booth's body, saw what the Rune Killer had done to him... I felt relief, James. For the first time in years, I felt like my sister could finally rest in peace."

I closed my eyes, the extent of Jones' confession hollowing out my insides. His anguish was palpable, I understood his pain, his desire for vengeance. But to forge an alliance with a murderer, to stain his own hands with blood - that was a line I couldn't cross, a decision from which there was no turning back.

"Jones," I said, opening my eyes to meet his. "What you've done... it's not justice. It's murder, and no amount of rationalizing is going to change that."

He flinched at my words, but I continued. "I get it, okay? I get the anger, the helplessness. But this? This isn't the answer. We're supposed to be better than that. We're supposed to uphold the law, not take it into our own hands."

Jones shook his head, a bitter smile on his lips. "The law? The law failed my sister, James. It fails people every day. Maybe it's time for something new. Something that actually works."

I stared at him, feeling like I was looking at a stranger. The Marcus Jones I knew, the one I trusted with my life... he was gone. In his place was a man consumed by grief and rage, willing to do anything for a chance at revenge.

"Marcus..." I began, threatening. "Tell me this is some kind of sick joke."

He held my gaze unflinchingly. "It is the truth. I'm not going to insult you by lying about it now."

I took a deep breath as I tried to control the shaking in my hands. The system's failures had torn him apart, I understood that. How far would I go for my own brother? How far was I about to go for O'Malley? But this path he wanted to take... it would destroy everything we stood for, everything we'd worked so damn hard to build. There had to be another way, something that wouldn't leave our badges tarnished and our honor in the gutter.

I fought to keep my emotions in check. Losing it now wouldn't help O'Malley. I had to stay focused.

"Why are you telling me this now?" I asked through clenched teeth.

Jones' expression turned grim. "Because Ward went off script. He took an innocent, James. Your partner and my friend. O'Malley was never part of the plan."

A cold fist clenched around my heart, seizing it in my chest. O'Malley was now a pawn in this psychopath's twisted game. And I was to blame. I had been too blind, too naive, to see the truth about Jones until it was too late.

"What do you mean, off script?" I demanded, my voice raspy with barely contained rage.

Jones shook his head, frustration etched into the lines of his face. "This was supposed to be about justice, about righting wrongs the system couldn't touch. But kidnapping a cop? That's not justice, that's insanity."

I barked out a harsh laugh. "Oh, so now you have a moral compass? Now that it's one of our own on the butcher block?"

He flinched at my words, but didn't argue. "I know I made mistakes, James. Unforgivable ones. But right now, I'm the only chance you have of finding O'Malley alive."

I locked eyes with Jones, a storm of thoughts swirling in my head. Bile rose in my throat as the bitter truth of his words sank in like a snakebite. As much as I wanted to pound my fist into his sanctimonious face until it was a bloody pulp, I needed him. Jones was my only link to the Rune Killer. The only flickering hope of finding O'Malley before her time ran out rested squarely on the hunched shoulders of the broken man before me.

"How?" I asked, hating the desperation in my voice. "How can you find her?"

Jones looked around as if checking for eavesdroppers. "I've been communicating with him through coded messages on the historical forum. I can contact him, try to arrange a meeting."

I nodded, a plan already forming in my mind. "Do it. Set up the meeting. But Jones..."

I leaned in closer, my voice dropping to a menacing baritone. "If anything happens to O'Malley, if she's harmed in any way... there will be nowhere on earth you can hide from me. Understand?"

He met my gaze unflinchingly, a flicker of the old Jones in his eyes. "Understood."

We shook hands, a gesture that felt like a mockery of the trust we'd once shared. But now I didn't have the luxury of pride or principles. O'Malley's life hung in the balance, and I'd make a deal with the devil himself if it meant bringing her home safely.

As Jones walked away, disappearing into the shadows of the alley, I leaned back in my seat, my head spinning from the unexpected turn of events. My partner, my friend, was in the hands of a psychopath. And my only ally in finding her was a man I could no longer trust, a man who had betrayed everything we stood for.

But I couldn't afford to dwell on that now. I needed to focus, to put all my energy and skill into the task at hand. O'Malley was counting on me, and I'd be damned if I let her down.

And as for Jones... well, that reckoning would come in time. But for now, we had a common goal, a shared mission. Find O'Malley. Bring her home.

Everything else could wait.

The order went out – haul Ward's sorry ass in here. His murderous rampage had come to an end, one way or another. Jones' betrayal was a lead weight weighing on me, but I pushed those feelings into a mental lockbox. They were just a distraction from what was important now. O'Malley was still out there, her life hanging by a thread, and the bastard Ward was our only breadcrumb to follow. I had to keep my head in the game.

Jones didn't argue when I gave the order, but he did suggest that Ward might have gone into hiding and might not be so easy to find. "We need a contingency plan," he said, his voice low but insistent. "We may need to lure him in as well."

I raised an eyebrow, not liking the sound of that. "What do you have in mind?"

Jones leaned closer, his eyes flickering around the station, searching for prying ears. "We're setting a trap for Ward. I'm going to send DeLuca an invitation to the forum, the kind of tempting bait that Ward won't be able to pass up."

A rush of memories flooded my mind at the mention of DeLuca's name. Vince DeLuca, a low-level dealer and serial felon. He was also a known spousal abuser, the kind of scum that slipped through the cracks of the justice system and was back on the streets in no time.

"You really think Ward's going to come for him?" I asked, my voice skeptical.

Jones nodded, a grim smile playing at the corners of his mouth. "I know he will. DeLuca is exactly the kind of target he looks for. Someone who has escaped justice, someone the system has failed to punish."

I chewed my bottom lip, weighing the options in my mind. Using DeLuca as bait was risky, but it might be our only chance to draw Ward out into the open. And if it meant getting O'Malley back safely, I was willing to take that risk.

"Okay," I said finally, my voice heavy with resignation. "Set it up. But Jones, if this goes sideways..."

He held up a hand, cutting me off mid-sentence. "It won't. Trust me, James. I know how this guy thinks. I can predict his every move."

I wanted to believe him, wanted to trust the bond we'd once shared. But the truth of his betrayal was too fresh, the wound too raw. I couldn't afford to let my guard down, not even for a moment.

We made our plans with uncomfortable haste, Jones providing inside information on the Rune Killer's methods and likely hideouts. He seemed to have an uncanny knowledge of Ward's mind, anticipating his reactions and strategizing accordingly.

It was unnerving to watch, to see the man I'd once considered a friend and mentor turn into something else entirely. A man consumed by his own thirst for vengeance, willing to blur the lines between justice and vigilantism.

As we finalized the details of the plan, I felt a sense of unease settle in the pit of my stomach. We were playing a dangerous game, one with no guarantees and no safety net. If we failed, if Ward slipped through our fingers... I didn't even want to think about the consequences.

But failure wasn't an option. Not with O'Malley's life on the line. Not if it meant the Rune Killer would continue their bloody war.

I took a deep breath, steeling myself for the battle ahead. It was time to end this once and for all. And heaven help anyone who got in my way.

I strapped on my bulletproof vest and checked the magazine on my Beretta before holstering it at my side. The weight was familiar, comforting even, a tangible reminder of my parents, who had given me the gun before they were taken from me in a fateful house fire. It was one of the few things I had left to remember them by, and I cherished it deeply. But even with my trusty sidearm, the tension in my gut remained. This was a mission like no other, a deadly tango with the devil himself, and the stakes had never been higher.

Jones set up next to me, his movements precise and methodical. I watched him out of the corner of my eye, trying to reconcile the man I'd known for years with the stranger who now stood in his place.

We'd set the trap, dangling DeLuca as bait for the rune-killer. It was a risky gambit, one that could backfire in a thousand different ways. But it was also our best chance to draw Ward out into the open and force a confrontation on our terms.

Jones had sent the invitation through the forum, a thinly veiled message promising retribution for DeLuca's crimes. We knew Ward wouldn't be able to resist, that his twisted sense of justice would force him to act. And when he did, we'd be waiting.

We pored over maps of the city, marking potential ambush sites and escape routes. A game of chess at work, anticipating our opponent's every move.

But even as we worked out our plans, I found myself second-guessing his suggestions, questioning his motives at every turn. Was he truly committed to bringing Ward to justice, or was this all just another ploy in a twisted game? I couldn't be sure, and that uncertainty was eating away at me like a cancer.

As we finalized our plans, I caught Jones' eye across the table. For a moment, I saw a glimmer of the old Jones, the man who had been my friend and mentor. But it was gone just as quickly, replaced by a hardened mask of determination.

"We'll get her back, James," he said, his voice sure and intense. "I promise you that."

I wanted to believe him.

As we prepared to leave, I checked and rechecked my weapons, making sure everything was in working order. There could be no room for error, not when the stakes were so high. I caught Jones' eye again. "Marcus," I said, "if you double-cross me on this..."

He stopped me with a hand gesture. "I won't, James. I swear on my sister's grave. I'm with you on this, all the way."

I searched his face for any sign of deception, any hint of the betrayal that had shattered our trust. But his gaze was steady, unwavering. For better or worse, we were in this together.

I nodded, a brief jerk of my chin. "Okay, then. Let's do this."

We climbed into our respective vehicles, the silence broken only by the crackle of the radio. This was it, the moment of truth. We were going to end this once and for all.

The drive to the ambush site was a blur. Thoughts swirled in my head, an endless reel of what-ifs and worst-case scenarios playing out like a grim picture show. I tried to focus on the plan, each step meticulously planned, but the seeds of uncertainty had taken root. They clawed at the edges of my resolve, threatening to unravel it thread by thread.

What if Jones was leading me into a trap? What if this was all just another move in some twisted game, a ploy to throw me off the scent? I couldn't shake the feeling that I was walking into a viper's nest, and the only question was which one of us would strike first.

As we approached the location, I pushed those thoughts aside. I couldn't afford to be distracted, not now. O'Malley's life depended on me keeping a clear head and focusing on the mission at hand.

We parked our vehicles in a secluded alley, out of sight. The night was thick and heavy, the air thick with the stench of garbage and decay. It was the perfect place for an ambush, a maze of shadows and blind corners.

CHAPTER SEVENTEEN

COUNTDOWN

DeLuca paced back and forth in the dimly lit alley, his hands wringing nervously as he looked around, as if expecting someone to leap out of the shadows at any moment. Thoughts raced through his mind, reminding him of the sheer insanity of his current situation. He knew he shouldn't be here, willingly putting himself in danger like this. But the detectives had leverage over him, and he was all too aware that this was his only ticket to getting his assault charges reduced. A Faustian bargain he felt powerless to refuse.

With a heavy sigh, DeLuca leaned back against the grimy brick wall, his trembling fingers fumbling as he pulled out another cigarette. He brought it to his lips, the cherry glowing brightly in the darkness as he took a long, anxious drag. His heart pounded in his chest, the thumping pulses echoing in his ears like a drumbeat of impending doom. The reality of his agreement to be bait for this half-baked operation still hadn't fully sunk in.

DeLuca knew he was many things – a lowlife, a junkie, a failure – but he wasn't stupid. He was all too aware of the risks, the very real possibility that he could end up with a knife in his back or a bullet in his brain. But he also knew that if he didn't cooperate, he was in for a rough time, and that wasn't an option. Not again. He couldn't bear the thought of being locked away again, his freedom taken away by the cold, unforgiving bars of a prison cell.

The sudden creak of a nearby door made DeLuca jump, the cigarette falling from his fingers as his heart leapt into his throat. Detective Black emerged from the shadows, his trench coat billowing slightly in the night breeze that carried the scent of decay and despair. DeLuca exhaled shakily, the sight of his handler coming to prepare him doing little to calm his frayed nerves.

"Are you ready for this?" Black asked gruffly, his piercing blue eyes seeming to bore right through DeLuca, taking his measure in a single, penetrating glance.

DeLuca laughed humorlessly, the sound hollow and brittle in the oppressive silence of the alley. "As ready as I'll ever be to be live bait for a fucking serial killer," he replied, his voice tinged with a bitter edge of sarcasm.

Black's expression softened slightly, a flicker of understanding crossing his weathered features. "Look, I know this isn't ideal-"

"That's a hell of an understatement," DeLuca snorted, cutting him off with a dismissive shake of his head.

"But if we want to catch this psycho, we need someone who fits the bill," Black continued, undeterred by the interruption. "Someone he can't resist. From what we know of his M.O., you check every box, something you shouldn't be proud of."

DeLuca grimaced, his stomach churning at the thought of being described as "prey." But as much as he hated to admit it, Black had a point - the mysterious Rune Killer did seem to target those like him, the dregs of society who kept slipping through the cracks.

Black's hand rested on DeLuca's shoulder, a source of warmth amidst the pervasive chill that seeped from the weathered bricks and unyielding concrete. The touch conveyed protection, reassuring DeLuca that he would not face the impending danger alone.

"We've got you covered, Vince," Black said, his voice steady with conviction. "My team will form a perimeter around the location, weapons at the ready. If this bastard even thinks about making a move, we'll take him out on the spot. Your only job is to wait for him to reveal himself. Leave the rest to us."

DeLuca nodded, swallowing hard as he tried to quell the rising tide of fear that threatened to overwhelm him. He was still far from convinced that this wasn't an elaborate plan to get him killed, a convenient way for the cops to get rid of another deadbeat junkie. But he was out of options, backed into a corner with no way out. "Yeah, yeah, fine. Let's just get this shit over with," he muttered.

Black squeezed his shoulder tightly before letting go, a silent gesture of support that did little to loosen the knot of fear in DeLuca's gut. "Atta boy. Now go wait at the east entrance, near the streetlight. Jones and I will be in position. It's showtime."

DeLuca watched as the detective disappeared back into the shadows, presumably to rendezvous with Jones somewhere nearby. He took a few more long puffs on his newly lit cigarette, the nicotine doing little to calm his nerves as he flicked the smoldering butt to the pavement. Then, with a sense of resignation that bordered on despair, he reluctantly shuffled toward the designated spot, his hands buried deep in his pockets as if seeking some small measure of comfort or protection.

The whole area was eerily quiet, the kind of heavy, oppressive silence that heralds impending doom. The warehouse loomed overhead, a hulking behemoth of corrugated metal and broken windows. DeLuca's ratty sneakers crunched on shards of glass and other debris as he took up position in the sickly pool of light cast by the flickering streetlamp, the feeble illumination doing little to dispel the darkness pressing in from all sides. He glanced around cautiously, his eyes straining to penetrate the shadows as he wondered where Black and the others were hiding. Were they watching him through a sniper's scope right now, he thought, just a twitch away from putting a bullet through his head?

A convulsive shudder ran through DeLuca's body as the pervasive chill emanating from the dilapidated surroundings seeped into his marrow. The crawl of time mocked him, each passing second ticking away with excruciating slowness, an unbearable eternity as he waited for some sign that the sting operation was underway. A sign that he wasn't just a sacrificial lamb to be left to his fate.

But only the wild, desperate pounding of his pulse echoed in his ears like a taunting reminder of his own mortality. And as the minutes dragged on with no sign of the killer or his supposed backup, DeLuca began to wonder if he had made a fatal mistake in trusting the detectives. Had he sealed his own fate by agreeing to this harebrained scheme and signed his own death warrant?

As the night wore on, the chill in the air seemed to seep into Detective Black's bones, numbing his extremities and clouding his breath with each exhale. He checked his watch again, scowling at the unmoving hands as if he could make time speed up by sheer force of will. Hours had passed since they'd set up this sting operation, and there was still no sign of their quarry. The Rune Killer, it seemed, was content to let them stew in their own anticipation and fear, toying with them.

Black shifted his weight, trying to ease the cramps in his legs from squatting for so long, his muscles protesting the prolonged inactivity. Next to him, Detective Jones was a silent, motionless presence, his eyes fixed on the distant figure of Vince DeLuca, unwavering in his vigilance. He looked small and vulnerable out there, illuminated by the flickering streetlight like a moth drawn to a flame, his silhouette casting long, distorted shadows on the cracked pavement. Black couldn't help but feel a pang of guilt for putting him in this position, even though DeLuca was far from an innocent man, his rap sheet a testament to his own misdeeds.

As the minutes ticked by with no sign of their target, Black's frustration began to boil over, bubbling up from the pit of his stomach like magma seeking release. He turned to Jones, his voice a harsh whisper in the darkness, barely audible over the distant hum of the city.

"This is pointless," he hissed, his words dripping with venom. "We're wasting our time out here. The killer's probably long gone by now, laughing at us for being stupid enough to think he'd take the bait, mocking our futile efforts."

Jones didn't even look at him, his eyes still on DeLuca, his focus unwavering. "Patience, Black. He'll show. He always does, in the end, drawn to the promise of another kill like bees to honey."

Black snorted derisively, the sound harsh and grating in the stillness of the night. "And what makes you so sure? Because from where I sit, this whole operation feels like a wild goose chase, a fool's errand with no end in sight."

Now Jones turned to face him, his expression unreadable in the shadows, his eyes glaring with an unspoken challenge. "He'll show up, he always does."

Black's eyes narrowed as he studied Jones, a flicker of suspicion sparking in his gut. "You seem awfully confident, Jones."

Jones' expression remained impassive, his voice even and controlled. "I've been feeding the Rune Killer information for some time now, Black. I know how he works, how he thinks. Believe me, he won't be able to resist the bait we've laid out for him."

Black shook his head, a humorless chuckle escaping his lips. "Trust you? That's a tall order, considering the circumstances. I mean, let's face it, Jones. This whole setup, tempting this madman with DeLuca as bait, it's a risky move. And for what? Who's to say he won't go after some other poor soul whose name you gave him?"

Jones' jaw tightened, a hint of irritation creeping into his tone. "It's a calculated risk, one I believe will pay off. We're close, Black. Closer than we've ever been to catching this guy."

Black's gaze never left Jones' face, searching for any sign of deception. "Or maybe this is all just an elaborate game, a way to buy time for Ward to disappear into the wind. I've considered that possibility, Jones. That maybe you're the one playing us like a fiddle?"

Jones' eyes flashed with anger, his voice dropping to a throaty growl. "Watch yourself, Black. You're treading on dangerous ground."

Black leaned forward, his voice filled with accusation. "Am I? Because it looks like you're more concerned with protecting Ward than finding O'Malley. Tell me, Jones, do you even want her back, or is she just another pawn in your twisted little game?"

Jones' hands clenched into fists. "Don't you dare question my commitment to O'Malley, Black. I want O'Malley back as much as you do, she's like a second sister to me."

Black scoffed, his tone dripping with sarcasm. "Do you? Because right now it feels like you're more interested in making us play cat and mouse with a serial killer than saving one of our own."

For a long moment, the two men stared at each other, the tension between them crackling like electricity, the air heavy with unresolved grievances. Black could see the muscle in Jones' jaw twitch, as he considered his response while calculating his next move.

But before Jones could speak, a distant sound shattered the silence around them, cutting through the veil of tension like a knife. It was a scream, high and panicked, followed by the unmistakable sounds of a struggle, of bodies colliding and grappling in the darkness. Black's head whipped around, his eyes widening as he saw a shadowy figure struggling with DeLuca near the warehouse entrance, their silhouettes merging and separating in a frenzied dance.

"Shit!" he cursed, already moving, his body propelled forward before his mind could catch up. "It's him! Move in, now! Go, go, go!"

Black's footsteps pounded against the cracked pavement as he sprinted towards the struggling figures near the warehouse entrance, his breath coming in ragged gasps. Adrenaline coursed through his veins, narrowing his focus to the single goal of reaching DeLuca before it was too late. Jones followed close behind, his longer strides allowing him to overtake Black despite his desperate rush.

As they drew closer, the scene came into ghastly focus under the dim light of the flickering streetlamp. DeLuca was pinned against the brick wall of the warehouse, his eyes wide with terror, his mouth open in a silent scream. A dark figure was pressed against him, a gloved hand clamped over DeLuca's mouth, muffling his screams.

DeLuca continued to struggle until the killer drove the hilt of his knife sharply into his temple. DeLuca's body went rigid, his screams were cut short. Stunned by the brutal blow, his eyes lost focus and rolled back as he slumped dazed against the wall.

"Police! Freeze!" Black roared, his gun raised as he closed the remaining distance in a few steps. Beside him, Jones had his gun drawn as well, the two of them closing in on the killer like hounds on a fox.

At the sound of Black's voice, the Rune Killer's head snapped up, eyes glaring malevolently from behind his mask. Without hesitation, he grabbed the limp DeLuca and spun him around as a human shield. DeLuca's head lolled back, oblivious.

"Drop it! Let him go!" Black ordered, gun pointed at the pair.

In response, the killer plunged his knife into DeLuca's stomach, ripping downward to spill his guts. DeLuca convulsed uncontrollably as his insides oozed from the yawning cavity.

The Rune Killer flung the sagging, disemboweled body forward. Jones tried to stop or dodge, but DeLuca's body slammed into him with the force of a freight train, sending them both sprawling. Jones' gun skittered across the pavement as he struggled to free himself from the tangle of limbs and entrails.

"I got him!" Black yelled, already spinning toward the fleeing killer. He fired a shot, but it ricocheted off the warehouse wall as the Rune Killer rounded the corner. Without hesitation, Black took off after him. "Stay with DeLuca!"

Cursing under his breath, Jones scrambled to steady DeLuca, who lay crumpled on the ground. DeLuca's breath came in wet, choking gasps as blood and guts spilled from the deep lacerations that bisected his abdomen, the damage irreparable. DeLuca's breath came in weak, wet gasps as his hands feebly grasped at the protruding coils of his intestines as he tried to pull himself back together.

"No, no, no," Jones muttered, pressing his hands over the yawning wounds in a futile attempt to stop the catastrophic bleeding. DeLuca whimpered weakly, eyes wide with shock and disbelief at the sight of his own entrails spilling out of his body.

Jones kept up a stream of desperate encouragement, telling DeLuca over and over that help was on the way, that he'd make it. But the pallor of death was already claiming DeLuca's features. His lips moved soundlessly, forming words he no longer had the strength to utter.

Jones leaned down and put his ear close to DeLuca's face. "S-sorry..." DeLuca rasped, so soft it was almost inaudible. "I didn't know...he was..." His words trailed off as the light faded from his eyes, his brutalized body going limp.

Jones rocked back on his heels, his blood-soaked hands falling away from DeLuca's still form. Everything around him felt muted and distant, memories of his sister flooding back to him, his hands covered in her blood. His vision distorted, his deceased sister slowly fading away until all he could see was DeLuca's mutilated body before him. They had failed. He had failed. And DeLuca had paid the price.

The sound of approaching footsteps jolted Jones from his spiraling thoughts. He looked up to see Black coming toward him, shaking his head grimly.

"He slipped into the shadows near the loading docks," Black said bitterly, holstering his gun. "I couldn't keep up once he hit the back alleys. He's gone." Black's voice sounded hollow, devoid of his usual confidence.

Kneeling beside DeLuca's lifeless body, Black surveyed the horrific wounds with a clenched jaw. "Even after we arrived on the scene, this monster still managed to finish what he started," he muttered angrily. "Damn it all!"

Black slowly rose to his feet, swaying slightly as the delayed shock set in. "This is on us, Jones," he growled through gritted teeth. "We never should have used him as bait, not like that. It was a death sentence."

Jones's face was grim, his mouth set in a hard line. "Maybe so. But we had no way of knowing the killer would get away and do this kind of damage. I thought we could end this tonight."

Black stepped closer and jabbed an accusing finger into Jones' chest. "But we didn't finish it, did we? And now another man is dead because of our failure." He waved an angry hand at DeLuca. "This... this is on our hands now, Jones. His blood is on both of us."

Jones bore Black's anger stoically, making no move to defend himself. When Black finally fell silent, his chest heaving with emotion, Jones spoke softly. "What's done is done, Black. We can't change it now. All we can do is continue to hunt this bastard down before he kills again." His eyes hardened with conviction. "And we will find him. I swear we'll make him pay for this."

Black held Jones' unwavering gaze for a long moment before giving a short, terse nod. As much as he hated to admit it, Jones was right.

Wallowing in guilt wouldn't bring DeLuca back or undo this tragedy. The only way forward was to doggedly pursue the killer, using every resource at their disposal to prevent more blood from being spilled.

Black turned to look down at DeLuca one last time, memorizing every detail of the gruesome scene. He suspected that this image would haunt his dreams for many nights to come, a grim reminder of the terrible evil they hunted and the high price paid by those who stood in its path.

When he turned around, Jones was watching him intently, as if trying to gauge his mental state and stability. Black met his assessing gaze directly. "Let's get back to the station and go over everything we know with fresh eyes," he said firmly. "We're missing something, some clue or pattern we haven't seen yet. And we're not leaving that briefing room until we have a solid lead on where to pick up the trail."

Jones searched his face for a moment before nodding. "Agreed. We'll take this case apart piece by piece if that's what it takes. The Rune Killer's days are numbered."

The two detectives stood in solemn silence amidst the carnage and darkness, united in grim purpose. Around them, the wail of approaching sirens grew louder as reinforcements finally arrived on the scene. But the hunter had already claimed their prize and were long gone, vanishing into the night like ghosts.

The crackle of Detective Black's radio shattered the tense silence that had settled over the crime scene. The disembodied voice of the dispatcher, tinny and distant, carried a chilling message: another body had been discovered, bearing the same grisly signs of the Rune Killer's handiwork.

Black and Jones exchanged a look of disbelief and frustration, their expressions reflecting the confusion and anger that coursed through their veins. Black's brow furrowed as he processed this new development, his mind racing to make sense of the seemingly impossible situation.

"What the hell is going on here?" he demanded, his voice raspy with barely contained anger. "I just had the target in my sights. There's no way he could have killed anyone else in that time."

Jones shook his head, equally baffled by the turn of events. "It doesn't make any sense," he agreed. "We had him cornered, and yet he somehow managed to elude us and strike again."

A dark shadow passed over Black's face as his mind grappled with the ominous implications. His eyes narrowed, a storm of suspicion and fear swirling in their depths. The unfinished thought hung in the air, heavy and oppressive, as if the very words could unleash an unspeakable horror upon them all.

"Unless..."

CHAPTER EIGHTEEN

UNDER THE LENS

The precinct doors slammed behind me as I barged in, my mind a whirlwind of frustration and anger threatening to consume me. Electricity seemed to crackle through the bullpen, my fellow officers sensing the storm brewing within. I scanned the room for one person in particular. There, in the sea of desks and officers, stood Isabel Reyes. She stood like an island of calm amidst the chaos, her pen dancing across the pages of her notepad.

My feet devoured the distance, purpose driving each step. The words ripped from my throat, guttural and seething. "Reyes." Her name was gravel on my tongue. "You and I are going to have a little talk. Right now."

She looked up, her hazel eyes widening slightly at the intensity of my gaze. "Detective Black, I was just-"

"Save it," I snapped, grabbing her elbow and leading her into an empty interrogation room. The door slammed behind us with a resounding thud, the sound echoing through the cramped room like a gunshot.

I turned on her, my voice rising with each word. "What the fuck were you thinking, Reyes? Releasing those details about the coins? Do you have any idea what you've done - the shitstorm you've brought down on our heads?"

She straightened her posture and met my gaze with a defiant tilt of her chin. "I'm a journalist, Black. It's my job to report the truth, to inform the public..."

A harsh hiss of laughter escaped my lips. "Informed? You put lives in danger, Reyes. Your little scoop has spawned a wave of copycats, each more desperate than the last to mimic the Rune Killer's style."

My fists clenched as I paced the cramped office, frustration boiling in my veins. "The department's resources were already stretched thin, chasing ghosts and shadows, desperate for any shred of a lead. But now?" I spun around to face her, jabbing an accusing finger. "Now, thanks to you, we've got a plague of would-be vigilantes swarming the streets, muddying the waters, and leaving fresh bodies for us to clean up."

Reyes flinched, her eyes dropping to the ground. For a moment, I saw a flicker of uncertainty cross her features, a crack in her armor of self-assurance. "I... I didn't think-"

"No, you didn't," I snapped, slamming my palm against the metal table. The sound reverberated through the room, sharp and jarring. "You didn't think about the consequences, about the lives you put at risk. All you cared about was your byline, your shot at glory."

Her breath quivered as she inhaled, the words coming out as a faint whisper. "I'm sorry, Black. I never meant for things to get so out of hand."

I shook my head, my anger giving way to a bone-deep weariness. "Sorry doesn't bring back the dead, Reyes. It doesn't undo the damage you've done."

I turned away from her, my gaze fixed on the one-way mirror that dominated the far wall. In its reflective surface, I caught a glimpse of my own face, haggard and haunted, the toll of the investigation etched into every line and shadow.

"I don't know what to believe anymore," I murmured, more to myself than to her. "Is Ward the killer, or just another pawn in this twisted game?

Are we dealing with a single psychopath, or a whole network of them, each more depraved than the last?"

Reyes took a tentative step forward, her voice soft and hesitant. "Black, I... I want to help. I know I screwed up, but let me make it right. Let me use my resources, my contacts, to dig deeper, to find the truth."

A harsh, bitter sound escaped my throat, a mockery of laughter. "The truth? The truth is we're chasing shadows, Reyes. Every lead, every suspect, it all slips through our fingers like smoke. And with each passing day, the body count rises and the city descends further into chaos."

The possibilities swirled through my mind in a dizzying maelstrom of unease, each scenario a nightmare more terrifying than the one before. The immense pressure crushed down on my shoulders - the duty, the responsibility, the sickening certainty that time had already run out, that the Rune Killer had outmaneuvered us.

What of the copycats, the vigilantes who had taken up the mantle of the Rune Killer? Were they misguided souls seeking justice in a world that had failed them? Or were they something darker, a manifestation of the evil that lurked in the shadows of Silvergate's streets?

I had no answers, and the uncertainty was eating away at me, bit by bit. All I knew was that I had to keep going, keep fighting, even if it meant descending into the heart of darkness itself.

I turned back to Reyes, my voice firm. "If you want to help, do your job. Report the facts, not the sensationalism. And leave the police work to us."

With that, I pushed past her, my footsteps echoing through the precinct as I walked toward the exit.

The next day, the bullpen was a hive of activity, the air thick with tension and the clatter of keyboards. But even the clacking of keys couldn't drown out the screams of the victims that echoed endlessly in my head, a haunting soundtrack to the horrors we were trying to unravel. I sat hunched over my desk, my eyes bleary from staring at the endless sea of reports and case files.

Suddenly, the room fell silent, as if every breath in the precinct had been stolen in unison. I looked up, an inexplicable force drawing my gaze to the entrance of the station. There stood a figure framed in the doorway, an ominous silhouette against the fluorescent glare.

It was Ramirez, and standing beside him was none other than Ethan Ward, his wrists cuffed and his eyes downcast.

I felt a surge of adrenaline coursing through my veins, a mixture of shock and anticipation. Could this be it? Had we finally caught the Rune Killer?

Ramirez strode forward, his footsteps echoing through the silence. The room erupted with excited murmurs, officers, and detectives crowding around to get a better look at the man who had terrorized Silvergate for so long.

Ramirez held up a hand, silencing the chatter. "I tracked Ward to a cabin on the edge of town. He didn't put up a fight, just let me bring him in."

A faint flame of hope sparked within me, illuminating the shadows that had haunted my soul these long months. I barely dared believe that this could be it - the moment we would emerge from the suffocating darkness into the light of a new day, a day free from the influence of the Rune Killer.

But even as the thought crossed my mind, I couldn't shake the feeling that something was wrong, that there was more to this than met the eye.

I watched as Ramirez led Ward through the bustling precinct, the historian's head bowed and his shoulders slumped in defeat. Officers and detectives alike paused in their work, their eyes drawn to the man who had become the focus of our investigation.

My pulse raced as I followed Ramirez and Ward into the processing room. Ward's face was an inscrutable mask, betraying no hint of emotion as the booking officer began the intake process. I stood back, observing every detail, a tightness gripping my chest. Something about Ward's impassive demeanor unsettled me, like the eerie calm before a storm.

The booking officer, a grizzled veteran named Miller, began the process with a sense of grim efficiency. He snapped Ward's mug shot, the camera flash illuminating the historian's gaunt features. Ward barely flinched, his eyes staring straight ahead as if lost in his own world.

Next came the fingerprinting, the black ink staining Ward's fingertips as Miller rolled them on the card for their impression. The historian remained a cipher, his face betraying nothing throughout the process.

As Miller moved on to the search and inventory, I found myself studying Ward more closely. If I had found him disheveled and unkempt when we first met, it was nothing compared to the broken man who sat before me now. His hair, usually only slightly tousled, was a wild, greasy mess, sticking out at odd angles as if he had run his hands through it repeatedly. The dark circles under his eyes had deepened to a bruised purple, a testament to countless sleepless nights spent poring over ancient texts and artifacts.

Even his clothes, which had always been an afterthought at best, seemed to be in a state of total disarray. His shirt was buttoned haphazardly, the tail half tucked into his wrinkled pants. The cuffs of his sleeves were frayed and stained with what looked suspiciously like dried blood, though whether it was his own or that of his victims I couldn't tell.

But it was the look in his eyes that really stopped me in my tracks. The once bright spark of intellectual curiosity had been replaced by a dull, feverish glow, a hint of madness lurking just below the surface. It was as if the weight of his obsession, the burden of his self-appointed holy mission, had finally taken its toll, stripping away the last vestiges of the man he had once been.

I watched as Miller patted him down efficiently, removing his personal belongings with clinical detachment. Whatever had driven Ethan Ward to this point, whatever twisted belief had consumed him so completely, there was no denying that he was a man utterly shattered by the force of his own convictions.

Miller methodically emptied Ward's pockets and placed the contents on the table in front of him. A wallet, a set of keys, a few crumpled receipts - all the mundane fragments of an interrupted life. But it was the last item that caught my eye, a small, battered photograph that fluttered to the ground as Miller pulled it from Ward's jacket.

I bent to retrieve it, my fingers trembling slightly as I turned it over. It was a picture of a woman, her face radiant with laughter and love. She had the same once-piercing blue eyes as Ward, the same sharp intelligence in her gaze.

"Amelia," Ward said softly, his voice barely above a whisper. They were the first words he had spoken since his arrest, and they hung in the air like a confession.

Miller looked up, his expression unreadable. "I have to log this as evidence, Dr. Ward."

Ward's eyes widened, a flicker of emotion breaking through his stoic facade.

For a moment, I felt a pang of compassion for the man before me. I knew all too well the pain of loss, the pain of a loved one taken too soon. But then I remembered the victims, the lives cut short by the Rune Killer's blade, and my resolve hardened once more.

"Everything has to be documented," I said.

Ward seemed to deflate at my words, his shoulders slumping as he nodded in resignation. Miller finished the inventory, his movements precise and efficient, before leading Ward out of the processing room and down the hall to the interrogation room.

I followed, my mind racing with questions and doubts. What secrets lay behind those haunted eyes, what demons drove him to commit such atrocities?

As Miller secured Ward in the interrogation room, I felt a sense of anticipation building within me. I paced outside, my heart pounding in my chest as I tried to collect my thoughts. This was it, the moment I had been waiting for, the chance to confront the man who had become the focus of our investigation.

I could see Ward through the one-way mirror, his hands cuffed to the table and his head bowed. He looked smaller somehow, diminished in the harsh light of the interrogation room. But I knew better than to underestimate him, to let my guard down even for a moment.

I took a deep breath, steeling myself for what lay ahead. I had faced countless criminals in my time on the force, stared into the eyes of murderers and psychopaths without flinching. But there was something different about Ward, something that made my nerves tingle and my skin crawl.

Perhaps it was the way he seemed to anticipate our every move, always one step ahead as we chased him through the shadows of Silvergate. Or maybe it was the cold, calculating intelligence that lurked behind those piercing blue eyes, the sense that he was playing a game that only he understood.

I shook my head, pushing these thoughts aside. I couldn't afford to let my doubts and fears cloud my judgment, not now, not when we were so close to the truth.

I glanced over at Ramirez, who was leaning against the wall with his arms crossed, his expression unreadable. He had been the one to bring Ward in, to finally end the reign of terror that had gripped the city for so long. But even he seemed unsure, his confidence wavering in the face of the man sitting just a few feet away.

"Are you ready for this?" he asked gruffly.

I nodded, my jaw clenched. "As ready as I'll ever be."

I took one last deep breath, then pushed open the door to the interrogation room, the metal cool beneath my fingertips. Ward looked up as I entered, his gaze meeting mine with a flicker of recognition.

"Detective Black," he said, his voice soft and cultured. "I was wondering when you would come to see me."

I felt a surge of anger at his words, at the casual way he spoke, as if this were just another academic debate, another intellectual exercise. I slammed my hands down on the table, the metal ringing with the force of the impact.

"Cut the shit, Ward," I growled, my voice brash and threatening. "You know why you're here, you know what you've done."

He leaned back in his chair, his expression calm and unflappable. "Do I? Enlighten me, Detective."

I felt my temper flare, my patience wearing thin. "The murders, Ward. The Rune Killer. We know you are responsible, we have the evidence to prove it."

He raised an eyebrow, a hint of amusement playing at the corners of his mouth. "Evidence? And what evidence would that be, exactly?"

I reached into my jacket and pulled out the photo of Amelia that we had confiscated. I slammed it down on the table and watched as his eyes widened in surprise.

"Your wife, Ward. Amelia. She was murdered, wasn't she? Murdered by a criminal who got off on a technicality. Is that what this is about? Some twisted quest for revenge?"

He stared at the photograph, his fingers trembling slightly as he reached out to touch it. For a moment I saw a flicker of pain in his eyes, a glimpse of the man he had once been, before the darkness had consumed him.

But then it was gone, replaced by a cold, hard rage. He looked up at me, his gaze boring into mine with an intensity that took my breath away.

His whispered words sliced through the air like a razor, sharp and biting. "You have no idea what you're talking about, Detective."

He fixed me with a stare that could've frozen hell itself. "You think you understand, but you don't. You can't."

I leaned closer, my face inches from his. "Then enlighten me, Ward. Tell me what I'm missing, what I don't understand?"

Then he smiled, a twisted, mocking grin that made my hair stand on end. "You're missing the truth, Detective. The truth about justice, about the world we live in. You think you're on the side of the angels, but you're just as blind as the rest of them."

I felt my anger rise, my fists clenching at my sides. "And what truth is that, Ward? The truth that justifies murder, that makes it okay to take the law into your own hands?"

He shook his head, his expression almost pitiful. "The truth that the law is a lie, Detective. A children's tale we tell ourselves to make sense of the chaos, to pretend there is order in the universe. But there is no order, no justice, no purpose. There is only power and those willing to use it."

I leaned forward, my eyes narrowing. "Well, if power is the only thing that matters, Ward, what's to stop me from using my power right here and now?"

With a deliberate motion, I unholstered my weapon and placed it on the table between us, the metal gleaming dully under the glaring lights. Ward's eyes widened almost imperceptibly, a flicker of uncertainty crossing his features for the first time since he entered the room.

I let the silence stretch between us for a moment, the weight of an unspoken threat hanging heavy in the air. When I spoke again, my voice was deep and dangerous. "What's to stop me from using this gun to end you, right here in this room? No judge, no jury, just the executioner's bullet. Isn't that the world you believe in, Ward? Where the strong do as they will and the weak suffer as they must?"

Ward's eyes darted from the gun to my face, searching for any hint of hesitation or weakness. But I remained impassive, my hand resting lightly on the gun, a silent reminder of the power I held over him at this moment.

Finally, he spoke, his voice strained and uncertain. "You wouldn't. You're bound by your oath, by your precious laws and regulations. You don't have the stomach for true justice."

I leaned back in my chair, a mirthless smile playing at the corners of my mouth. "Don't be so sure, Ward. You said it yourself – there is no order, no justice. Just power. And right now, I have all the power I need to end this, to end your twisted crusade once and for all."

I let the words hang in the air between us, a challenge and a threat all at once. In the end, I knew I wouldn't pull the trigger, that I was still bound by the very laws and oaths Ward so despised. But at that moment, with the weight of the gun in my hand and the madness in his eyes, I wanted him to feel the same fear and uncertainty that his victims must have felt in their final moments. I wanted him to understand the true nature of the power he so craved and the terrible responsibility that came with it.

His soft chuckle broke the tense silence, mocking my bravado. Ward's eyes burned with a fevered intensity as he spoke. "I have peered behind the veil, Detective. The truth hidden there has been revealed to me in all its glory."

I shook my head, my voice cold and unyielding. "There was no truth there, Ward. Just the delusions of a broken, resentful shell of a man. You saw whatever helped you make sense of your shattered world, nothing more, nothing less. And I'm going to make sure you never hurt anyone else ever again."

He leaned forward, his eyes glowing with a malevolent light. "You can try, Detective. But you'll fail, just like everyone else. Because you don't understand, you haven't seen the truth that I've seen. You can't stop me, any more than you can stop the rising of the sun or the changing of the seasons."

I stood abruptly, the scrape of my chair against the floor startling him into silence. "We'll see, Ward. We'll see what a jury has to say, what the evidence proves. And then we'll see who's left standing when the dust settles."

The cool steel of my service weapon felt reassuring as I holstered it and walked toward the door. My fingers had just brushed the tarnished brass knob when Ward's grating voice slipped through the air and wrapped around me, stopping me in my tracks.

Ward spoke in a low, eerie cadence. "Ira divina expergiscitur, ecce eius furor."

A bitter fear seeped into my bones as I slowly turned to face him. The foreign words, spoken with such gravity, echoed through the dingy interrogation room. I fought to keep my voice steady, but an icy tingle crept under my skin. "What are you talking about, Ward? What did you just say?"

But he just smiled, the same twisted, mocking grin that made my blood boil. "Just a friendly warning, Detective. Take it or leave it, the choice is yours."

And with that, he fell silent, his eyes drifting back to the photograph of Amelia that lay on the table in front of him.

As I left the interrogation room, his words echoed in my mind. Was his intention to irritate me, to throw me off balance? Or was there something more to his warning, some deeper truth that I had yet to uncover?

Before I could take a moment to collect myself, I nearly collided with Officer Chen, her eyes filled with concern and anticipation. "Black, what happened in there? Did Ward break? Did he confess?"

I shook my head, my voice hoarse and tense. "No... he just kept rambling like a madman. It's like he's playing games with us, but I can't figure out his angle."

Her brow furrowed and she asked me to explain further. I took a breath and repeated the strange phrase Ward had uttered. "Ira divina expergiscitur, ecce eius furor." The words felt strange and ominous on my tongue as I repeated them to Officer Chen. "I have no idea what it means, but the way he said it... It was unnerving."

Recognition flashed in her eyes and she translated, "It's Latin. It means 'Divine wrath awakens, behold its fury. It sounds like a threat, a warning of sorts."

I turned to her, my brow furrowed in surprise. "You know Latin?"

Chen shrugged, a hint of a smile playing at the corners of her mouth. "I grew up Catholic. Went to mass every Sunday, took all the classes. Latin was one of the few things that really stuck with me."

I nodded, impressed with her unexpected knowledge. "I never would have guessed. You don't strike me as the religious type."

She laughed, a short, sharp sound that echoed in the quiet of the hallway. "I'm not, not anymore. But some things stay with you no matter how hard you try to shake them."

I understood this sentiment all too well. My own past, the ghosts that haunted my every waking moment, were a testament to the indelible mark our experiences can leave on our lives.

I returned to my desk, my mind still reeling from the confrontation with Ward. I couldn't shake the feeling that we were missing something crucial. As I slumped into my chair, Officer Reynolds approached me with a grim expression.

"Black, we got another victim," he said, handing me a report. "And this one's the real thing, not another copycat."

I flipped through the pages, my heart sinking with each gruesome detail. The Rune Killer's signature was unmistakable, the ancient symbols carved into the victim's flesh with chilling precision. But how could this be? We had Ward in custody, and the evidence against him was overwhelming.

I looked up at Reynolds, my voice cracking with frustration. "This doesn't make any sense. If Ward is the Rune Killer, then who the hell did this?"

He shook his head, his own confusion obvious. "I don't know, Black. But we need to find out, and fast. The city's on edge, and the media will be all over this."

"Any chance this murder happened before we arrested Ward?" I asked.

Reynolds met my gaze, his doubt mirroring my own. "I'll let you know as soon as I have that information."

I nodded, my jaw clenched. The coroner's report would tell us the time of death, but until then I was grasping at straws. "I need to talk to Jones."

I found Jones in the break room, drinking a cup of coffee and looking like he hadn't slept in days. When he saw me coming, he straightened up, his expression guarded.

"Black, what's up? You look like you've seen a ghost."

I slammed the report down on the table in front of him, my anger boiling over. "How many names did you feed this guy, Marcus? I thought you said Ward was the Rune Killer."

He flinched at my tone, his eyes darting away from mine. "He is."

I leaned closer, my tone measured and stern. "Don't lie to me, Jones. Has Ward ever contacted you directly?"

He hesitated for a moment, then sighed, his shoulders slumping in defeat. "He always contacted me anonymously, over the Internet. I never saw his face, never heard his voice."

I stared at him, my mind racing. "So why did you bring Ward? Why were you so sure it was him?"

Jones shrugged, his expression helpless. "I don't know, Black. It's just... the way Ward confided in me after his wife's case fell apart, the things he said, the anger and desperation in his voice. It all matched up so perfectly with the words the Rune Killer used when they contacted me. It was like a mirror..."

He paused, his gaze distant and haunted. "Then when the Rune Killer mentioned the Ordo Iustitiae, it felt like a confirmation of everything I had suspected. Ward was the only other person I knew who even knew about it. I guess I just assumed... "

I felt a shiver run down my spine, a sickening realization dawning on me. "What if Ward isn't the Rune Killer, Jones? What if he just believes in what the Rune Killer is doing, so much so that he's willing to take the fall for it? To let the real killer continue their work, to get revenge on all the other Amelias out there?"

Jones looked up at me, his eyes wide with horror. "Jesus, Black. Do you really think that's possible? That Ward would go that far?"

I shook my head, my mind spinning with the implications. "I don't know, Jones. But we need to find out, and fast. Because if Ward isn't the Rune Killer, then that means the real killer is still out there, and they're not going to stop until they finish what they started."

Pain shot through my skull as consciousness returned, the throbbing pain a stark reminder of my predicament. Blinking away the fog, I found myself in a cramped, musty room, the air thick with the smell of mildew and decay. Dim light filtered through a small, dirty window, barely illuminating the room.

I tested my bonds, the rough rope biting into my wrists and ankles. Panic threatened to overwhelm me, but I forced it down, drawing on my training to assess the situation with a clear head. This wasn't just about me - Black and the others would be walking into a trap if I didn't find a way out.

Gritting my teeth, I worked at the knots, my fingers numb and clumsy. The killer had been thorough, but I refused to give up. I'd faced tough situations before, and I certainly wasn't going to let this bastard use me as bait.

My mind raced as I tried to piece together how I'd ended up here. The last thing I remembered was investigating the warehouse alone, like a damn fool. I cursed myself for not waiting for backup, for letting my determination cloud my judgment.

The ropes chafed against my skin, but I kept at it, twisting and pulling with every ounce of strength I could muster. Sweat beaded on my forehead, my breath came in short, sharp gasps. I had to break free, warn the others before it was too late.

CHAPTER NINETEEN

JUDGMENT DAY

T he computer screens flickered with volumes of data as my fingers flew across the keyboard, lines of code scrolling by at a dizzying pace. The low hum of the servers faded into a familiar white noise, the background soundtrack to my digital explorations. This was my domain, my theater of operations, where the intangible became tangible through sheer analytical skill. The faint scent of ozone and heated electronics permeated the air, a byproduct of the intense computations taking place inside the machines.

Sifting through the endless trails of digital breadcrumbs was like breathing for me. I inhaled terabytes of raw data and exhaled patterns that revealed the hidden narratives buried in the noise. My mind was operating at a higher frequency, processing logic gates, and conditional statements with fluidity most couldn't comprehend. The rapid-fire click-clack of my keystrokes formed a disjointed rhythm, a digital symphony that only I could fully appreciate.

A slight shift in the alphanumeric sea caught my eye, an anomaly that didn't quite belong. Instinctively, I traced its source, peeling back layers of obfuscation until the core truth was exposed. A triumphant grin spread across my lips as the last string of numbers dissolved into a coherent IP address. The thrill of the chase coursed through my veins, a heady mix of adrenaline and intellectual satisfaction.

"Gotcha," I muttered under my breath, allowing myself a brief moment of satisfaction before jumping back into action. The word felt good on my tongue, a verbal manifestation of the small victory I had just achieved.

With a few deft keystrokes, I pulled up the relevant service records, revealing a flood of information tied to that elusive digital fingerprint. Slowly, the pieces began to fall into place, painting a disturbing portrait of meticulous planning and cold calculation. The glow of the screens cast an eerie light across my face as I delved deeper into the twisted maze of data.

My eyes widened as I cross-referenced the data streams and linked the IP address to an unlikely name - Lucas Parker. The same Lucas Parker who had assisted Ethan Ward with his academic theories on ancient ritualistic cults. Bingo. The revelation stirred a whirlwind of emotions within me-relief at the discovery mixed with a shock that settled uneasily in the pit of my stomach.

The speed of my keystrokes increased as I dug deeper, uncovering a meticulously crafted digital trail that stretched back months. Unsealed court records, criminal databases, personal profiles - Lucas had systematically gathered information on his victims, carefully curating selection criteria that grew more chilling with each new revelation.

Gritting my teeth, I compiled the damning evidence into a neat package, complete with maps, timelines, and cross-referenced data points that left no doubt as to Lucas's twisted obsession and murderous intent. This was the break we'd been desperately searching for, the linchpin that could potentially crack this case wide open. My heart raced with a mixture of excitement and trepidation as I prepared to share my findings with the team.

I grabbed my headset and quickly patched into the secure channel I shared with Black and Ramirez. "Listen up, Black. You're going to want to see this..." My voice was calm, masking the emotions swirling inside me.

Over the next few minutes, I methodically laid out my findings, walking them through the intricacies of Lucas's modus operandi with cold, hard facts. The digital paper trail didn't lie-this was our man, the elusive mastermind who had been playing us all along. Each piece of evidence I presented felt like a hammer blow, driving home the inescapable truth of Parker's guilt.

The line went dead quiet after I finished, so quiet I swore I could hear Ramirez's heart pounding through his kevlar from here. Or maybe that was my own pulse pounding in my ears, an irregular thumping fueled by the adrenaline still coursing through my veins. The things I'd uncovered about Lucas, what he'd done, and what he was planning to do, shook me in a way few things could these days. That stunned, leaden silence emanating from Black and Ramirez told me I wasn't alone in grappling with the gravity of it all.

Ramirez was the first to respond, his words laced with a strange combination of awe and disgust. "So Parker used Ward's research as an excuse to carry out his own deranged brand of 'justice' through these sadistic murders. Clever son of a bitch..." His voice dripped with a mixture of grudging respect and utter disgust.

"More like a cold-blooded psychopath," Black snarled. The raw anger in his tone sent a shiver down my spine, a stark reminder of the high stakes we were dealing with.

The gnawed skin around my thumbnail throbbed, a dull ache compared to the storm raging in my mind. Parker's face swam before my eyes, his once benign features now twisted into a grotesque mask of cruelty. This so-called pillar of the community, a man we had trusted, had orchestrated a symphony of suffering right before our very eyes.

The road ahead promised only dark depths and treacherous turns. Exposing Parker was only the first fraying thread in this tapestry of horror. Who was Lucas Parker? What demons drove him to such depravity? And perhaps most importantly, what kind of unspeakable endgame was he working toward? These questions swirled in my mind, an endless loop of speculation and fear that threatened to consume me.

The computer screens flickered around me, their harsh glow casting an ethereal glow over my workspace. Somewhere out there in the streets of the city, a twisted mind was pulling the strings, fully convinced of his righteous duty to cleanse the world through blood and ancient dogma. And we were the only ones standing in his way. Game on, you piece of shit. This is only the opening salvo... The words echoed in my mind as I dove back into the digital fray, ready to unravel the next thread in this twisted tapestry of madness.

The air hums with electric excitement and vindication as I realize we finally have irrefutable digital evidence of the Rune Killer's true identity. Lucas, an unlikely person who greeted me with a smile the last time I met him, is even more unassuming than Ward. My heart races as the pieces fall into place, the puzzle finally complete after countless hours of investigation and frustration.

I stare at the monitor, the glow illuminating my face in the dark office, as I review the data Chen has uncovered. The IP addresses, the forum posts, the meticulously collected personal details on each victim - it all points to one person. Lucas Parker. The evidence is damning, painting a picture of a deeply troubled individual who has been hiding in plain sight all along.

Lucas Parker. Memories flash through my mind – his gentle smile, his soft-spoken manner the few times we crossed paths. I had dismissed him as nothing more than Ward's gentle, unassuming assistant, barely a blip on my radar. But the clues had been there all along, just waiting for me to open my eyes.

His uncanny knowledge of ancient rituals and practices. His unrestricted access to all of Ward's confidential research and data, the way he always seemed to slip away. Bile rises in my throat as I realize the extent of my oversight, the wool he had pulled over my eyes with his clever facade of harmless passivity. Some detective I am.

I think back to my last visit to Ward's office, Lucas shuffling in the background, eager to please his mentor. I had sensed something wrong in that cluttered room of obscure tomes and artifacts. But I had focused my suspicions on the wrong man. The memory now ignites a surge of anger in me, knowing how close I had been to the truth without realizing it.

Jones and I were convinced that Ward was behind the murders that led us astray. While Ward fit our profile, he was simply escaping into a fantasy world to cope with the unresolved murder of his wife. The truth is both a relief and a bitter pill to swallow.

It was never Ward who guided the Rune Killer's hand. It was Lucas who had truly embodied the dark vision planted in his psyche by Ward's nihilistic teachings. Lucas who had taken it upon himself to become the executioner, empowered by perverted notions of divine justice.

I remember Ward's erratic behavior when we interviewed him, the wild look in his eyes as he spoke of avenging his wife's death. He was unhinged with grief and obsession, but not a killer. No, it was the quiet, unassuming Lucas who had taken Ward's academic interests to their deadly conclusion. The thought is chilling, a reminder of how easily madness can hide behind a mask of normalcy.

But the question remains: how deep does Ward's connection to Lucas really run? Were his rants about archaic punishment and retribution more than just hypothetical musings with his star pupil? Did he, in his own Machiavellian way, deliberately mold Lucas into an instrument of vengeance? The possibilities are deeply disturbing, a tangled web of manipulation and twisted ideals.

I stare at the photo of Lucas pinned to the evidence board. Such an ordinary, forgettable face hiding a deeply troubled mind. Lucas had taken Ward's passions and disillusions and violently manifested them in the real world. But did Ward plant the seeds? Does that make him complicit in Lucas' crimes? The questions swirl in my head, a moral morass with no easy answers.

I meet with Jones and fill him in on the latest revelations. To my surprise, he seems genuinely shocked to learn that Lucas is the killer. I study his face for any hint of deception, but find none. The fact that even Jones was fooled is a testament to Lucas's skill at deception.

Lucas has clearly been playing us all, cleverly hiding his madness behind a harmless facade. But if what Jones told me is true, Lucas has now gone rogue, deviating from whatever twisted mission they were on together. By taking O'Malley, he crossed a line, and violated the code. The thought of my partner in his clutches fills me with a seething rage.

Jones suggests we start at the old Hollowbrook Asylum on the outskirts of town, a place Lucas had become strangely fixated on during his time with Ward. The asylum's sordid reputation precedes it - a monument to the cruelty and pseudoscience that masqueraded as psychiatric treatment in a less enlightened era. Even now, the ghosts of the asylum's dark past seem to seep from its crumbling walls, a tangible aura of suffering and despair. I can't help but shudder at the thought of the unspeakable horrors that took place in those forsaken halls.

The chances are slim, but right now it's our only lead.

We waste no time, hastily gathering the case files and rushing down the precinct hallway to Chief Thompson's office. The adrenaline already pumping through my veins, my heart racing, we burst through the door without warning, startling the Chief from his paperwork.

"Black, Jones, what the hell?" Thompson demands gruffly, his brow furrowed in annoyance as he looks up from his desk.

"Sir, we have irrefutable proof," I say, struggling to keep my voice steady despite the whirlwind of emotions swirling inside of me. "Lucas Parker is the Rune Killer."

Thompson's eyes narrow as he processes the bombshell I've just dropped. "Lucas Parker? Ward's assistant?" he asks, confusion evident in his tone. "I thought we were going after Ward as our prime suspect. What the hell happened?"

I take a deep breath and try to organize my racing thoughts. "Sir, we were wrong about Ward. He's not our killer. It's been Lucas all along, hiding right under our noses."

Thompson leans back in his chair, his expression a mixture of skepticism and curiosity. "All right, Black, you have my attention. But you better have some damn convincing evidence to back up that claim."

I nod, pulling out the case files and spreading them out on Thompson's desk. "Officer Chen was able to track down the IP addresses associated with the historical forum where our victims were targeted. One of those addresses belongs to Lucas Parker, and it shows him accessing detailed public records on each victim before they were killed."

Thompson's eyes widen as he scans the documents, the pieces beginning to fall into place. "Jesus Christ," he mutters under his breath. "How did we miss this?"

"Lucas was clever, sir," Jones chimes in. "He played the role of the quiet, unassuming assistant perfectly."

I nod in agreement, "Lucas used his position with Ward to gain access to his research on ancient rituals and punishment. He took those twisted ideas and made them a reality, carrying out his own sick version of justice."

Thompson rubs his temples, deep in thought as he absorbs the information. "And what about Ward? Is he involved in this?"

I hesitate for a moment, pondering the question. "Frankly, sir, we're not entirely sure. Ward's teachings and obsessions certainly influenced Lucas, but whether he actively encouraged or aided in the murders is still unclear."

Thompson sighs heavily, the lines on his face seeming to deepen with the burden of this new information. "All right, so what's our next move? We need to bring this bastard in before he can hurt anyone else."

I nod solemnly, "You're right, sir. Lucas has already proven that he's willing to go to extreme lengths to carry out his twisted mission. If he has O'Malley..." I trail off, unable to finish the thought, a knot forming in my stomach.

Thompson leans forward, his gaze intense. "We have to be careful. If we frighten Lucas, there's no telling what he might do. He's already deviated from his pattern by taking O'Malley. The man has become unpredictable."

Jones clears his throat, a hint of hesitation in his voice. "Sir, I may have an idea where Lucas might be holding her. The old Hollowbrook Asylum on the outskirts of town. Lucas had a strange obsession with that place during his time under Ward."

Thompson raises an eyebrow at the information. "Hollowbrook Asylum? That place has been abandoned for decades. It'd be the perfect place for someone like Lucas to hide out."

I feel a surge of determination, my resolve hardening. "Sir, we need to act quickly. Every minute we waste, O'Malley is in greater danger. I say we assemble a tactical team and hit the asylum tonight."

Thompson nods, his jaw set. "Agreed. But we have to be smart about this. Lucas is intelligent and methodical. He'll expect us to come after him. We have to catch him off guard. Gather a small, lean team and head to Hollowbrook immediately. Use unmarked cars and cut the lights on your vehicles a mile out, I don't want him to know you're coming. I want that son of a bitch in custody and O'Malley back safe."

I feel a surge of gratitude for Thompson's decisiveness. "Yes, sir. We'll get them both back no matter what it takes."

As Jones and I turn to leave, Thompson shouts a final warning. "Black, Jones... be careful out there. If Lucas is as deranged as he seems, there's no telling what he might do when cornered."

I meet Thompson's gaze, my own eyes blazing with conviction. "We'll be ready for him, sir. This ends tonight, one way or another."

With that, Jones and I leave the office, our minds already racing ahead to the confrontation that awaits us at Hollowbrook. The weight of the case files in my hand serves as a tangible reminder of the twisted path that has led us to this moment.

As we make our way through the precinct, I can feel the eyes of our colleagues on us, the tension in the air. Word of O'Malley's kidnapping has spread like wildfire, and everyone knows the stakes are higher than ever.

I catch a glimpse of Officer Chen as we pass her desk, her face etched with worried optimism. She gives me a small nod, a silent acknowledgment of the battle ahead. I know she'll be working tirelessly to support us on the digital front, searching for any additional clues or evidence that might aid our mission.

Jones and I waste no time in assembling a team of our most trusted officers, each hand-picked for their skill and dedication. We quickly brief them on the situation, the urgency in our voices leaving no room for doubt or hesitation.

Strapping on my tactical vest, a surge of adrenaline rushes through me, fueling my mind into a raging inferno. Jenna's face flashes through my mind - the terror in her eyes, the unimaginable torment she must be enduring at the hands of this sadistic monster, Lucas. A crimson mist descends over my vision, raw rage boiling up from some primal depth, threatening to break free. Through clenched teeth I fight it back, forging the molten rage into an iron determination that covers me like an impenetrable armor. Every ounce of my consciousness is now bound to a single, all-consuming purpose - to return with O'Malley unharmed.

The drive to Hollowbrook is tense, my mind racing with a thousand questions and doubts. Even if we manage to bring Lucas in, even if we save O'Malley from his clutches, what then? How do we begin to unravel the tangled web of deceit and betrayal that has brought us to this point?

I look over at Jones, his face lit by the passing streetlights. The man I once trusted with my life, who I considered a friend, now sits beside me as an accomplice to unspeakable horrors.

Can he ever truly atone for what he's done? For the lives he helped destroy, the families he shattered in the name of some twisted sense of justice? Part of me wants to believe there's still a shred of the man I once knew buried beneath the lies and manipulation. But another part, the part that has seen the depths of human depravity, knows that some sins can never be washed away.

Jones shifts in his seat as if sensing the turmoil raging within me. "Black, I know what you're thinking," he says, his voice low and tense. "But you have to understand, I never meant for things to go this far. I thought I was doing the right thing, helping Lucas bring justice to those who had escaped it."

Jones stares at the floorboards, his eyes downcast. "I know I can never make it right," he says, his words almost lost in the white noise of the engine. "But I want to try. I want to help bring Lucas down, to make sure he never hurts anyone else."

I sigh deeply, "And what about after that, Jones? What about the families of the victims, the lives you helped destroy? How can you ever make that right?"

The silence stretched between us, and Jones' guilt burned into the lines of his face. "I don't know," he finally admits, his voice breaking. "But I have to try. I have to do something to make amends, to try to balance the scales."

I shake my head, the anger and betrayal still burning hot in my veins. "It's not that easy, Jones. You can't just wash your hands of this and walk away. There will be consequences and you'll have to face them, just like Lucas."

Jones nods, his shoulders slumping in defeat. "I know. And I'm ready to take whatever punishment is necessary. But first, we have to stop Lucas. We have to save O'Malley and put an end to this madman."

I take a deep breath, trying to center myself amidst the chaos swirling inside of me. He's right, of course. As much as I want to rage against Jones, to make him suffer for his betrayal, I know that our first priority is to stop Lucas and save Jenna. I'm going to make sure that Lucas pays for every moment of pain he's caused her and countless others.

But even if we succeed, even if we bring Lucas to justice and save O'Malley, I know the scars of this case will run deep. The betrayal, the loss of trust, the knowledge that someone I once considered a friend could be capable of such heinous acts - these are wounds that will take a long time to heal, if they ever do.

As we approach Hollowbrook, the old asylum looms in the distance like a dark specter. I look over at Jones one last time, my eyes hard and unyielding. "When this is over," I say, my voice deadly serious, "you and I are going to have a long talk. But for now, let's just focus on getting the job done."

Jones nods, his face grim with determination. "Understood. Let's take this bastard down and get O'Malley home."

I turn my attention back to the road, my mind already racing ahead to the confrontation that awaits us. Whatever happens, I know that this night will change everything - for me, for Jones, for the entire city of Silvergate.

Chapter Twenty

CONFRONTATION

T he crumbling facade of Hollowbrook Asylum looms before us, a decaying monument to the forgotten and the abandoned. As I step out of the car, the cool night air chills me to the bone. We're walking right into the lion's den, and I can only pray that we make it out unscathed.

Jones' stoic expression betrays an unwavering determination as we stand shoulder to shoulder. Despite everything that's happened between us, I'm grateful for his presence. We may have our differences, but for now, we're united in our goal - to stop Lucas and bring O'Malley home safely.

We approach the entrance, guns drawn, our footsteps echoing on the cracked and weathered pavement. The rest of the team falls in behind us, a silent but powerful force. We've been through hell to get here, and we're not leaving without our own.

As we cross the threshold into the asylum, the air seems to grow thicker, heavier. The smell of decay and neglect coats my tongue and throat until I choke on the taste of despair. The walls are stained with dark stains that could be mold, could be blood, could be the inky residue of madness seeping from the cracked plaster. The cries of the damned echo in my skull, a discordant chorus that threatens to shatter my resolve as we push forward into the heart of this abandoned place.

We move deeper into the building, our senses on high alert. Every shadow seems to hold a threat, every creaking floorboard a potential trap. But we press on, driven by our shared conviction to see this through to the end.

And then, without warning, his voice fills the air, a sickening, twisted sound that seems to come from everywhere and nowhere at once.

"Welcome, detectives," Lucas sneers, his words dripping with malice. "I've been expecting you."

I feel my heart skip a beat at the sound of his voice, my grip on my gun tightening. Next to me, Jones tenses, his eyes scanning the shadows for any sign of movement.

"It's over, Lucas," I yell, my voice steady despite the adrenaline coursing through my veins. "Let O'Malley go and turn yourself in. There's nowhere to run."

His laughter echoes through the halls, a sound that unleashes a primal fear in me. "Oh, but you're wrong, Detective Black. This is only the beginning. You see, I've been chosen to bring justice, to right the wrongs that your beloved system has failed to address."

I shake my head in disgust, my anger rising to the surface. "You call this justice? Murdering people, torturing their families? You're nothing but a monster, Lucas."

"A monster?" he sneers, his voice growing louder and more unhinged. "No, Detective. I'm a savior. I'm doing what needs to be done, I'm bringing balance to the world, one sinner at a time."

"And what about O'Malley?" Jones demands, his voice thick with barely contained anger. "What did she do to deserve this?"

Lucas laughs again, a sound that grates on my nerves like nails on a chalkboard. "Oh, she's just collateral damage, a means to an end. I had to get your attention, to show you how serious I am about my mission. And what better way than to take one of your own?"

I feel my entire body seethe at his callousness, at the way he so casually dismisses Jenna's life - she's not just a pawn in his sick game - she's a person, a friend, someone I care about deeply.

"Enough of this," I growl, my patience wearing thin. "Where is she, Lucas? Tell us now and maybe we can end this without more bloodshed."

He laughs again, a sound that echoes through the decrepit halls of the asylum. "You need to find her, Detective. But I warn you - I've left a few surprises along the way. Consider it a test of your dedication to the cause."

And with that, his voice fades, leaving us alone in the oppressive darkness of Hollowbrook.

I take a deep breath, trying to calm the rage and fear that are fighting inside of me. We have to stay focused, stay alert. Jenna's life depends on it.

I turn to Jones and the rest of the team, my eyes full of single-minded focus. "All right, listen up. We're going in, but we're doing this by the book. Pairs of two, single file formation. Keep your partner in sight at all times and maintain constant communication. We don't know what kind of surprises Lucas has in store for us, so stay alert and watch your step."

The rotten floorboards groan beneath our feet as we cautiously make our way into the main building of Hollowbrook Asylum, our formation tight and disciplined. The air is thick with the stench of mold and decay, and the only light comes from the beams of our flashlights, casting eerie shadows on the crumbling walls.

I take the lead, Jones close behind me. The rest of the team follows, each pair watching each other's backs, their eyes scanning the darkness for any sign of movement or danger.

Suddenly there's a sharp snap, followed by a sickening crunch. The ground beneath the last pair in line gives way and they fall into the darkness below, their screams echoing for a moment before they are swallowed by the void.

"Hold formation!" I yell, throwing out an arm to stop the rest of the team from advancing. My heart pounds in my chest as I peer into the gaping hole where the floor used to be, trying to catch a glimpse of the fallen officers.

"Jenkins, Morales, do you copy?" I call into my radio, praying for an answer. But there's nothing but static on the other end.

Jones curses under his breath, his face pale in the dim light. "He set traps for us," he says, his voice tight with anger and fear. "That bastard's going to pay for this!"

"Jones, call it in, request immediate backup and medical assistance," I say.

He nods, already reaching for his radio, his face grim with the knowledge that our fallen comrades may already be beyond help.

I nod bitterly, my mind racing as I try to come up with a plan. We can't afford to lose any more officers, but we can't turn back now.

I turn back to the rest of the team, my voice low and urgent. "New plan. We spread out and stick to the walls. Keep your partner in sight, but give each other some space. We can't afford to put too much weight on any one spot."

They nod, their expressions a mixture of fear and confidence, and we continue. Each pair hugs the walls on opposite sides of the corridor, our flashlights searching the darkness ahead for any sign of danger. We've all seen the horrors the Rune Killer is capable of, but we're not going to let that stop us from doing our job.

We press on, moving deeper into the asylum with a newfound sense of caution. Every squeaky floorboard, every gust of wind through a broken window makes my nerves tingle. I can feel the tension radiating from the other officers, their fingers twitching on the triggers of their guns.

As we approach a set of double doors at the end of the hallway, I feel a sense of dread wash over me. Something tells me that whatever lies behind those doors will test us in ways we could never have imagined.

I take a deep breath, steeling myself for whatever horrors await us on the other side of those doors. And then, with a nod to Jones and the rest of the team, I push them open, ready to face the Rune Killer and whatever twisted games he has in store for us.

Suddenly there's a low groan as a chunk of the ceiling comes crashing down inches from Jones' head. We jump back, our hearts racing as dust and debris fill the air. "Watch your step," I hiss, my voice cracking with fear and adrenaline. "This whole place is falling apart from the inside out."

As we round a corner, I catch a glimmer of light reflecting off something metallic on the ground. "Hang on," I whisper, holding out a hand to stop the team. I crouch down and shine my flashlight on the object. It's a tripwire, thin and almost invisible in the dark.

"Good catch," Jones mutters, his eyes scanning the hallway ahead. "Who knows what kind of hell that would've unleashed."

I nod, my mouth set in a grim line. We've already lost too many good men to the Rune Killer's sadistic traps. I'll be damned if I let him take any more.

I disarm the tripwire with a steady hand, my breath catching in my throat. As we push forward, the shadows of the asylum grow teeth, looming and hungry. Every footstep echoes too loudly in the silence. The darkness thickens with every corner we turn, until it feels like wading through ink, cold and clinging. My nerves press against my skin, raw and electric.

Suddenly there's a scream from the back of the group, followed by a sickening crunch. I whirl around to see one of the officers writhing on the ground, a sharpened spike sticking out of his leg. "Officer down!" someone shouts, and the team rushes to his aid.

I curse under my breath, my fists clenched in anger and frustration. The Rune Killer is playing with us, picking us off one by one like flies in his twisted web. But I won't let him win, not while I still have breath in my body. We patch up the wounded officer as best we can and press on, our drive only strengthened by the horrors we've witnessed.

We find ourselves at another set of heavy metal doors, and with a deep breath, I push the doors open. The hinges groan in protest, the sound echoing through the empty halls like a death knell. As the doors swing open, we're hit with a blast of cold, stale air that chills me to the bone.

The room beyond is shrouded in darkness, the only light coming from our flashlights as we cautiously step inside. Rays of light dance across the walls, revealing a scene of utter chaos and destruction. Furniture is overturned, papers and debris litter the floor, and a thick layer of dust and dirt covers every surface.

But it's the smell that hits me first, a sickening mixture of decay and something else, something darker and more sinister. It's the smell of death, of suffering and despair, and it makes my stomach churn with disgust.

We sweep the room, weapons at the ready, but there's no sign of the Rune Killer or O'Malley, just a disturbing silence. Suddenly there's a flicker of movement in the corner of my eye. I turn quickly to face the movement, only to see a rat scurry across the floor and disappear into a hole in the wall.

I let out a shaky breath, my nerves frayed to the breaking point. Every shadow seems to hold a threat, every sound a potential warning of danger. And then I see it, a glint of metal in the darkness, a flash of something that shouldn't be there.

I take a step closer, my flashlight beam zeroing in on the object. It's a coin, ancient and tarnished, with strange symbols etched into its surface. The mark of Malthor, the god of punishment, retribution, and balance.

I hesitate, remembering the traps and tricks Lucas has left for us so far. I can't afford to take any chances, not now, not when we're so close.

Kneeling down, I carefully examine the area around the coin, looking for any signs of disturbance or tampering. I run my gloved fingers along the edges of the floorboard, feeling for any wires or pressure plates that might trigger a hidden mechanism.

Finding nothing, I gently reach out and tap the coin with the tip of my knife, ready to spring back at the slightest hint of movement or resistance. But the coin remains still, inert, just a harmless piece of metal lying in the dust.

I let out a breath I didn't realize I was holding and carefully picked up the coin, turning it in my hands. It feels heavy, weighted with the lives it represents, the horrors it has witnessed.

I put the coin in my pocket with trembling hands. We're close, so close to catching this bastard and ending his reign of terror. But at what cost? How many more lives will be lost, how much more horror will we have to endure before it's over?

I shake my head and push these thoughts aside. We can't afford to dwell on the what-ifs, not now. I signal Jones and the rest of the team and we move out, deeper into the bowels of the asylum.

Suddenly there's a deafening explosion, followed by a blinding flash of light that sends us stumbling backwards. I feel a searing pain in my leg and look down to see a jagged piece of metal embedded in my thigh, blood already soaking through my pants.

"Black!" Jones yells, his voice barely audible over the ringing in my ears. "You all right?"

I grit my teeth, the pain in my leg almost unbearable. "I'm hit," I manage to get out, my voice cracking with pain.

Jones is at my side in an instant, his strong hands grabbing my arm and helping me to the ground. "Let me see," he says, his voice calm and steady despite the chaos around us.

I lean back against the wall, my breath coming in short, ragged gasps as Jones examines my wound. The metal shard is still embedded in my thigh, blood oozing from the jagged edges of the wound.

"This is going to hurt," Jones warns me, his eyes meeting mine with a fierce intensity. "But we need to get the metal out before it does more damage."

I nodded, bracing myself for the pain. I grab a small piece of wood from the rubble around us and place it between my teeth, a makeshift bite block.

Jones grabs the shard with both hands and, with a quick, decisive motion, rips it from my flesh. The pain is blinding, a white-hot agony that sears through every nerve in my body. I bite down hard on the wood, my screams muffled by the improvised gag as my vision swims and my ears ring with the force of my own screams.

The piece of wood falls from my mouth as I gasp for air, my chest heaving with the effort of breathing through the pain. I can taste blood on my tongue, but whether it's from the wound or from biting too hard, I can't be sure.

But Jones is already moving, his hands pressing down on the wound to stop the flow of blood. He reaches into his vest and pulls out a pack of QuikClot, ripping it open with his teeth.

"This is going to hurt like hell, Black," he warns, his voice tight with tension. "But it's the only way to stop the bleeding."

I nod, clenching my teeth as he pours the granules into the wound. The pain is immediate and excruciating, a searing agony that feels like a thousand hot needles piercing my flesh. I can't hold back the scream that rips from my throat, my body convulsing involuntarily as the QuikClot does its work.

It feels like an eternity, but in reality, it's only a matter of seconds before the bleeding slows and finally stops, the clot forming a thick, sticky seal over the wound. I'm left gasping and shaking, my skin slick with sweat and my vision blurred at the edges.

Jones works quickly and efficiently, tearing strips of cloth from his shirt to make a makeshift bandage. He wraps it tightly around my thigh, securing it with a knot that he pulls tight enough to make me gasp.

As he ties off the bandage, I take a moment to catch my breath, my heart still pounding from the adrenaline coursing through my veins. The pain in my leg throbs in time with my pulse, a constant reminder of how close I came to death.

I look around the room, taking in the devastation that surrounds us. The other officers are either dead or incapacitated by the Rune Killer's traps.

I pat myself down, looking for my sidearm, but it's nowhere to be found. A quick glance at Jones confirms that he's in the same predicament, his holster empty and his expression grim.

"Damn," I mutter, the reality of our situation sinking in. "We're sitting ducks."

Jones nods, his eyes scanning the room for anything that might serve as a makeshift weapon. "We're going to have to improvise," he says, his voice tense.

I know he's right, but the thought of facing the Rune Killer without a weapon is frightening. This is a man who has proven himself to be cunning, ruthless, and utterly merciless. And now we're on his turf, playing by his rules.

"We have to keep moving," I say, my voice hoarse with pain and exhaustion. "O'Malley's still out there."

Jones nods, his face grim. "You're right," he says, helping me to my feet. "But it's just the two of us now."

I take a deep breath, trying to steady myself. "More than enough."

My leg throbs with every movement, but I force myself to push through the pain. Driven by the knowledge that we're the only ones left who can stop the Rune Killer.

We move forward cautiously, Jones taking the lead as we navigate the twisting corridors of the asylum. The air is thick with the stench of death and explosives, making every breath a struggle.

Suddenly, Jones holds up a hand and tells me to stop. He points to a tripwire strung across the hallway, almost invisible in the dim light. "Careful," he whispers, his voice tense with warning.

We tiptoe around the tripwire, our hearts pounding with each step. I can feel the sweat beading on my forehead, my hands shaking with a mixture of fear and adrenaline.

As we navigate the labyrinthine corridors, the air grows colder and more oppressive with each step. Suddenly, we stand before a set of massive, ornate doors.

"This is it," Jones whispers, his voice tense with anticipation. "The central chamber. If he's got O'Malley anywhere, it'll be in here."

I nod as I reach for the door handles. The metal is cold and smooth under my fingers, and it takes all my strength to push the doors open.

The chamber is a living nightmare, stretching out before me in grotesque proportions. Vaulted ceilings tower above me, disappearing into the shadows, while eerie symbols and twisted sculptures stare down from the walls. Candlelight flickers across the room, flames thrashing as if to an unseen rhythm, casting a demonic shadow that capers and crawls. My breath mists in the cold air, and a primal fear wraps around my neck like a noose.

But it's the figure standing in the center of the chamber that grabs my attention. Tall and gaunt, his face hidden beneath a hood, the Rune Killer exudes an aura of malevolence that freezes me in place. And there, at his feet, lies Jenna, bound and gagged, her eyes wide with terror.

"Welcome, detectives," the Rune Killer says, his voice a rasping whisper that echoes through the chamber. "I've been expecting you."

Jones and I exchange glances at the hooded figure. "It's over," I say, my voice steady despite the fear coursing through my veins. "Let her go and come quietly. No one else needs to get hurt."

Lucas laughs, a sound that begins faintly and builds to a crescendo, bouncing off the walls and filling the chamber with its sinister echo. "Oh, but where's the fun in that?" he asks, his voice dripping with malice. "We're just getting started, Detective Black. And before this night is over, you will wish you had never set foot in this place."

He takes a step forward, his hands outstretched, and I feel a wave of terror rise in me. Whatever he has planned, I know it won't be good. But I stand my ground, my grip tightening on the rusted pipe I managed to salvage from the rubble, ready to do whatever it takes to save Jenna and put an end to the Rune Killer's reign of terror.

His laughter grows louder and more insane, echoing through the chamber until it feels like the walls are shaking with its power. And as I stare into the depths of his hood, I know that the true horror is just beginning.

CHAPTER TWENTY-ONE

FINAL SHOWDOWN

The eerie sound of the Rune Killer's laughter hangs in the air, a haunting reminder of the madness we face. Despite the fear coursing through my veins, I refuse to let it shake my resolve, holding my ground, my hands steady. Next to me, Jones stands firm, his eyes narrowed and his grip on the makeshift weapon in his hands tight.

"Lucas," I say, my voice carrying through the cavernous room. "This is only going to end badly for you!"

But Lucas just grins, a twisted, unhinged expression distorting his features into a demonic mask. He holds up the ancient coin, its surface glistening in the flickering candlelight. "You don't understand, Detective," he says, his voice rasping and shrill. "This is only the beginning."

As he speaks, the coin begins to glow, a sickly green light pulsing with otherworldly energy. Lucas' eyes take on the same eerie glow, and I feel a wave of fear wash over me. Whatever dark forces he's tapping into, it's beyond anything I've ever seen before.

I risk a glance at Jenna, bound and helpless at Lucas' feet. Her eyes are wide with terror, but there's also a spark of defiance, a strength that gives me hope. I know she won't go down without a fight.

"Lucas, listen to me," Jones says, his voice calm and steady. "You're surrounded, backup is on the way as we speak, there's no way out. Release

Jenna and surrender peacefully or end up like one of your victims, dead and broken."

But Lucas just laughs, "You still don't get it, do you?" he asks, his voice dripping with contempt. "This isn't about me or Jenna or any of you. This is about sending a message, about exposing the hollow promises of a broken system."

He leans in closer, his eyes blazing with fanatical intensity. "I'm giving you one last chance, Detective," he says, his voice deep and menacing. "Do your job with impunity, or I will. And believe me, my methods are far less forgiving than yours."

I feel a wave of anger rise inside me, hot and fierce. "Fuck your last chance," I spit, my grip on the pipe tightening. "I'm not playing your twisted games anymore. This ends now."

Lucas' eyes narrow, his lips curling into a sneer. "So be it, Detective."

He takes a step forward, the coin pulsing with an even brighter light. The shadows on the walls surge toward him, swirling around his feet like a living thing.

"The spirits of the Ancients guide me now," Lucas says, his voice taking on a deeper, more resonant tone. "They demand retribution, and I am their instrument."

He raises the coin higher, and the candles flare with a blinding, white-hot intensity. The sudden burst of light is searing, almost unbearable, like the glare of a magnesium flare. I squint against the brightness, my eyes watering from the intensity.

In the dazzling radiance, Lucas' form seems to waver and distort, the very fabric of reality is bending around him.

"And now," Lucas says, his voice barely human, "you will witness the true power of the Ancients."

The coin hums with unnatural energy as a wave of malevolent power washes over me, sapping my strength and filling my mind with visions of horror. Beside me, Jones staggers, his weapon trembling in his hand.

But I force myself to stand firm, to push back against the darkness that threatens to overwhelm me. I won't let Lucas win, I won't let him hurt anyone else. Whatever it takes, I'll stop him.

Even if it means sacrificing everything.

The coin flips through the air, glinting in the eerie light that fills the chamber. As it lands in Lucas' outstretched hand, his body suddenly contorts, twisting and jerking as if possessed. His eyes roll back in his head and a guttural, inhuman sound rips from his throat.

A choked gasp escapes my throat as I watch in horror as Lucas' body continues to convulse. His limbs jerk and flail at unnatural angles, manipulated by the unseen hands of a sadistic puppeteer. The shadows on the walls mirror his tortured movements, their shapes growing more monstrous and twisted with each passing second.

Beside me, Jones mutters a curse under his breath, his gaze inexplicably drawn to Lucas' convulsing form. "What the hell is happening to him?" he asks, his voice cracking with fear and confusion.

But I barely hear him as the pieces in my mind click together like the chambers of a loaded gun. Samuel's ramblings, his cryptic warnings about a "hollow soul" - it all makes sense now. He wasn't ranting about some abstract concept or metaphor. He was talking about Lucas.

A realization claws its way into my mind, one that defies all logic and reason. Lucas isn't himself anymore. He's become a vessel, a conduit for something dark and ancient. The way his body moves, the otherworldly quality of his voice - he's been possessed by powerful, vengeful spirits.

And then it hits me. The coins, the ancient relics he leaves at each crime scene - they're not just symbols or messages. Each one represents a different spirit, a different entity from the ancient cult that was obsessed with sacrifice and retribution, just like Dr. Kensington said.

I feel a wave of disbelief washed over me, followed by a sinking sense of dread. This can't be happening. It goes against everything I've ever known, everything I've ever believed in. But the evidence is right in front of me, undeniable and terrifying.

We're not just dealing with a serial killer anymore. We're dealing with something far more ancient and malevolent, something that's been waiting for centuries to exact its revenge on the world. And now it has found its perfect vessel in Lucas.

Lucas' body finally stops, his head lolls forward, and his strings finally cut. For a moment there is only silence, broken by the sound of our own ragged breathing.

Then, slowly, Lucas raises his head, his eyes glowing with an unearthly light. When he speaks, his voice is different, deeper, and more resonant, as if several voices are speaking through him at once.

"You think you can stop us, Detective?" he asks, his lips curling into a cruel, mocking smile. "You think you can stand against the power of the Ordo Iustitiae?"

I swallow hard, my mouth dry with fear. But I force myself to meet Lucas's gaze, to stare into those glowing, inhuman eyes.

"I don't know what you are," I say, my voice shaking slightly. "But I know you won't hurt anyone else. Not on my watch."

Lucas laughs, "You have no idea what you're up against, do you?" he asks, his voice dripping with contempt. "We have waited centuries for this moment, for the chance to bring bloody penance to a world that has forgotten the old ways. And now, with this vessel as our instrument, we will have our reckoning."

He raises his hand, the coin glowing even brighter in his palm. The shadows on the walls merge into a gnashing, snarling, rabid beast. I can feel its malevolence, its hunger for blood and suffering.

But I stand my ground, unwavering. I look over at Jones and see the steadiness in his gaze. We both know this is a fight we cannot afford to lose.

"Right here, you bastard," I growl, my voice filled with anger and fury.

And then, without warning, the monstrosity lunges forward, a mass of writhing, twisting shadows. I try to dodge, but I'm too slow. The creature slams into me, sending me flying across the room. I hit the floor hard, the air knocked out of my lungs.

For a moment I am dazed, my vision blurred at the edges. I can feel the creature looming over me, its presence dark and oppressive. But then, out of the corner of my eye, I see Jones spring into action.

He charges at Lucas with a fierce battle cry, his eyes blazing with fire. The creature turns, its attention drawn away from me to this new threat.

I struggle to my feet, my body aching with every movement. I watch as Jones engages Lucas in combat, their forms blurring together in a whirlwind of movement.

Jones is a skilled fighter, his moves were precise and deadly. But Lucas is something else entirely. He moves with an inhuman grace, his body shifting and flowing like liquid smoke.

With a flick of his wrist, Lucas sends Jones flying across the room like a rag doll. He slams into the stone wall with a sickening thud, cracks spiderwebbing from the impact as dust mushrooms outward in a chalky cloud.

I rush to Jones' side, my heart pounding in my chest. He's still breathing, but there's a deep gash across his chest, blood seeping through his shirt. Lucas' blades gleam in the eerie light, dripping with crimson.

"You disappoint me, Jones," Lucas says, his voice cold and mocking. "I had such hopes for you. I thought you understood the true nature of things, the need for vengeance. But it seems you lack the conviction to see it through."

Jones coughs, blood splattering his lips. "I thought I did," he rasps, his voice weak and strained. "But this... this isn't it. It's madness."

Lucas pauses, " Madness? No, this is the only sane response to a world that has forgotten the old ways, that allows the guilty to walk free while the innocent suffer. The Ordo Iustitiae understands this. We are the instruments of divine retribution, the bearers of the one true, inevitable equalizer, death."

He lunges forward, the coin clenched in his fist. I barely have time to react before he's on me, his eyes blazing with otherworldly fury.

I dodge to the side, barely avoiding his first blow. But he's fast, faster than any human should be. He spins around, his fist connecting with my jaw in a burst of blinding pain.

I stagger back, my vision swimming. I can taste blood in my mouth, feel it dripping down my chin. But I don't have time to think about it. Lucas is already coming at me again, his movements a blur of speed and precision.

I block his next attack, my forearm absorbing the impact. I counter with a swift jab to his ribs, feeling a surge of satisfaction as he grunts in pain. But it's short-lived. He retaliates with a vicious kick to my knee, sending me stumbling back.

We exchange blows back and forth, our movements growing more desperate and erratic with each passing second. I can feel my strength waning, my muscles screaming in protest. But I can't give up. I won't let him win.

Out of the corner of my eye, I see Jones struggling to his feet, his face contorted in pain. He's clutching his chest, blood seeping through his fingers. But there's a determination in his eyes, a fierce will to see this through to the end.

"Black!" he shouts, his voice hoarse with pain. "The coin! You have to get the coin!"

I nod, I know he's right. The coin is the key to everything. If I can just get my hands on it...

I lunge forward, my fingers reaching for the ancient relic. But Lucas is too quick. He pulls his hand back, the coin just out of reach.

"Not so fast, Detective," he taunts, his voice dripping with contempt. "You think you can stop me? You think you can stand against the power of the Ordo Iustitiae?"

I meet his gaze, my eyes blazing with anger. "I don't think, Lucas. I know."

Jones tries to join the fight, but the lurking creature is on him in an instant, its claws raking across his leg. He cries out in pain, feeling the warm rush of blood soaking through his pants.

But he refuses to give up. With a burst of strength, he lunges forward, his fist connecting with the creature's jaw with a satisfying crunch. It staggers back, its form rippling and distorting.

Pressing his advantage, he rains down blows on the creature with all the strength he can muster. It howls in pain and rage, its movements growing more erratic and desperate.

Suddenly I catch a glimpse of O'Malley, struggling desperately to free herself from her bonds. With one last determined effort, she breaks free and jumps to her feet, lunging at Lucas, her eyes blazing with fury. She lunges at him with all her might, knocking him off balance and sending him stumbling backward.

I see Lucas stagger, caught off guard by the attack. The shadows around us flicker and fade for a moment, his concentration disrupted. The monstrous creature he conjured from the darkness lets out an eerie shriek, its form beginning to fizzle and dissipate.

Taking advantage of the opening, I charge forward, unleashing a barrage of punches into Lucas' face and torso. My fists connect with a sickening crunch, and I feel a savage satisfaction as I watch Lucas recoil, blood spurting from his nose and mouth. Each blow is fueled by a potent mix of desperation and burning rage.

Lucas staggers back under the onslaught, his concentration shattered. The shadow beast flickers like a dying candle flame, its once terrifying presence now little more than wisps of fading darkness.

I press my advantage, driving Lucas back with a relentless series of blows. I can feel the tide of battle turning, the scales tipping in our favor.

But even as the shadow creature dissipates, Lucas remains a formidable foe. His eyes blaze with an unearthly light, and he growls like a cornered animal. With a swift motion, he hurls Jenna across the room, her body slamming into the chamber wall.

I roar in rage and redouble my efforts, raining down blows on Lucas with all the strength I can muster. But he weathers the onslaught as if my attacks were nothing more than a gentle rain. I can feel the dark energy surging through him, the spirits of the Ordo Iustitiae giving him unnatural strength and resilience.

Jones comes in from the side and knocks Lucas to the ground. Both men hit the floor hard, the impact reverberating through the chamber. I see Jones' eyes flicker to the coin in Lucas's hand - the ancient talisman that binds him to the spirits that give him power.

"Black, get the coin!" Jones shouts, grabbing Lucas's free arm to keep him from moving.

I dive for Lucas's hand, fingers clawing to pry the coin from his grasp. Lucas lets out a guttural growl, thrashing violently beneath us. His strength is terrifying, an unnatural force driving his movements. My heart pounds as I concentrate on the coin, fingers digging into Lucas' flesh, trying to break his grip.

A surge of dark energy pulses from the coin, coursing through Lucas and jolting my hand back with searing pain. Undeterred, I push forward, ignoring the agony. I glance at Jones, his face contorted with determination.

"Hold him still!" I grunt through clenched teeth.

Lucas' eyes are wild, rabid with desperation. He bucks and twists, his otherworldly strength making the task almost impossible. Jenna, unsteady but determined, pulls herself up from the rubble and staggers over to join the fight. She clings to Lucas' arm, using her weight to keep him pinned down.

"You're finished, Lucas!" she shouts, her voice strained but fierce.

With Jones pinning Lucas's arm and Jenna adding her weight to the fight, I find an opening. I channel all my focus and strength into one hand and strike Lucas' wrist with a precise, bone-crunching blow. Lucas lets out a howl of pain, his grip on the coin finally weakening. In that split second, I seize the opportunity and rip the coin from his fingers.

The coin pulsates in my hand, throbbing white-hot with latent energy. I resist the urge to drop it, knowing it must be contained.

A howl of tortured souls fills the chamber as a thousand damned voices wail in unison. Lucas writhes on the floor, his body racked by violent convulsions. Tendrils of shadow, once wrapped possessively around him, now flee back into his body like rats abandoning a sinking ship. Whatever dark force bound Lucas has been severed, the unnatural bond broken. He shudders and convulses, his hands clawing at the air as waves of excruciating pain wash over him.

The air around Lucas' crumpled form begins to bend and distort. A swirling whirlwind of primal darkness explodes from him, an unholy storm of hellish energy that feels ancient beyond reckoning. The vortex rages, threatening to engulf the entire chamber and drag us all into oblivion.

I can only watch in horror as the maelstrom expands, its tendrils of shadow lashing out like whips. Jones is pulled into the vortex, his body seized and tossed around as if he were nothing more than a toy in the hands of a cruel child.

He bangs against the stone walls, his screams of pain echoing through the chamber. I try to reach him, to offer some kind of help, but the swirling shadows keep me at bay.

A chilling silence falls as the swirling vortex implodes, the shadows evaporating into wispy nothingness. Amidst the settling dust, I see Lucas kneeling motionless, his body intact but his eyes hollow and without a spark. The spirits that once held him so tightly seem to have been violently torn from him, leaving only an empty shell, a mere shadow of the man he once was.

But the price of this victory is high. Jones lies crumpled on the ground, his body broken and bleeding. I rush to his side, my heart pounding in my chest as I cradle his head in my lap.

"Jones," my voice is hoarse with emotion. "Stay with me, buddy. We'll get you help."

But even as I say the words, I know it's too late. Jones's breaths are shallow and labored, his eyes glazed with pain. He looks up at me, a faint smile playing on his lips.

"We did it, Black," he rasps, his voice strained but still with a hint of his characteristic wit. "We stopped him."

I nod, my throat tight. "You did it, Jones," I say, my voice breaking. "You saved my life and O'Malley's."

Jones' smile widens, and for a moment I see a glimmer of the man he once was - the brave, determined detective who always fought for what was right, even when the odds were stacked against him.

Jones winces, a look of deep regret settling over his features. "I know I made mistakes, I let my anger, my pain, cloud my judgment. I thought I was doing the right thing, but I only made things worse."

He coughs, a trickle of blood running from the corner of his mouth. "But in the end, I tried to do the right thing. I tried to make things right."

I nod, my vision blurred with tears. "You did, Jones," I say, my voice shaking. "You made things right."

Jones smiles, a look of peace settling over his features. "Good," he whispers, his voice fading. "That's good."

And then he's gone, his body going limp in my arms. I bow my head, tears streaming down my face as I clasp his hand in mine.

Jenna kneels beside me, her own eyes glistening with tears. She puts a hand on my shoulder, a silent gesture of comfort and support.

We stay like this for a long moment, keeping watch over our fallen comrade. My mind is a whirlwind of emotions - sadness, anger, guilt, and a deep, aching sense of loss.

But underneath it all, there's a glimmer of something else – a sense of respect and admiration for the man who gave his life to end the Rune Killer's reign of terror. Jones may have been flawed, but in the end, he found a measure of peace in his final moments.

As I kneel there, holding his hand in mine, I make a silent vow. The world will remember Jones as the hero he truly was, the man who gave his life to stop a monster. I'll keep his secret, make sure his mistakes and his past die here with him. What he did today, the lives he saved - that will live on.

I squeeze his hand, one last gesture of friendship and understanding. A single tear slides down my cheek, splashing on our joined hands. I promise to continue to fight for justice and truth, to honor his death. It's the least I can do for the man who sacrificed everything to set things right.

CHAPTER TWENTY-TWO

AFTERMATH

The world as we knew it changed forever the moment the news broke. Every media channel, from the 24-hour news networks to the endless sea of social media, was focused on a single, groundbreaking story: the existence of The Soulscape. It was a revelation that shook the very foundations of our understanding of life, death, and the nature of reality itself.

As I sat in the precinct, my eyes glued to the television screen, I couldn't help but feel a sense of stunned disbelief. The images flashing before me were almost too surreal to comprehend - ethereal landscapes of shimmering light and shadow, ghostly figures drifting through an endless void, and glimpses of a realm that seemed to defy logic and reason.

Beside me, Jenna stood in silence, her face a mask of shock and awe. The flickering light from the TV danced across her face, accentuating the intensity in her eyes. I could see her mind racing as she grappled with the overwhelming implications of the scenes unfolding before us. For years, we had been on the front lines of fighting crime, dealing with the darkest aspects of human nature on a daily basis. But this... this was something else entirely.

As the news anchors droned on, speculating about the nature of the Soulscape and its potential impact on the world, I found myself thinking back to our confrontation with Lucas. The memory of those final, terrifying moments was still fresh in my mind – -the shadow beast, the swirling vortex of darkness, the otherworldly screams, and the sense of pure, unadulterated evil that had emanated from his body. At the time, I was too focused on stopping Lucas and saving Jenna to fully process what I was seeing. The scene was so surreal, so out of the ordinary, that I couldn't even bring myself to include it in my official report. To do so would have jeopardized not only my career, but O'Malley's as well. Instead, I tried to block the moment from my mind, burying it deep in my psyche with the other traumas and horrors I had experienced over the years. Deep down, however, I knew that I would eventually have to come clean with the Chief and file an updated report.

Now, with the benefit of hindsight, I realized that we had caught a glimpse of something truly extraordinary—the realm beyond the veil of death, where the spirits of the departed roam free. This realization left me feeling both exhilarated and terrified. On the one hand, the idea that there was something beyond this mortal coil, that death was not the end but merely a transition to another state of being, was a comforting thought. On the other hand, the implications of the Soulscape's existence were staggering.

If the dead could communicate with the living, if they could influence the world of the living in ways we had never imagined... what did that mean for the future of humanity? How would we cope with the knowledge that our loved ones were not truly gone, but merely existing in another form? And what of the darker aspects of the Soulscape, the malevolent entities that lurked in its shadows, waiting to prey upon the unwary? Was the Rune Killer just a preamble to greater evils?

As I pondered these questions, I felt a sense of unease settle over me. The world had changed in ways we were only beginning to understand, and I knew that the road ahead would be filled with challenges and dangers beyond anything we had ever faced before.

But I also knew that we had a duty to meet these challenges head-on. As law enforcement officers, it was our job to protect and serve the public, to stand as a bulwark against the forces of chaos and darkness that threatened to engulf us all. And with the revelation of The Soulscape, that job had taken on a new and terrifying dimension.

As the news continued to play on the screen before us, I caught O'Malley's eye, and a silent understanding passed between us.

We were about to plunge headlong into the unknown, to face whatever horrors lurked in the shadows of the Soulscape. Together, we would stare into the darkness, knowing that it would stare back.

The precinct buzzed with newfound energy, the weight of the Soulscape revelation still heavy in the air. Months had passed since that fateful day, yet the repercussions continued to ripple through every facet of our lives. As I sat at my desk, my mind wandered to the countless questions that now plagued our every waking moment.

Dr. Kensington's soft footsteps echoed through the bullpen, drawing my attention away from my thoughts. She was clutching a stack of files to her chest, her forehead furrowed in deep concentration. Since the unveiling of the Soulscape, her work had taken on even greater significance. The ancient texts she had dedicated her life to studying now held the potential to unlock secrets we had never dared to imagine.

As she approached my desk, I couldn't help but notice the dark circles under her eyes, a testament to the countless hours she had spent poring over our case files on the Rune Killer. "Detective Black," she said, her voice filled with a mixture of excitement and trepidation. "I think I found something."

I leaned forward, my interest piqued. "What is it, Dr. Kensington?"

She spread the files out on my desk, her fingers trembling slightly as she pointed to a series of symbols etched across the pages. "I've been cross-referencing the Rune Killer's markings with the ancient texts I've been studying. And I think I've discovered something significant."

I watched as she traced her finger along a particularly intricate set of runes, her eyes glowing with newfound understanding. "These symbols," she said. "They speak of a concept known as a 'vessel' or a 'Hollow Soul.'"

The words hit me like a bolt of lightning, making the hairs on my arms stand on end. "Hollow Soul," I repeated, my mind racing back to a conversation I had almost forgotten. "My brother... Samuel. He warned me about the Hollow Soul."

Dr. Kensington's eyes widened and her gaze locked with mine. "Your brother mentioned this?"

I nodded, "He was always sensitive to things beyond our understanding."

My thoughts turned to Lucas, the young man at the center of the Rune Killer case. I had seen the emptiness in his eyes when we had finally apprehended him, the hollow shell of a person who had been used as a vessel for something far greater than himself.

I made my way to the state penitentiary, passing through the rigorous security checks before being escorted inside by a stone-faced guard. As we descended into the depths of the prison, my footsteps echoed off the concrete walls. The guard led me down a row of cells, pausing at one near the end.

When I reached Lucas' cell, I found him sitting on the edge of his bunk, his head in his hands. He looked up as I approached, his eyes devoid of the malevolent presence that had once possessed him.

"Detective Black," he said, his voice tentative. "I..." His words trailed off, unable or unwilling to put his thoughts into words.

I looked at him for a long moment, trying to reconcile the young man before me with the monster we had faced in that final, terrifying confrontation. "Lucas," I said, my voice calm. "I need you to tell me what happened. How did you become... what you became?"

He shook his head, tears in his eyes. "I don't know," he said, his voice breaking. "It was like... like I was trapped inside my own body, watching someone or something else take control. I could see everything that was happening, but I couldn't stop it. I couldn't..."

Lucas paused, his breathing uneven, and wiped the tears from his cheeks. "Andrew and Ward had just returned from a major discovery, a cache of coins. They were all in a frenzy, analyzing their find, theorizing about their origin and meaning. They were like children on Christmas morning, their eyes wide with excitement. They could hardly contain themselves, discussing the possibilities and implications late into the night.

"That evening, after they left for the night, I stayed behind. I wanted to do some last-minute inventory. I was also curious. These coins... something about them attracted me. So I retrieved the cache and started cataloging each piece. That's when I picked up one of the coins. It was cold and heavy in my hand, and then it spoke to me.

I watched as Lucas's expression changed, a haunted look replacing the earlier sorrow. "The coin... it read my mind," he continued. "It knew about Ward's wife, her murder, and the injustice that followed. It asked me if I wanted to help ease the pain of all those who had suffered as Dr. Ward had. I had been with Ward as he struggled with his grief. I saw how it had destroyed him, made him the disillusioned man he was.

"I thoughtlessly said yes. I wanted to help him, to right the wrongs that plagued our world. But that's when my nightmare began. The coin... it took over. I was no longer in control. I was a passenger in my own body, watching in horror as it... as it did unspeakable things in my name."

His voice trailed off and he looked away, unable to meet my gaze. The room felt colder, a heavy silence hanging between us. It was clear that he was a victim in all of this, a pawn in a much larger game that we were only beginning to understand. The notion of possession challenged the very foundation of our legal system, which rested on the fundamental precept of individual agency and intent. How could we, in good conscience, hold him responsible for actions that were not his own?

Yet the pragmatic reality could not be ignored. Releasing him posed an undeniable threat. If he was susceptible to possession once, there was no guarantee it wouldn't happen again. The potential atrocity hung over us like a dark cloud, whispering of future tragedies that could only be averted by preemptive action. The safety of the community was paramount, and the fragile balance between justice and security was on a razor's edge.

There were also broader societal implications to consider. Setting a precedent for leniency in possession cases could open the floodgates to a range of supernatural-based defenses, complicating an already overburdened judicial system. The courts were ill-equipped to navigate the murky waters of metaphysical influence, and the prospect of mixing ancient mysticism with modern legal codes presented an initiative of unprecedented proportions.

I thought of the victim's family, their grief raw and untempered by time. They deserved closure, a sense of justice that only a conviction could bring. But how could we reconcile their need for retribution with the young man's obvious victimhood? The fabric of our moral landscape seemed to unravel with each passing moment, leaving us to question the true definition of justice.

In the end, the decision would not be mine alone. It would rest on the shoulders of courts, judges, and perhaps even lawmakers, who would have to consider new statutes and legal frameworks to address this bewildering intersection of the supernatural and the legal. But as I looked into the young man's eyes – haunted, pleading, and undeniably human – I couldn't shake the feeling that we were all caught in a web of shadows,

struggling to discern the contours of right and wrong in a world where
the lines had blurred beyond recognition.

The sterile scent of the care facility clung to my nostrils as I walked
through its labyrinthine corridors, each step an effort under the crushing
weight of recent revelations. The implications of the Soulscape's existence
had shattered my understanding of reality, haunting my every thought,
an ever-present specter. However, my brother Samuel was the only
person who could possibly provide some insight into the mysteries that
now filled every part of my life.

I found him sitting in his usual spot by the window, his gaze fixed on
a distant point beyond the horizon. As I approached, he turned to me, a
flicker of recognition in his eyes. "James," he said, his voice soft but clear.
"You came."

I nodded and took a seat beside him. "I have," I said, my voice thick
with sentiment. "Samuel, I need your help. The things you warned me
about, the Hollow Soul... it's all real. I've seen it with my own eyes."

Samuel's gaze sharpened, a clarity I hadn't seen in years settling over
his features. "I know," he said, his voice calm. "I've always known. The
Soulscape... it's not just a realm of darkness and danger. There's light there
too, wisdom and knowledge beyond our understanding."

I leaned forward, my heart pounding in my chest. "What do you
mean?"

Samuel's eyes drifted to the window again, a faraway look settling
over his face. "The spirits that dwell in the Soulscape... they're not all
evil. Some of them want to help us, to guide us through the challenges
that lie ahead. They have knowledge and power beyond anything we
can imagine."

"How can we reach them?" I asked.

Samuel's eyes locked with mine, a knowing smile tugging at the corners of his mouth. "You already have," he said, his voice filled with a quiet certainty. "The Soulscape is all around us, James. It's in the air we breathe, in the ground beneath our feet. It's in the hearts and minds of every living thing on this earth. All you have to do is open up to it and let it guide you."

I sank back in my chair, my mind reeling with the implications of Samuel's words. If what he said was true, then we had barely scratched the surface of the mysteries that lay before us. The Soulscape was not just a realm of darkness and danger, but a source of wisdom and guidance, a tool we could use to navigate the challenges that lay ahead.

As I looked into my brother's eyes, I saw a glimpse of the old Samuel, the brilliant mind that had been lost to us for so long. At that moment, I knew I had to trust him, follow his lead, and see where it led.

My throat tightened as I met Samuel's gaze. "Thank you, Samuel," I managed, my words wavering. "I don't know what the future holds, but I do know that we will face it together." I took a shaky breath. "And with the Soulscape to light our way, maybe, just maybe, we'll find a way to fix this broken world."

Samuel nodded, a small smile playing on his lips. "I know you will, James. You've always been the strong one, the one who never gives up. And with The Soulscape on your side, there's nothing you can't accomplish."

I left the care facility that day with a renewed sense of purpose, a fire burning in my chest that I hadn't felt in years. The road ahead would be long and treacherous, but I knew I was not alone. I had my team, my brother, and the wisdom of the Soulscape to guide me.

That night, I found myself standing on the rooftop terrace of my apartment building, gazing out at the cityscape below. The lights of

Silvergate stretched before me, a glittering tapestry of life and energy that never failed to take my breath away.

As I stood there, my thoughts turned to the challenges that lay ahead. The Rune Killer may have been stopped, but I knew that he was only the beginning. The Soulscape had opened up a world of possibilities, both wondrous and terrifying, and it was up to us to navigate the uncharted waters that lay ahead.

I thought of Dr. Kensington and her tireless work, of Officer Chen and her unwavering commitment to the truth. I thought of O'Malley and the sacrifices she had made, the scars she now bore inside and out. Of Jones, who had strayed from the path but found his way back through sacrifice. And I thought of Samuel, my brother, who had been lost to us for so long, but who now offered a hopeful perspective on a new, frightening world.

As I turned my gaze back to the city below, I felt a sense of excitement mingled with the cloak of responsibility. Silvergate was a city on the brink of a new era, one in which the living and the dead coexist in a delicate balance. It would take time for us to adapt, to find our footing in this strange new world, but I had faith in the resilience of the human spirit.

The future was uncertain, but it was also full of promise. With each passing day, we would learn more about the Soulscape and the spirits that inhabited it. We would forge new alliances, discover hidden truths, and unravel the mysteries that had eluded us for so long. And through it all, we would stand together, united in our determination to protect the innocent and preserve the fragile peace between worlds.

As I breathed in the crisp night air, I felt a renewed sense of purpose settle over me. The Soulscape may have changed the rules of the game, but it also gave us the opportunity to be something more than we ever thought possible. And I, for once, was ready to embrace that challenge with open arms and an unwavering heart.